MW00769994

THE
LORDS OF
OBLIVION

THE
LORDS OF
OBLIVION

A SAN FRANCISCO FANTASY

PETER W. BLAISDELL

To Daniel:

Merry Christmas 2021.

Mom + Dad Gillespie

THE LORDS OF OBLIVION. Copyright © 2017 by Peter Warren Blaisdell. All rights reserved. Printed in the United States of America. No part of this book may be used or reproduced in any manner without written permission except for brief quotations used in reviews. For information, contact Blasidell Literary Enterprises at blaisdellliteraryenterprises.com

Interior book design by Alissa Theodor
Cover design by Heidi North

ISBN: 978-0-9992205-1-1
E-ISBN: 978-0-9992205-2-8

Please visit the publisher's website, blaisdelllitteraryenterprises.com
First Edition

Library of Congress Control Number: 2017912780

To my parents who showed me what educated people should be and to my wife, Shikha, and daughters, Anne and Shraya, who never hesitated to provide perceptive (and occasionally snarky) critiques of my writing efforts.

AUTHOR'S NOTE

Discerning readers of The *Lords of Oblivion* may notice, but hopefully will allow, my occasional lapses in describing the Bay Area's geography accurately. Rarely, I've rearranged landmarks or sight-lines to create more dramatic scenes or arresting vistas in service of the story. For example, in the novel, the Nike missile pad on Angel Island occupies the tallest island promontory. In reality, it has a bit less elevated location. Further, Angel Island's Immigration Station renovation is described as more extensive than it actually is at the time of this writing. Perhaps the city and park planners would make the same alterations if given a storyteller's license.

The Quatrain in the dance club scene is from the Edward Fitzgerald translation of the *Rubaiyat* by Omar Khayyam.

THE
LORDS OF
OBLIVION

Tintagel's Shadows

Blood fell like tears, rosy droplets that hit the flagstones below. This charmed everyone. Everyone except the dead.

Among the corpses hanging head-down from the rafters, Bradan curled upward to reach the chains knotted around his ankles. He tried to stifle grunts of exertion. When did the Druids and warlords sitting below intend to kill him?

Holding onto the chain with one hand to take stress off his stomach muscles, he worked at his fetters with the other, jamming a thumb between the rusted links and his ankles, trying to loosen the chains just enough to slide his feet out of the metal noose, but the bonds had been tied tightly enough to numb his ankles. He ripped a nail off and almost vomited down on the company.

As he fumbled, Bradan caught glimpses of the hall's oak rafters, the wood so aged and charred that it resembled black iron supporting a ceiling almost lost in the shadows and hazy smoke above. The long, rectangular hall appeared to be a subterranean cavern carved by geological forces from solid granite over eons. Symbols from rival tribes decorated the walls with newer signs overlaid on defaced carvings from generations gone by. The fortress, Tintagel, had changed hands several times after the Romans' departure, with Arthur and his British knights taking possession for a time. Now the Druid priest, Cynbel, and his Saxon allies controlled it. How long this situation lasted would depend on who won the looming battle.

All this Bradan saw while hanging with blood pushed into his brain. He smelled smoke and death drifting down from the rafters.

Wrenching himself about, Bradan saw that there must be a hundred beams, and from every one dangled a body. The nearest, a young woman, limned by a fireplace's glow, her dead brown eyes lit by the blaze, hung close enough to caress his face. Gray had replaced the girl's once ruddy skin. The corpses were of both sexes and all ages. Gravity had drained many of the bodies, though some still bled through deep, almost decapitating, gashes in their necks. They hadn't been dead that long. Directly beneath them, broad crimson splashes discolored the floor where their blood had fallen.

"Cynbel, they look good up there," the priestess Aennati said, standing below Bradan. She ran her hand down her gown. The dress matched her eyes. Her eyes were the color of coal. She stretched her arms upward, pulling the gown taut over her breasts as her reaching fingers almost touched one of the dangling bodies.

Cynbel raised one hand to deflect his peers' murmured approbation. Their praise echoed within the hall and sounded small as the voices created whispered conversations in the dark, badly lit recesses. However, Bradan guessed that plaudits weren't why Cynbel had gathered his colleagues together. He wanted to crush Merlin and Arthur so thoroughly that their memories would be fainter than the hall's echoes, and he needed his fellows' collective strength to act on that strategy.

Aennati stared upward at the corpses. Did she see him?

Bradan recognized the priestess and Cynbel's other comrades, Calder, Arthfael, Drust, Ake, and two dozen Saxon tribal warlords, seated around a table laden with ale, wine, and venison, warming themselves before a fire set into the north wall. Near the hearth, skulls had been haphazardly arranged, inverted to serve as planters for herbs to grow in. A small, balding man acting as a scribe sat unobtrusively on a bench a little away from the main table. Amazingly to Bradan, the man wrote on vellum rather than simply memorizing what transpired; Roman practices intruded even into this war council. He wondered if his own death would be important enough to record.

The blaze sent orange sparks spiraling upward toward the bodies to meet the falling blood. However big, the fire barely kept the frigid midwinter's night at bay, and chill drafts swirled about the room's occupants in sympathy with gusts outside. Snowflakes drifted in through a gash in the roof for the fire's smoke to escape.

Could there be a rawer, bleaker place than the North Cornish coast midwinter?

Cynbel, Aennati, and their followers once again controlled Britain's forests and meadows, the ever expanding wild places that encroached on cities, little puddles of culture evaporating before the hot blaze of war in the chaos following the Roman legions' departure. Dozens of invading barbarian tribes from the continent, Saxons, Angles, and Jutes, fought with one another and the British Celts over the remnants of civilized wealth while Irish pirates and painted Picts from Caledonia attacked from the north. Most of the coastal towns had been torched, and cities in the interior would soon burn too. Cynbel had allied himself with one large band of Saxon attackers heading westward to pillage. While the Saxons' motives were entirely acquisitive and mercenary, Cynbel wanted to sweep the land clean of Roman-Celtic civilization and allow the worship of nature to reestablish itself. Arthur's knights and Merlin's spells were all that stood in his way, preserving order during the interregnum.

The utter stupidity of trying to sneak into Cynbel's council hall hit Bradan. He'd had free rein of Arthur's camp and, though no one had ever confided in him, his hearing was excellent and he'd overheard Arthur and Merlin's plans. He wanted to help the cause that had inspired tonight's foray into Cynbel's hall. The possibility of being caught and tortured hadn't occurred to him.

Bradan noticed that the group below looked fatigued, perhaps because of their efforts to destroy Arthur and Merlin. Ake pillowed his head on his arms and slept on the table, ignoring the conversation around him. Would their lassitude give Bradan a chance to escape? If he couldn't free himself with main strength, was there another way to break his fetters?

Cynbel slammed his wine goblet onto the table. Everyone jerked upright on their benches and the drowsy murmurs died away. The winter wind quieted, too. The priest's rapport with the elements was legend.

"To business." Cynbel stood at the head of the table. He wore a woolen robe the color of pine needles and a gold torc of braided strands about his neck that glowed auburn in the firelight. The priest was tall and had shoulder-length black hair combed straight back from a broad forehead. His eyes were the color of the polar sea just before a blizzard hit. The other men, now wide awake and watching him intently, all had full blond or red beards, but Cynbel was clean shaven and youthful, seemingly no more than thirty years old, though his gravitas suggested great age. Merlin had once told Bradan that Cynbel, like Merlin himself, had discovered the runes and rituals needed to delay aging. Merlin had also said that Cynbel and Aennati were native-born Britons from the Celts' almost extinct Druid priest class, though they'd formed an alliance of expediency with invading barbarian tribes in pursuit of power.

"They're good ornaments." Cynbel pointed up at the bodies. "They're useful, too. My magic, fed by their deaths, will kill Merlin and the chieftain, Arthur, along with his knights."

"It'll be a fight," said Calder. He pulled his cloak closer about him. "Merlin is the best magician in Britain." He paused and stared at Cynbel. His face whitened. He'd been too frank. "Excepting you, Cynbel."

"Stop flattering me. Merlin will put up a battle going down, but go down he will."

"Our fighters—" Ake began.

"Your fighters are of uncertain mettle," Cynbel interrupted. "Since their rout at Mount Badon, you've hesitated to challenge Arthur's horsemen. That's why I'm not relying only on you. Besides my spells, we have another advantage."

Cynbel now looked up directly at Bradan. Mortified, the boy saw everyone stare at him. He stopped tugging at his chains.

"We have an unexpected helper," the priest said.

"Who's he?" Calder asked. He drank ale and wiped his mouth on a sleeve. "Some shopkeeper's son?"

"Merlin's apprentice," Cynbel said.

There was a collective intake of breath around the table.

"Why let him live?" Aennati asked flatly.

Bradan stopped breathing. If the woman had any soul, her eyes didn't show it. Despite his resolve to keep calm, he instinctively redoubled his efforts to break free, only to crash into neighboring corpses. A dead hand slapped his cheek. The limb was cold as winter. The Saxon fighters laughed hugely. Aennati smiled faintly. Cynbel stayed expressionless.

"The little shit isn't more than fourteen," Drust said. "Aennati's right. Merlin's confidante or not, why let him live?"

"Look at his filthy clothing," Aennati said. "You can see his ribs."

Bradan was smeared with blood as well as dirt. He'd fought hard when the priest's guards had discovered him some hours before. Ribs did show through his pale skin where his disheveled tunic exposed them, hardly surprising given the troubled times; no one got fat with pagans warring with Arthur's supporters.

"He belongs to a village near Glastonbury," Cynbel said. "I also thought the boy was just a peasant, a thief maybe, until I noticed the small scars cut onto his left forearm. They protect him from aging—a gift from Merlin. They show that the boy is close to Merlin and knows his tactics."

The scars encircled one of Bradan's skinny wrists, a snake around a branch. The bold symbols etched into his skin were alive with meaning; as long as he wore them, his body would age only one year in every century.

"He was sent to spy on us. Maybe Merlin wasn't up to that himself."

"Not true!" Bradan shouted. "I came on my own."

"No lie there," Calder said. "Merlin wouldn't have been stupid enough to send a naïf we'd be sure to catch and wring information out of."

"You have a name?" Aennati addressed him. "It's no fun hurting a stranger."

"The scars on your wrist keep you young," Cynbel said. "They won't keep you alive. Talking to me keeps you alive."

Bradan quickly spoke several rhymed couplets. A rusted link

in the chain binding his ankles snapped, sending him falling to the table below, crashing into plates and scattering the seated warlords. Simultaneously, the fire in the hearth doubled in size, provoking more chaos in the hall. Bradan, exhausted by the effort needed to create these distractions, rolled awkwardly off the table, in the process squashing an oily roasted goose on a tray. He ducked an ax thrown by a Saxon clan chief and staggered toward the hall's main door.

Cynbel and Aennati remained calm. Aennati brushed long hair away from her eyes and intoned her own spell. The fire reverted to its normal size. She continued speaking rhythmic stanzas and the words cut through the commotion. Bradan couldn't breathe as a viselike force contracted around his windpipe. He pitched headlong onto the floor. He tried to suck air in, but his throat froze and didn't respond. Bright spots shifted before his eyes to be replaced by black fog, then this and everything else faded.

Cynbel walked over to Bradan's body on the floor.

He said to Aennati, "You wanted your fun, but he could have told us things, useful things we need to know. Is it a wonder that Merlin and Arthur with just a handful of warriors have been able to keep all of us at bay for a generation?"

He prodded Bradan's body with his boot.

"Tonight we had a way to improve our odds if we'd used our brains; too late for that now."

"The boy was a distraction," Aennati said. "He tried to escape, so he's dead."

The warlords talked quietly among themselves, seeming to ally with the priestess. Cynbel folded his arms across his chest. He might be a match for any one of them alone, but together they could crush him. Persuasion, not confrontation, was his best strategy.

"What you might have, could have, should have gotten from him doesn't matter," Aennati said. "He's gone."

Cynbel regarded Bradan's corpse. "If I can bring him back—a big if—let's ask a question or two of our boy-guest. After I'm done, kill him again if you want. Scribe, I don't use this enchantment often so my memory is hazy. If I ever need this again, I'll use your text."

Cynbel spoke metered rhymes. Periodically he paused at a particular verse, then resumed. Nothing happened.

"I see my mistake. So a small amendment . . ."

The mage rearranged the phraseology. He seemed tentative. The scribe wrote and edited in a fever trying to keep up. Aennati turned away and stared up at the rafters. The Saxon warlords all looked bored.

As if his ears were blocked by layers of wool, Bradan heard someone say, "Do I have it right?"

Cynbel toed Bradan's body again.

Air rushed into Bradan's lungs like water pouring through a ruptured earthen dike. Coughing, he knew he could breathe again. His throat hurt massively. Dimly, he was aware that he'd simply not existed for some period of time. There had been nothing whatever to experience, no darkness, no pain or remembrance. Now his heart skipped beats then resumed its normal cadence. Stimuli crashed against his sight, hearing, smell, and touch, but then his brain regained control of the disordered sensations.

"Scribe, you have this?" Cynbel asked.

The scribe nodded and held up a velum scroll as proof.

Cynbel hauled himself onto the table with effort, scattering cups and plates to the floor. "I will hear him out."

He turned his back on them all, daring a concerted move

against him. Calder glanced briefly at Aennati, then at Arthfael, but no one wanted to collude against Cynbel. Bradan sensed the warlords' defiance defusing like a summer shower blowing past. Cynbel must have also felt the challenge to his leadership dissipating. He turned around and nodded to a huge braided warrior to retie the chain around Bradan's ankles and hoist him back up among the dead—whom he'd almost just joined.

Cynbel addressed Bradan. "Where will Arthur and his men attack us?"

"Traitor!" Bradan shouted down at the priest.

"That isn't an answer. Talk in Celtic. That's your mother language, not Latin."

"You invited outsiders to pillage our homes!" Bradan remembered the Saxon raiders wielding axes who had crushed the skulls of his family and burned his home two years earlier. Merlin had adopted him then.

"I'm friends with whoever I need to be to purify Britain," Cynbel said. "The Romans murdered Druid priests when they took this land generations ago. Roman cities and cultivation have eaten away the trees and streams. Nothing authentic remains of Celtic culture. Merlin and Arthur support that blasphemy. They're trying to keep the remnants of something that should never have been in the first place. So, since you're in their camp, I'd say you're the traitor, not me."

"You don't have to justify yourself to him," Aennati said.

Cynbel waved this support aside. "It feels good to be angry. How many are left in Arthur's forces?"

Bradan didn't respond. Now he wished Cynbel hadn't been able to reverse Aennati's death incantation before they wrested anything useful from him. Bradan tried to hold himself with as much dignity as possible given his awkward position.

"What spells will Merlin use to help Arthur?"

"The boy must have grit," Calder said. "Merlin wouldn't have apprenticed just anyone. He won't break easily."

Apparently thinking the same thing, Cynbel jumped off the table and walked over to the fire. A thin iron bar that could be used either as a poker or a spit lay on the stone hearth with one end immersed in the coals beneath burning logs. Cynbel wrapped a cloth around his hand and gingerly picked up the bar. The blaze emitted a shower of sparks, reluctant to release it. Cynbel shifted it from hand to hand. Even the cloth barely made the poker holdable.

"Why not use potions or a spell?" Arthfael asked. "That would make him talk."

"And what he'd say might or might not make sense. We won't turn his mind to ashes yet."

Cynbel hefted the poker and climbed back onto the tabletop. He now stood at eye-level with the bodies.

"A hot iron is more direct," Aennati said. She walked over to the table near Cynbel, apparently his ally again.

"Your name?" Cynbel asked.

Bradan guessed that trying to pry this small, harmless, information from him would begin the interrogation . . .

"Bradan," he muttered. His name didn't matter. He wouldn't tell them anything else.

"At least we've got you speaking Celtic. Bradan is a hero's name. Why say it so softly? Where is Arthur's camp, Bradan, and how many soldiers does he have?"

"You won't win. You've given away your position. Merlin will have noticed the magic you used to resurrect me."

"Let him notice. I'm stronger. How many are left with Merlin and Arthur?"

"You don't have surprise with you anymore."

The priest moved the poker's glowing tip toward the boy's face. Bradan squeezed his eyes shut and twisted away as far as the chains allowed, but he felt Cynbel shift the poker nearer. Bradan began to cry. *He's almost got me talking,* he thought, despairing. *He'll wring every bit of information out of me.*

The priest jabbed a corpse next to him. The dead woman's flesh sizzled. Bradan jerked upward as if he'd been seared himself.

"Arthur plans to attack you at Camlann tomorrow evening." His thin voice forced its way through his tears. "I don't know how many knights the king has. He lost many when he beat you at Badon. He hasn't been able to recruit replacements since then. Times are hard."

"How many soldiers does he have left?" Cynbel repeated, hardly raising his voice; the poker provided all the emphasis needed by moving inexorably closer to Bradan's face.

Bradan writhed away. "Five hundred." The words felt torn from his throat. He cried in earnest now, and tears dropped to the floor just as blood had earlier.

Cynbel let the poker droop for a moment. "So few . . . even with his foot soldiers, he has only a small force remaining. Without the element of surprise . . ."

"He'll lose," Aennati stated. The assembled Saxon warlords nodded agreement.

Cynbel pointed at the scores of hanging bodies surrounding Bradan. "And sacrificing them helps us make spells that defeat armies."

"Stupid, so stupid to fight us," said Aennati. "We were nature's steward before the Romans came and we will be again."

"What's Merlin planning next, Bradan?" Cynbel said. His use of Bradan's name made it seem that this was really just a personal conversation of no consequence shared between the two of them.

"He plans magic tomorrow that will distract and confuse you and keep you from working your own spells." Bradan's words were cinders in his mouth. "I don't know exactly how he'll do it."

Cynbel shrugged. "I know the ritual and how to defeat it." He jumped off the table and tossed the poker toward the hearth, where it clattered against a skull and sent it rolling. Bradan watched him. The interrogation was over and Cynbel seemed disinterested in him. They'd kill him now.

"So we have what we need," said Arthfael. "I'll kill the kid, no spells needed." The clan chief unsheathed his sword.

There was a commotion outside, horses stamping followed by ringing swords and shouts growing to an uproar. The hall's main door buckled inward with a splintering crash. A slender figure moved through the debris into the hall, walking straight at the Saxons. Bradan recognized Merlin. Other figures, in mail and leather armor and indistinct in the night, followed him forward, Arthur's men.

Arthfael sat nearest the remnants of the door. As he turned toward the invaders, a spear erupted from his throat. Other Saxon warlords and their soldiers scrambled to meet the intruders. Calder hurled his ax, which burst through a shield in a shower of splinters and smashed into the face of a Briton warrior next to Merlin.

Bradan hung above the melee unnoticed. Below, Cynbel pulled Aennati close, as if embracing a lover. The two stood apart from the vicious fighting, a calm island in a flooding river, but about to be engulfed.

"Reviving the boy alerted Merlin," Cynbel admitted. "We lost surprise and wasted the power of these deaths." He nodded upward at the bodies. "We'll win tomorrow with what the boy told us, I foresee that, but neither we nor Merlin survives tonight. I see that, too."

"So we die," Aennati said. "Because of the boy."

"The scribe recorded my rituals. Someone may bring us back."

"When?"

CHAPTER 1

All Hallows' Eve on the North Beach

An Asian kid on a skateboard paused at Filbert Street's summit, a skier perched on Everest's peak.

"No," Bradan said. "Don't be a fuckup."

If the skater moved forward another millimeter, he'd be committed to a steep four-block run. He'd be going at lightspeed before he was halfway down.

The kid had set himself an insane challenge. Filbert descended Telegraph Hill with an incline so sharp that stairsteps had been cut into the sidewalk to allow pedestrians to scale its flank. Cars parked perpendicular to the street's direction to avoid pitching headlong down the hill if their brakes failed.

If sheer velocity didn't make the skateboarder crash hard, he'd be pulped by a car barreling obliviously up the street. There'd be no room to evade the vehicle. Cars had parked legally on the left and illegally on the right, reducing Filbert to a narrow slot.

The kid regarded the near-vertical descent before him and seemed to perform the same analysis. He wore a threadbare white T-shirt several sizes too big for him and no protection from the shredding asphalt if he took a tumble. No helmet; the boy's only concession to safety was a pair of heavy work-gloves.

Suspecting he had an audience, the skateboarder looked up,

noted Bradan's presence on a fifth-floor balcony above him, flipped dark hair out of his eyes, and flashed a thumbs-up sign. Bradan shook his head, but the idiot was going to go for it.

All in.

The boy pushed off hard and immediately began zigzagging down the slope, gaining momentum every microsecond. Now he hurtled forward, crouching down over the board to keep his center of gravity low, with his hands outstretched and bent slightly at the elbow. He had almost enough speed for lift-off.

One block further down Filbert, a Mercedes as big as a tank swung onto the street and accelerated up the hill. In seconds, the car was on top of the skateboarder. Bradan leaped up, leaned far over the balcony railing, and shouted a warning. He judged that there couldn't be more than a meter between the Mercedes and the parked cars flanking it, not enough room for even a small skateboarder to zip past.

The Mercedes's driver saw the little missile aimed directly at his front grill. With a screech of tires, the car stopped dead in the middle of Filbert. Angry horn blasts echoed off the buildings.

The kid, absorbed in the geometry of his run, didn't see the car until its horn sounded. Suddenly realizing the shit he was in, the boy swung the board perpendicular to the street's direction and leaned into the hill, one of his gloved hands almost touching the asphalt. The board wasn't rolling now; it slid with a loud rasp as its wheels and the board itself scraped down Filbert's rough surface, wooden splinters and sparks cascaded upward. The kid balanced phenomenally well and he had the board doing the right thing, but he wasn't scrubbing off speed fast enough.

Bradan snapped off four rhymed verses.

The skateboarder jerked to a halt as if he'd reached the end of a tether. He still had enough momentum to bang into the

Mercedes's right front headlight, but not hard. In fact, the kid stayed upright and pushed himself off the vehicle and rolled around the Mercedes, giving the dumbfounded driver the finger as he slid past. Beyond the obstacle and standing fully erect now, the boy cruised his battered board down the last block in controlled, undulating curves until he hit flat terrain; cool, it was no big deal. He obviously thought he'd done it all himself. The skateboarder turned and waved up at Bradan then rolled off across Washington Square.

With a sigh of relief and weariness, Bradan sat down heavily on the balcony next to an agave plant, breathing in. He'd once been as crazy rash as the kid on the board. How else to explain his idiocy in attempting to spy on Cynbel, Aennati, and their followers? What possible chance had his self-appointed mission had of succeeding against individuals as malign as the priests? Youth was a time for absolutes; with age, came shades of gray and, long since, he'd learned that longevity and caution were joined at the hip. Now he prided himself on an existence carefully arranged to avoid risks. Today he'd been the guardian angel bailing out the Asian kid from a lethal crash, just as Merlin had helped him at Tintagel fifteen centuries ago.

For several moments Bradan inhaled deeply, slowly recovering. Amazing how even a small bit of magic could be so exhausting. The most he'd been able to do was slow the boy— elementary stuff. Anything more dramatic would have been beyond him on such short notice, but it had been enough today.

"A neighbor is here to see you," his condo's melodic female voice informed him. He'd programmed it with a BBC announcer's urbane British accent. "Should I let them in?"

Emphasizing the point, someone knocked on his front door. Bradan heaved himself upright, ambled across the living room.

"Wow, what a racket on Filbert." Claire Chan stood in the hall. She had brushed aside her bangs and secured them under a headband. Beauty was the exceptional feature that made a pretty face unique; Bradan thought Claire's mahogany-colored eyes were singular.

"Can't they keep it down on a Saturday morning?"

"There was almost an accident," Bradan said. "No one hurt."

He wandered back across his living room and plopped down again on his balcony, talking to his neighbor through the open sliding door. "Grab a seat. I'd offer a glass of cabernet, but it's early and you're ready for a run."

"Never too early for a cab. And I can run when I'm buzzed. By the way, you look exhausted."

Bradan stood back up, sighing inwardly at the effort, and moved to his kitchen. He debated a moment, then opened a bottle of Caymus. It was a really good vintage and pricey, but he wanted to impress Claire.

"Where's Julie?" Claire asked. "She's usually here on weekends. Say hi to her for me."

"She hasn't been around much lately." Bradan hoped Claire would read between the lines and change the topic.

"You've got a history."

Bradan saw that Claire had walked into the hallway connecting the front door to his living room and now stood looking at a painting on the wall, hands on hips, challenging the piece.

"We've been neighbors in the building for a while, but I haven't really seen your place before." She nodded thanks, accepting a glass of cab from Bradan. "Nice artwork. Over my pay grade."

"It'd be over my pay grade, too, if they were original. They're not. Just good copies."

"Amazingly good reproductions." She turned away from the art to look at him. "I'm the classic nosy neighbor. If you don't mind my asking, you've got the damnedest accent. It's from everywhere and nowhere. Sounds British sometimes, then it doesn't."

"I've lived all over." He'd learned and forgotten more languages than he could count over the centuries. However, despite his accent, he'd become comfortable with modern English, ironic given the loathing he'd once harbored for all things Anglo-Saxon. He'd kept his Celtic and Latin too.

"Misspent youth, *creatio ex nihilo*," he said.

"You started from nothing? You're getting mysterious on me, Bradan. Is that what happens on Halloween?"

"Mysterious? Never." Ennui shaded his tone. "Nihilistic and cynical, even a little self-protective. So, I lead the most staid life you can imagine. Nothing exciting *ever* happens to me."

He waved her further into his home and watched her hesitate briefly before venturing onward. Ah, the caution of a modern concerned about intruding on personal space.

"Where'd you get all this stuff? I took some art history at Stanford. That one's a Raphael? The colors have even darkened with age."

"It's a Correggio . . . a reproduction of a Correggio. The original would have been painted in the early sixteenth century. His vision was eroticism and theology intertwined, definitely the male gaze. He was a sensualist, but with a real flair for religious subjects, too. Look at the face of Saint Catherine."

Bradan watched Claire earnestly studying the piece. He tried to hide a smile. It was no copy. Bradan had known the painter and recollected buying the work right out of the artist's studio. He remembered seeing it being finished, a nude peasant girl from the Tuscan countryside posing unselfconsciously as the saint while the artist deftly worked on the canvas, hardly looking at the model, driven by an inner image of carnality blended with godliness. A bishop in Siena had commissioned the piece, but the diocese had run out of money before it was finished, allowing Bradan to make an offer.

A jolt shook the building, accompanied by a crash in Bradan's kitchen. The world seemed to flex for an instant. Car alarms sounded and someone laughed on the street below.

"Shit—a quake! We were about due," Bradan said.

Claire said, "This one wasn't bad, but one of these days . . ."

". . . one of these days. The price of paradise. Check that your quake insurance is current. I think my cab just bit the dust. I left the bottle open on the kitchen island. Too bad. It was a strong vintage."

Bradan moved through his condo assessing damage.

"What was the magnitude?" he asked his home.

"About 4.6. There was no damage to gas or water lines."

"Very helpful," Bradan said. When he communicated with his home's artificial intelligence, he had to resist the urge to thank it for providing routine information or doing some basic housekeeping function.

"Any significant destruction?" Claire asked from his main room. She seemed only mildly anxious. "I should check my own place, but almost everything breakable is secured. I'm such a native here that I sleep through smaller temblors."

"A vase with roses fell in my second bedroom/study. Other than that, and the wine, *status quo ante*."

In his kitchen, the Caymus was now an expensive crimson-purple puddle with a thousand glass shards and bits of label smeared across his tile floor. That seemed a pointless waste of an excellent wine. Bradan considered for a moment. Claire was out of sight. Then he quietly recited six rhyming couplets. He blinked and the Caymus bottle now stood intact on his kitchen island. It had even been re-corked. Bradan slumped against a countertop holding himself upright with both arms. It never got any easier.

"Bradan, you okay?"

"Fine. I was ready to mourn the loss of a good cab, but it was another bottle that fell."

"Well, hallelujah. Can you bring me a refill?"

Refreshed glass in hand, Bradan watched Claire return to earnestly studying his Correggio, then she moved over to a tall, seven-paneled screen painting that divided the room into halves. Surprisingly, this still stood after the quake. The life-size cranes preening along the edge of a forest were drawn with spare brushstrokes and looked untroubled by modern concerns.

"How do I get on your Christmas list?" she asked. "What's this? Edo period?"

Claire showed real interest in his collection; he needed to be guarded.

"Who knows? I bought the screen because it works with my other pieces. And, before you ask, the little limestone tablet on the stand next to it with the weird carved symbols in it, that's got to be a fake. The antique dealer claimed that it was a pre-Christian Celtic carving, but they can do anything with modern 3-D printers."

"Doesn't look fake at all. Looks really old. The glyphs are quite worn, but they're carved with real flair."

"You're full of aperçus this morning."

Bradan momentarily felt a lazy inclination to let his guard down and describe the pieces in real detail. Centuries of not having his façade punctured bred a sense of invulnerability; no one ever could see who and what he really was. Besides, he felt proud of his collection and he desperately wanted to talk about the art. However, almost unbidden, habit reasserted itself and he found himself becoming obscurant.

"The tablet with the glyphs comes from who knows where, some antique shop when I last visited Europe. I can't remember. All this stuff is just to impress clients when I do counseling sessions in my home. Think of it as marketing. They love coming over. And they see me as some kind of shaman—it's all mumbo jumbo, but it makes them happy so I keep it on display."

Was Claire a closet art aficionado? He'd been a little too forthcoming about the Correggio. With mild concern, he watched as she stared at another painting hanging close to the fireplace, a Reynolds portrait of a young Georgian-period woman wearing a broad-brimmed hat with the bloom of an English spring on her cheeks. The picture also was original. In this case, he'd known both the painter and the model.

"It all goes with your space," Claire said. "You worry about what outside air will do to the pictures?"

"I've got a high tech moisture control system. Works even with the windows open. Also, none of the art is in direct sunlight."

"It's almost a museum. You've got an extra bedroom? My floor plan only has one. The market value for this place must be enormous. Your New Age counseling gig has really taken off."

"My clients are rich. Stupid, but rich. I bill them accordingly."

He despised his vocation and felt utter contempt for his patrons. He'd lost track of the number of credulous wealthy clients for whom he dispensed platitudes about "finding one's inner pagan" and "locating a spiritual center amid the clutter of your soul," but it definitely paid the bills. Sandalwood permeated his condo. Two little teak incense holders held the smoking nubs of aromatic sticks. He smiled in self-mockery. Well, he had to fit the part of an intuitive counselor.

Claire sat down on a sofa sectional—she'd made herself right at home—talking to him across his airy, high-ceilinged living room while he'd gone back to sitting outside in the sun. The little steel platform doubled as the building's highest fire escape landing. The view was gorgeous, with the entire northern edge of the city seemingly at his feet, mind-fucking splendor right outside the floor-to-ceiling windows. Bradan occupied the top story of the old five-floor building now converted to condos because he enjoyed the sight lines. He looked up to see Coit Tower at the top of Telegraph Hill just above him surrounded by a cluster of pines and eucalyptus. Their fragrances floated down to him. The last of the dawn's fog still wreathed the fluted concrete tower and hung about the trees cloyingly as the ocean breeze and sun nibbled away at it.

Claire now stared at a small parchment in a clear Lucite case on his coffee table.

"You're into old manuscripts, too? The writing is Latin? There are symbols, too, though I can't guess what language they're in. This should be in a museum. Won't the paper degrade?"

"The case protects it from humidity and temperature extremes. It's clear but virtually bulletproof. And the parchment isn't paper; it's vellum, so it's a lot more durable. It's never on display. I keep that in my wall safe, had it out this morning because it reminded me of someone, old memories. I need to put it back. "

"It is Latin? I'm right about that, aren't I? Is it an illustrated Bible page from way back?"

"It's Latin, but definitely not biblical. It's sort of about superstitions and folklore. Going to any Halloween parties tonight?"

"All right, I get the hint. Keep your secrets. Hopefully, you're not wanted for art theft. Anyway, no parties for me. I'm working all weekend. I've got a presentation Monday for some start-up in Palo Alto. They're a biotech working on extreme longevity. I'm not a molecular biologist, but as I understand it, if the control elements of certain genes can be edited, aging slows way down. We can all live to be a thousand. That's scary enough without adding long-dead spirits. You?"

"I was planning on hitting Formentera—great beaches and more rustic than Ibiza—with Julie, but she's not going, so instead I'm flying to see family in Miami. Maybe the kids and I will do some fishing and snorkeling. Should be a quiet time."

It had been anything but quiet when he'd lived in Miami during the 1970s and '80s helping to handle transportation for cocaine cowboys, getting powder up from Columbia to South Florida. Merlin wouldn't have been proud. However, at the time, Bradan needed money.

"You seem kind of young to have a bunch of kids. Want me to check on your place while you're out? If you're not kenneling your dog, I can jog with him in the evenings when I'm back from work."

"Thanks, with Julie gone, that's appreciated. The front door is alarmed, but I'll program my condo to recognize you and let you in. There's a motion detector, too. My dog is also a good deterrent against thieves."

"Thought you said that this artwork is fake. Why all the security?"

"It's fake, all right, but it's got sentimental value and I don't want to lose the stuff, including the parchment. The detector recognizes the dog's movements so it shouldn't be set off when he comes and goes with you, and I think the condo's smart enough to recognize your movements, too, now that you've been inside, if I tell it to, but I'll leave you my number and the security service's contact info in case there are issues while I'm in Florida. I don't give my number to clients or they'd be bothering me while I'm away."

"I think your home is smarter than mine," she said.

"Honestly, this place runs itself better than magic," Bradan said. "I had it updated last summer. Let's see, what else . . . if you get tired of minding my dog, you can leave him with a friend over in Sausalito. He lives on a boat sometimes. I think he has a place in the city, too, somewhere in the Haight. His name is Wally. He's bartender in a south of Mission club. I'll give you his contact info."

Claire walked down the hall to the front entrance and paused to push against the doorframe, stretching her hamstrings.

"I could use a vacation, too, something far away and enchanting. How can life be so stale in a city this interesting?" She held up her hands to forestall a reply. "Sorry, rhetorical question. I don't mean to quiz you on existential matters on a weekend morning. But don't you ever feel a need for a little adventure?"

Bradan stood lazily savoring the lack of a schedule today. "Is that another rhetorical question? No? I'm not daring. I've had my adventures in life. Too many. Now I spend my money on things that make me happy." He gestured at his artwork. "And I go to bed early with the covers tucked under my chin. The quake was enough adrenaline for me."

"So, Tintagel—can I borrow the wonder puppy for a jog? He's good company."

"Sure. Take him. He enjoys a good run." Bradan whistled.

His pet stalked out of the study. The animal moved with neither haste nor hesitation. His claws clicked on the hardwood. Tintagel's paws were as big as a large man's fist and his black fur had hints of gray at the hair tips as if frost dusted his coat. Tintagel looked at Claire dressed in a Stanford University sweatshirt, maroon tights, and running shoes, seemed to understand the situation immediately, and nodded somberly, apparently signifying his assent to a run.

"There's a wild quality to him," Claire said. "He's gigantic, looks more like a wolf every time I see him."

"I'd keep a wolf in the North Beach? The homeowners association would love that. He fools people, but he's just a mix of shepherd and malamute."

Tintagel turned to stare at him with lambent blue eyes and growled, clearly angered by this description of a pedestrian pedigree. Bradan would have to make amends.

He lied out of habit about his pet. Even in San Francisco's ever more genteel North Beach, which tolerated—didn't notice, actually—tattoo parlors and assorted nude dancing clubs, remnants of a more raffish past, his neighbors would surely freak if they knew he owned a wolf. It was a singular wolf at that. He remembered Merlin telling him that Tintagel had once been part of Gwyn's pack, the hunter of souls, when that grim figure had set his animals loose among the corpses after a battle to gather dead warriors' spirits. The creature also might be related to Fenrir, the Norse demon-wolf. Tintagel had been Bradan's companion since youth, but, despite the wolf's centuries of loyalty to him, Bradan still shivered when he awoke at night to see the animal's sapphire eyes staring at him.

"Whatever he is, he scared the shit out of that creep in the

Presidio who tried to follow us when we went running last week."

"He can be scary when he needs to be. Can't you?" Bradan rubbed Tintagel behind his ears. The animal tilted his head to better show just where it itched. Bradan hoped they were friends again.

"What do I feed him when you're gone?" Claire asked. "Dog chow?"

"He takes care of himself. The condo lets him in and out. He doesn't get lost."

"What does he eat?"

"I've never inquired too closely."

"He won't snack on me?" Claire said, deadpan.

"He likes you."

"Good to know. Let's go, puppy. I've had my coffee this morning. You're in for a race."

"Want another glass of cabernet for the road?"

"I said I could run buzzed. I can't run drunk. Funny name, Tintagel. What does it mean?"

"He's named after a fortress, but it's been a ruin for about fifteen centuries. Enjoy your run. Watch for traffic. There may be signals out after the quake."

Bradan closed the thick oak front enterance behind her.

Two windows stretching from floor to ceiling flanked the balcony door. These were open, allowing a breeze off San Francisco Bay to waft long gossamer draperies into his room. This morning they reminded him of white burial shrouds. He stared out across the Bay at the Golden Gate Bridge. Every year, planners and developers confidently increased the urban area, covering more and more of the hills and green spaces, yet the whole city of crystal and stucco existed at nature's sufferance, Pompeii clinging to Mount Vesuvius's flank. The bridge's massive rust-orange towers stabbing up from the breakers were nothing if not organic to the technological twentieth century. Immense stressed-concrete abutments on the San Francisco and Marin County sides secured the cables that suspended the bridge's tons. Cars, barely visible in the distance, moved across the span sluggishly—the weekend's first traffic jam—completing the picture of tense modernity.

He shifted his gaze further north to Marin's hills partly obscured by fog. The grasses, burned brown by another dry summer, covered the rippling bluffs overlooking the bridge and transformed the hills into sensual, tan curves flaunted by a bikinied beauty reclining on a California beach. He shaded his eyes. Marinas in the rich, effete Marin towns of Sausalito and Tiburon sent forth weekend sailors intent on beginning a day on the water as early as possible. Everything was a little too vivid this morning, the hues too brilliant, an acid-induced vision.

Where not obscured by the remaining fog, the glare radiating from the Bay was intense, creating a vast, smooth pool, almost bright enough to mask the small boats close to Alcatraz. Their cream sails fattened as they moved away from the island's shelter, becoming pregnant with the breeze as the vessels heeled over in the wind, cutting clean arcs through the waves. They resembled Celtic fishing boats. Bradan almost wondered if an Irish pirate or a Saxon corsair might lie in ambush ready to fall upon the vessels.

Here we go again, he thought angrily, castigating himself for not keeping tighter rein on his memories. Today the juxtaposition of modern scenes and ancient reflections was jarring.

Beneath him, across from Washington Square, sat the Saints Peter and Paul Church. Bradan smiled. The Italians, once the North Beach's major ethnic group before the Chinese arrived in force, felt they'd needed patronage from two saints to bless their neighborhood. Britain's ancient Christians had also tried to comfort themselves with multitudes of saints. However, ecclesiastical protection didn't always ward off darker powers during those primitive times.

A few older Italians and Chinese with skin more brown and leathery than a pterodactyl's mixed with younger, professional types relaxing on the benches and lawn soaking up the sun. A street person shuffled systematically among them, stopping to demand money with an aggressively outstretched hand. The Italians and Chinese ignored him while the professionals gave the panhandler lengthy explanations, but no spare change. Eventually the crowd's parsimony enraged the street person and Bradan watched him halt his fruitless quest and scream invective at the loungers and the heavens, one fist raised at the laughing sky.

"Oh hell, somebody give the man a fiver," Bradan said.

He pulled out his wallet, withdrew a bill, and held it delicately between thumb and forefinger. He declaimed six Latin stanzas. The money vanished from his hand. Simultaneously, he saw the beggar stop mid-harangue and slowly, wonderingly, lower his fist that now clenched a bill. The man whirled around, staring at the other park denizens, but none sat close by. The beggar shrugged off his Wagnerian gloom, stuffed the money in a pocket, and sauntered off toward Columbus Avenue, a supplicant no more.

Bradan smiled. He was just a conjuror, not a real magician. Modern life never really demanded potent tricks even on Halloween, just little bits of enchantment to smooth life's coarse edges. Technology took care of everything else. But, as always with good magic, however small, he felt a peculiar, pleasurable sensation of oneness with the universe at once cerebral and erotic. He'd just peered into its core and seen chaos, but by a delicate manipulation managed to elicit symmetry amid the disorder. The essence of a spell was to apply that symmetry to the local situation you wished to influence by using the appropriate metered phrases. He wondered if magic was related to quantum entanglement. Hadn't Einstein described this phenomenon as "spooky action at a distance"?

Against all appearances, he wondered if Einstein had actually been a Druid priest.

Theoretically, anything the mind conceived could be realized with the right spell. However, there was a cost: fatigue proportional to the enchantment's result, as if a psychic battery had been drained. He could no more change a sand grain into a mountain than he could lift a mountain—unless he amplified his innate power with human sacrifice. Cynbel and Aennati did that. He wouldn't. The manuscript in the Lucite case was a testament to that. He'd managed to recover the scribe's pages during the tumult in Tintagel's hall when Merlin had attacked Cynbel and Aennati 1,500 years ago. In a savage battle of mutual destruction, Merlin as well as Cynbel and Aennati had died that night, allowing Bradan to slip his chains and escape the chaotic hall. The scribe had recorded the proceedings of Cynbel's conclave, including the spell's meters by which the priest had revived Bradan. However, the scribe had dropped the vellum parchment in his flight from the hall, allowing Bradan to recover it. With the parchment in his possession, Bradan had naively planned to use the same resurrection spell to bring back Merlin. However, the energy needed to restore Merlin—or anyone else—to life would have required spilling a lot of blood synchronized with the spell's recitation.

He wouldn't trade one soul for another.

The spell was far too long to memorize with complex rhythms and rhymes. He kept the tattered fragment as a tribute to his long-dead mentor and on the remote chance that he could somehow determine how to make it work without bloodshed; at the moment, the parchment had as much practical worth as foolscap covered in random scribbles.

Tired from the morning's third spell, Bradan slouched against the iron balcony railing, regarding his airy home, then wandered into the condo's study and called out, "Lights." The room responded with diffuse illumination as though he'd cast a spell. He stared down at his tiny computer, elegantly black on an early-nineteenth-century maple desk. He told the computer to wake up and scanned his inbox, which kept him in touch with the world as easily as enchantment. The computer also was a wonderful bookkeeper that alerted him to clients in arrears on their payments. A screen full of unread messages had accumulated since he'd checked last night. He'd read them another time.

Sophisticated as it was, the computer was already an antique with ever more intelligent upgrades hitting the market monthly. The border between technology and enchantment was blurring fast—he kept Clarke's epigram in mind: advanced technology is indistinguishable from magic.

Rather than fight it, he had learned over fifteen centuries to adapt to changing circumstances. Moreover, Bradan found that magic and technology sometimes made strangely good bedfellows with the computer serving as a convenient repository of spells. He had them all indexed by key word and subject. Even if he forgot the exact phrasing of a given piece of enchantment, silicon memory complemented his own neurons.

The library of spells was mostly archaic and pointless in

modern times unless one needed to guarantee a stable against fleas for the coming season, but some of the incantations could be reimagined and adapted to modern circumstances, as his activities this morning had shown. The phraseology of magic resembled case law wherein a skilled practitioner could use precedent as guidance in creating a new incantation to address the current need.

Above the desk, a fin-de-siècle portrait of Arthur in full plate armor with regally furrowed brow stared down at the modern accoutrements of Bradan's profession. Merlin, in a hooded cape, with an impossibly long, gray beard, whispered presumably sage advice into the king's ear. Bradan laughed aloud at the picture. The real Arthur and Merlin would have sneered, too. Fortunately, Claire hadn't questioned him about this piece. Nothing about the work was right, not the clothing, not the men, not the attitudes. As folklore, the king and wizard weren't legends; they were mirrors reflecting back whatever baggage a given age chose to weight the historical reality with: chivalric ideals in medieval times, Victorian manliness in the nineteenth century, and feminist revisionism currently. Every era's projection of its particular narcissistic urges on the legend explained its appeal and longevity.

Bradan leaned against the wall with both arms, his chin sunk on his chest. Memories surfaced within his consciousness, luminous jellyfish rising out of the abyss. The Arthur whom Bradan had known in the late fifth century wasn't even a king; he'd been a chieftain leading a ragged band of horsemen only slightly less savage than the barbarians they'd fought. Few surviving chronicles of the time even mentioned him. Nonetheless, the man had been a charismatic leader with a keen sense of his culture sinking beneath waves of pagan invaders.

Merlin also had been both less and infinitely more than the wizened figure depicting wisdom incarnate. Wisdom would have cautioned against an obsessive fondness for nubile women. However, Merlin knew more than anyone about how to manipulate natural forces to the benefit of the communities he'd lived in. Like Arthur, he'd been a strong Celtic bulwark against seismic changes sweeping Britain. He'd also been Bradan's personal salvation.

Why keep the painting? His reactions were always the same: a smirk at its inaccuracies followed by lacerating guilt over betraying his mentor. Self-loathing fueled so much of who he was. However, forgetting Merlin altogether would be the final cut. So the picture stayed.

Besides memories, it was all sand, impossibly remote from his current circumstances.

CHAPTER 2

Broken Vase, Spilled Roses

S omeone knocked quietly but firmly on his door and, without waiting to be invited, entered the condo.

"Hi, Jules," Bradan said. "Happy Halloween."

"Hi, Brad." The tone was neutral. "I came to pick up the last of my stuff. It seems odd to knock. We shared this place for so long. It was my home, too."

Bradan knew the precise cadence of Julie's walk as she moved through the living room toward his office. She'd spent many weekends in his condo over the past seven years.

"The place won't be the same without you."

"How much damage from the quake?" she asked.

Without turning around from his desk, he pictured Julie's weekend morning dress, an old pair of sweatpants and a gray sweatshirt bearing her alma mater's emblem, San Jose State. She might be about to run a couple of kilometers through the hilly neighborhood, but sometimes good intentions met San Francisco's chilly mornings and steep slopes.

"I was picking up," he said. "Your stuff survived fine."

There were two bedrooms off the living room. An open door into one showed their futon—actually, his futon, since she was in the process of departing—sheets in disarray from a relaxed morning. The only things missing were his ex-girlfriend's. On a typical Saturday, one of Julie's sweaters might have lain next to his T-shirt where she'd thrown it after buying meats and cheeses at Molinari's or in-line skating in Golden Gate Park, but he'd slept alone for the last several weeks. Books lay scattered about on the blond hardwood floor next to a shattered vase and spilled white roses lying in a pool of water and porcelain shards, residue from the temblor. However, his big, comfortable chairs were undisturbed, a shirt tossed over one of them, a pair of slacks thrown on the other, the paraphernalia of his comfortable, quiet little life.

Bradan knew that Julie was only thirty-seven, but there was a settled look about her that came from a corporate job as a patent attorney and a gourmand's taste for food. On weekend evenings when she was over, fragrances from linguine, calamari, or a dozen other Italian dishes floated out of their home to permeate the complex. He'd miss that intensely. They ate out a lot, too; she kept up on the Bay Area's incessant changes in restaurants and, more often than not, judged well about which ones to visit despite their hyperexpensive prices.

"Staying in your condo?" he asked.

"Moving to the Marina. It's bigger than what I've got. There's a spare bedroom for kids—if I ever have any."

Bradan steered clear of the last remark. "Congrats. Pricey. I'll have to check out your new place."

She smiled slightly. "You're welcome anytime. I got a really good job opportunity. They gave me the offer letter two weeks back so I took a chance on a better home in spite of the insane mortgage."

"Terrific. Moving up was never going to be a problem for you. Want help getting your boxes down to the car?"

"Nope. I got 'em. There's not much."

She walked into the office and hefted a box off the floor then set it down again. "Brad, how do you look good this early in the morning?"

"It's already 9:30," Bradan said. "And actually, I feel pretty drained."

"That's early for Saturday. Look at me."

"Change out of the sweats and you'd be a million bucks."

Julie frowned at the flattery. "Thanks. You've seemed exactly the same during the years that I've known you. What's it been? Seven years? No lines. No weight. No gray hair. You look thirty. Permanently."

"Clean living. You know me, I exercise religiously. When you're not here, I eat raw vegetables and brown rice. Try it. The aging process stops dead. I fantasize about consuming food that will clog my arteries."

Julie ran a hand through her black hair with just a bit of gray, summer touched with autumn. "I've never even seen you sick."

"Broke my arm skiing at Tahoe last January. You were on that trip. I had it immobilized for weeks."

Bradan could be injured or killed as easily as anyone. Two-dozen-odd scars accumulated over the ages testified to his vulnerability; he just never got ill. He'd seen dozens of scourges in his long life: cholera, typhoid, bubonic plague, AIDS, Spanish flu. He hadn't even sneezed. Of the Four Horsemen, he could at least ignore Pestilence. Bradan ran his forefinger over the runic symbols Merlin had inscribed on his wrist visible as a faint pattern of scars. As long as he didn't efface them, he could snub the calendar.

"You do look tired this morning," she said.

His phone rang. What shitty timing. "Hey, Paul. Yep, I'm on the red-eye tonight. I'll get a car from the airport. You'll pick me up instead? Thanks. See you soon."

"I suppose that I shouldn't care at this point since I'm leaving, but who the hell was that?" Julie asked.

"Family in Miami."

"You've said that you had kids from a previous relationship, but you're too young to have a bunch of grown kids. Is that who's in Florida? Your kids?"

"I had them when I was younger." Strictly speaking, this was true. He'd sired them several decades ago when he'd lived in Key West. That would have made him about 1,480 years old at the time. It had been a good marriage until Trini had developed emphysema and died. Lifelong smoking hadn't helped. However, their two sons, Paul and Juan, had both gone on to the University of Florida and reasonably good careers. Their daughter, Juanita, was just finishing a graduate degree in fashion. A father could always want his children to go to better schools and accomplish even more professionally, but he was content with the way things turned out with his latest offspring. Paul himself was married with a young daughter and son, making Bradan a grandfather yet again.

He'd been married and had had families many times over the centuries of his *sui generis* existence. He remembered them all, though as the years and epochs passed, details became hazy for relationships long gone. He'd loved a lot, but the women were dust now with Trini being the latest. It was a lot of baggage to lug around in the recesses of his psyche.

He kept his longevity and the magical side of his life compartmentalized so as to blend in whenever and wherever he lived. The firewall hadn't been breached in fifteen centuries. Initially, women—including Julie—seemed to enjoy the mystery; ultimately they decided he was secretive.

"I'm sure there's a story that you're not going to share," she said.

"I'm not asking you to leave," Bradan said. "I wanted kids, just not yet; the ones I've already got need to get further along in life. I wanted a little space between them and new additions."

"I haven't got years to wait if I want my own."

"I'll miss you," he said.

"I'll miss Tintagel. Also, the view."

"Let's have you look one last time."

They stood together on the balcony.

"Gorgeous as always," he said. "But every time I check, there's some new building screwing up the sight lines. There used to be equilibrium between city and green spaces in the Bay Area, but now the balance has shifted to too much humanity. I wish that I could reverse the clock and dial in more nature."

"You're still a member of Greenpeace?"

"For all the good that it does."

"Ever the cynic."

"I resist that tendency," Bradan said. "Sometimes fighting the good fight is worth it. It wasn't cynical when we both rallied last August at the Transamerica Pyramid."

"To support the carbon tax," Julie said.

"There were the usual tedious speeches, but then someone somehow projected oil company CEO total pay packages tracking exactly with increasing global temperatures on the side of the Transam. The graphics were incredible and big enough that you could see it all over downtown. The crowd went crazy and the mainstream media couldn't ignore it."

"That was fun." She looked out at the city apparently remembering the protest. "Maybe I'll catch you at a march sometime. Don't lose that feisty bit of you."

"Never."

Bradan recalled imagining the juxtaposition of CEO compensation and warming temperatures while he stood amid the crowd. Suiting action to inspiration, he'd quietly mouthed a long string of verses, and the enormous visual effect materialized vividly on the building's white concrete. It must have covered thousands of square meters. Guerilla theater. When he did magic, he let the setting inspire the enchantment like a landscape painter; it was more efficient. Nonetheless, this effort had sucked so much energy out of him that he almost fainted, but the crowd's reaction was worth it.

"After today, you can reprogram the condo not to recognize me." This yanked Bradan back from his reverie. Julie let herself out. "Take care of yourself."

"And you as well," he said.

No parting kiss.

So be it.

This had all happened before.

CHAPTER 3

Folklore for the Forlorn

T he phone rang.

"New Age Counseling." He answered with his brisk business greeting by habit before recollecting that it was Saturday. "Hi, this is Bradan."

"Hey, Bradan, I'm glad I got you. I know it's the weekend and you need time to yourself, but I'm desperate."

"Hi, Danielle." Bradan recognized her voice. This client was always desperate. Hadn't she planned to be in England and Wales for the week attending some kind of conference? He recalled that the symposium would focus on intuitive empowerment. He'd decided to pass on that one. Danielle must have returned early. He wondered if she felt empowered. Certainly, she had no compunctions about bugging him early on a Saturday morning. However, she deserved attention as one of his regular patrons who paid his large fees promptly, more than could be said for many of his clients.

"Glad you're back. Hope you had a good trip to the U.K. What can I do for you today?" He adopted his professionally solicitous voice. Most of his clients expected him to manifest a calm sense of certainty about life in general and their personal problems in particular. The irony was delicious given the unsettled feelings he had about his own circumstances.

"I've been trying to follow your six-step plan for stress-free spiritual healing. It's outlined in one of your books, *Rituals of Healing*. We talked about that last Monday. It's helping, but I still feel upset. Is there something else that we need to consider in planning my meditation?"

"Maybe," Bradan said judiciously. "Advising someone as multifaceted and deeply committed to emotion as you is a complicated effort. In my experience, that process can take many sessions."

"Can we do one of those sessions today? I know it's not a business day for you, but I can pay double your normal hourly fee."

"That's not necessary, but if you insist . . ."

"I do."

"Then come on over to my place."

"Also, I need your help as a mediator," Danielle continued in hushed tones as if someone might overhear. "It's my husband, Dylan. He's been trying self-hypnosis, but it doesn't seem to help him and it's actually been screwing up the concentration that I need for my meditation." She paused. "Also, I think he's seeing someone. He's cheating with some neo-pagan witch—or should I say bitch—half his age. Can we talk, you, me, Dylan?"

"Conflict resolution without conflict is another one of New Age Counseling's services," he said blandly.

"By the way, Bradan, what are you doing tonight?"

"Tonight?" Momentarily he had an eldritch image of being trapped in Danielle and Dylan's ritzy Berkeley Hills home that night as he attempted to cool their marital difficulties.

"It's Samhain," she said.

Bradan winced, partly at her mispronunciation of the archaic

Celtic word, even more because of the memories it evoked. The festival was the traditional end of harvest and the holiday of the dead. The barrier between this world and whatever was on the other side was more porous and, with the right enchantment, omens of the future could be wrested from spirits. Sometimes worse things happened. During the Reformation in Europe, living foxes and cats were burned in bonfires. However, the animals were symbolic substitutes for still older practices. In pre-Christian times, during tribal rituals, men and women trapped in wicker baskets were cast into the flames. After the fires had died away, his people had danced among the ashes. Bradan felt the bonfire's heat, heard the chants, and saw the charred bone fragments mixed in with the burned logs. Halloween, the modern incarnation of old ceremonies, was a pallid festival in comparison.

"What are you up to, Danielle?" he asked.

"I and some friends of mine—Leah, Andrew, Joel, and Robert, we all went wine-tasting with you and Julie last July in Napa—are going to have a little celebration tonight. Dylan is coming, too—without his witch friend. We need to get in touch with something more authentic, find the natural savage within us. I think this will help."

Natural savage, Bradan almost sighed aloud in relief. How much trouble could these people get themselves into, after all? Danielle liked cats so presumably they wouldn't sacrifice anything live. Besides, they didn't know the appropriate rituals needed to invoke something dangerous. He suspected there wasn't much to invoke, anyway. Too much time had passed.

Mostly his clients' belief systems tended toward a benign spirituality that conveniently borrowed elements of folklore and mysticism from disparate global cultures and didn't require too much self-denial. Eating and good wine were cornerstones of their sanctity and the more ceremony and rite, the better. If anything, it was a bit passé, a holdover from the late '60s and '70s; his clients were mostly well into middle age. If he helped them find their true path, then he added value. At least his clients didn't equate piety with acts of terror as much of religion had throughout history.

"You want to join us?" Danielle asked. "I'm leading our annual ceremony to honor Samhain. Do you have anything that we could recite to set the mood?"

This gave Bradan pause. The morning became chillier. "The Celts didn't do a lot of writing," he said. "And never about their rituals. Those were sacred. We . . . they had an oral tradition for such things that even most Celts weren't privy to, just the Druids who were sort of the religious leaders, cultural historians, and teachers before Christianity became common. So, sorry, I can't give you anything to read from."

"Oh well, you sound so knowledgeable. But don't you have some old writing? I thought I saw something in a glass case last time I was over."

"It's just a fragment, very fragile. I keep it as a memento of a former mentor. It's not meaningful to anyone except me. How do you even know about it?"

"I only saw it once. You left it out. It is old, though? Way old?"

"Yep," he admitted. "Just being old doesn't make it enlightening."

"Join us this evening and tell me more. We're planning on docking Robert's sailboat at Angel Island and then finding an out-of-the way spot for the ceremony. We just improvise what we do. Usually, we light a bonfire and do some readings. We always have wine afterward."

"I'm only free this morning. I've got to be at the airport later; I'm flying out for a few weeks to see my . . . a relative." No reason to explain about visiting his grandson. Almost no one—certainly not his clients—even knew he had one. For that matter, he had great-grandchildren, great-great-grandchildren, and great-great-great-grandchildren, too. He looked younger than most of them.

Bradan massaged his temples. "How about you and Dylan drop by my place? We'll have some frank and positive discussions about your relationship. By the way, the Celts pronounced it 'Sow-in.'"

Gently, he clicked the phone off.

CHAPTER 4

Anthem to the Amphetamine Stars

A t dusk, the group of six reached the hill's summit. After trudging up the steep grade, they paused for a moment, out of shape, to admire the sight. This was the highest spot on Angel Island with an unrivaled view of the Bay. Directly west, backlit by the sun's last rose-violet tint, the Golden Gate linked the bulky, brown landmasses of San Francisco and Marin together with a string of lights. The evening's fog pushed into the Bay from the ocean, supporting the bridge's tons on a big pillow.

South of the group, across the water, San Francisco's downtown towers rose above the city's hills. The scene centered on the spiked Transamerica Pyramid's and Coit Tower's softer art deco lines. Lesser structures surrounded them in crowded, grayish-black clusters, turning the city into an enormous primordial forest. Even driven professionals, diligently working late on Saturday, had long since gone home, leaving most buildings dark except for the red warning beacon on top blinking with bloodshot demon's eyes.

In the foreground, Alcatraz sat with the sharp rust and gray outlines of the penitentiary blending into the island's rocks. An observer couldn't separate the hard architecture of man and nature.

North, elegant homes on Marin's hills surrounded Sausalito's and Tiburon's marinas with pinpoints of light. Sailboats and yachts slowly moved a few hundred meters out from the docks in a languid minuet, fireflies on the water's surface. There was no hurry to end the day. The sounds of Halloween partying aboard the boats echoed faintly over to Angel Island. Someone set off firecrackers, and a bottle rocket arched upward from a motorboat and out over the water before splashing into the Bay with a muted hiss.

All this sounded tiny from the hilltop. The six were at once detached and above prosaic holiday rituals. They moved to the center of the hill and stood on a concrete pad that had once been home to a battery of Nike missiles. The Cold War had never become hot and the weapons had been taken away long ago. Weeds broke up the pad. Without its armaments, the hilltop was a fangless old lion unable to defend itself from enemies. Martial hardware had been replaced by wood picnic tables, positioned haphazardly around the concrete. Pine and eucalyptus grew a little distance away, eerie abstracts in the twilight. Their smells wafted over the group.

"Let's get the fire going," Danielle said. "We're early, but why not? It's cold up here."

"I'm concerned about setting the whole island afire," Leah said. "There's a lot of loose pine needles and twigs around, all of it dry."

"That's why we're on this concrete," Dylan said. "And it won't be a big fire."

"It's supposed to be a bonfire," Danielle said.

"Think symbolically," Dylan said. He pulled on his mustache. "The actual size isn't that important."

"A smaller fire would be safer, Danielle," Joel cut in. "No

fighting tonight. I thought Bradan had worked all that out between you two this morning." He glanced at Andrew and rolled his eyes upward.

"How is Bradley?" Leah asked.

"He doesn't like being called that," Danielle said.

"I don't think he cares, given what we pay him in hourly fees. Couldn't he come? Isn't he interested in developing his pagan side? He's so knowledgeable about ancient rituals and faiths."

"He was busy with something," Danielle said. "Going out of town to see family. I'm sure he really wanted to be here, though."

"Firewood?" Dylan said.

"Joel and I will get it," Andrew said. He looked around. "There are a lot more trees on this hill than I expected. Last time I was up here, it was only little scrub pines and brush. These trees are big."

"That means more tinder for us," Joel said. "This feels like the Boy Scouts when I was a kid. Thank God my coworkers at Kleiner Perkins can't see me now." They moved off to the nearby pines, giggling.

"Won't the rangers jump on us for starting a fire?" Robert asked.

"Oh, stop being so cautious," Danielle said. "They're too busy with those kids docked off the marina. This whole island is a park and I don't think alcohol is allowed. They had at least a case of vodka or something. Drugs, too, for sure. They'll be raising hell tonight."

Joel and Andrew came back bearing a little pile of dead branches. Dylan and Danielle arranged it in the middle of the pad. A chill breeze blew intermittently off the Bay, whisking the leaves, needles, and twigs about into little piles, then, dissatisfied with the effect, rearranging them into new patterns. Danielle ignored the wind, pulled a lighter from her pocket, and held it close to the tinder underneath the bigger branches. Within a minute, they had a blaze going. Everyone moved closer. The evening had become cool after sunset. An explosion sounded from the far side of the island.

"You have the parchment?" Andrew asked Danielle.

"God no. Bradan keeps that under lock and key and hidden, too. I don't know where he puts it, but it's in a clear case and it was out this one time today, so I took a picture of it. It's here on my phone."

"Does he know that you have that?" asked Joel.

"No," Danielle said. "I feel a little guilty, but my motives were pure. The parchment has verses about Samhain folklore, I think. Reading them tonight makes our experience more authentic."

"Can I see?" Andrew cut in. Reluctantly, Danielle passed her phone over to him. She was possessive about her new lore. Andrew expanded the screen image. It was a picture of parchment discolored by a hundred stains and with a burned smudge on the left side. It appeared to be a page from the oldest book from the mustiest corner of the city library, but the lettering was legible.

"It's small on your phone," Joel said, looking over Andrew's shoulder. "Can you expand the lettering? This is supposed to have something to do with Halloween?"

"Careful." Danielle pulled the phone away from Andrew.

"It looks old, for sure," Leah said. "But didn't the Celts live way before printing?" The wind wafted back her long brown hair.

Danielle nodded. "You've done your homework. This parchment's evidently a transcription of some kind of oral ritual. Bradan didn't seem too interested in talking about it."

"This is Latin?" Joel said bemusedly. "Who understands that shit anymore? Even Catholic Masses have dropped it mostly."

Leah and Robert moved over to look, too.

"It's a poem in stanzas," Robert said. "Does it rhyme? It seems that it should."

"I know Hebrew, but not Latin," Leah said.

Danielle traced her finger gently down the phone's screen. "I went to a Catholic girls school until high school. My parents forced me to take a language so I picked Latin."

"Does Bradley read it?" Leah asked.

"I guess," Danielle said.

"Are we going to burn some things, too?" Robert asked. "To make the ceremony more true to life."

"We wouldn't burn anything living," Joel said. "We're all vegetarians."

"When did you stop eating meat?" Andrew asked.

"Five years ago."

"I've *never* eaten meat. I don't eat dairy products, either."

"That's good," Danielle said. "That's very good. No. Of course we're not going to burn something living. We're not savages."

She pulled a wicker basket the size of a bread loaf from her backpack. Inside the basket, there were thirteen painted wooden figurines carved into the shapes of various animals including wolves, foxes, bears, and cats. Close up, the carving was embarrassingly crude, but in the fire's shifting light, the little creatures seemed to struggle against their wicker cage.

Wispy puffs of mist nestled up against Angel Island's base. By now, San Francisco, including the downtown towers, had been engulfed in fog. The tips of the temples honoring finance and commerce floated on gray foam as their lower stories were completely hidden. The whole image had become one of massive, dark stone obelisks set into a raw, otherworldly landscape.

As darkness deepened, the surrounding trees hemmed in the missile pad as tightly as a noose, forming a small glade. Across the water, Tiburon had shrunk to a Dark Ages village, while above, a risen moon lit the encroaching trees, casting elongate shadows and, where the fog lay thick, the light created a diffuse, luminous haze. Sounds emanating from the forest's deeper reaches wafted up the hill toward them. At the edge of audibility, distant calls and screams seeped through the big trunks. The sounds evoked remembered times and other places that the trees dreamed of.

"Well, the atmosphere is right," Robert said.

"The trees look funny," Joel said. He stared at the encircling woods.

"Just trees," Dylan said.

"No, look. Mixed in with the pines, aren't those oaks?"

Dylan shrugged, but Leah pointed at a small stand. "I think you're right about the oaks—and that's mistletoe, too. I read that it was an important plant for the pre-Christians. Mistletoe isn't native to Angel Island."

"Really, we've all become botanists?" Dylan asked.

"Maybe they were planted for erosion control," Andrew suggested.

"I didn't see them when we hiked up the hill earlier," Joel said.

"What we'll burn in the fire is only symbolic," Danielle cut in. "But the wood animals *are* made of oak and rowan, which were woods prized by the ancient Britons. I think their priests didn't incinerate living people or animals. That's a modern allegation. It's only nowadays that we've taken to hurting each other with our wars and technology. Things were more peaceful back then."

Everyone in the group nodded.

"Let's gather in a circle around the fire," Danielle said. "Each Halloween we get together to reconnect ourselves with the gentle spiritual pagan that's inside all of us. Modern times have taken that away."

"Amen to that," Dylan said.

Danielle continued, "I try to make these ceremonies as genuine as possible, and this year we have a remnant of those innocent times in the form of the verses from Bradan's early English parchment."

She looked at her phone. "I'll do my best with this Latin. Truth to tell, I didn't read the parchment before taking a picture and Bradan was evasive when I asked what it was about, but he did say that it described rites of that period. He said it was linked to a particular time and place. The rest of you can try to follow along as I call out the words. I'm guessing that the rituals gain strength with more people participating."

She reached down and tossed several sticks into the blaze, sending a shower of sparks heavenward.

"Can your phone project an image of the parchment onto the concrete?" Joel asked. "That would help the rest of us follow along."

"I don't know," Danielle said. "I'll ask it."

"Yes, I can do that," the phone's pleasant, detached female voice said. "Do you really want me to?"

Danielle looked startled. "Yes, I really do. Does anyone else's phone talk back?"

The phone accommodatingly displayed the parchment's tiny screen image enlarged a hundredfold in bluish-white letters on the missile pad. The ancient phrases glowed vividly in the dark.

Danielle began the incantation, awkwardly holding the

phone above her head like a totem angled downward to project onto the concrete.

Andrew couldn't repress a giggle. "She's speaking in tongues," he whispered to Leah who ignored him.

Finding the verse's natural meter, Danielle's words metamorphosed into a chant. Only she understood the Latin, but others began reading along; the spell's alliteration and rhythm had been crafted skillfully and held them all rapt and guided their recitation. Suddenly, they all stopped.

"Feel that?" Leah asked.

"Jesus, a quake." Andrew sounded tense.

"A pretty big one, too," Leah said. The hill under them bucked for several moments, making Joel stumble and sit down heavily on his rump. A branch snapped among the trees and fell to the ground. Then the earth quieted. Leah helped Joel back to his feet and dusted him off.

"We didn't do that, did we?" Joel asked.

Across the Bay, in the city, several fires sprang up as incendiary pinpoints of light among houses in the Marina district.

"I wonder if anyone died," Robert said. "Maybe a gas main blew."

"Hope not," Andrew said.

"Look, besides the fires, there are no lights over in the city or up in Marin," Dylan said. "Power failure."

"We'll go on with the ritual," Danielle said. "The quake won't affect us. Modern culture is *so* dependent on its machines. Right now we've actually got more light and warmth with this fire here than anybody else in the Bay Area."

"It's pretty poetry," Dylan said.

"Now that I'm reading the full text, it isn't exactly what I thought originally," Danielle said. "It's a lamentation for a soul who died too early and a call to that soul to come back."

"Sounds appropriate for a Halloween ritual," Robert said.

"We're halfway through, let's finish," Danielle said. "The words are a conduit to a very particular time in ancient Britain."

She threw the basket with its imprisoned wooden effigies into the fire. The light wicker combusted quickly, but the figurines seemed to take a little longer. They succumbed eventually, though, charring and then burning to charcoal. The group read onward inexorably.

A wisp of dust and pine needles blew out of the trees, creating a diaphanous veil about the group standing on the old concrete pad. The wind fanned the fire, then almost made it gutter, leaving them all in darkness. The men and women shuffled in their sandals and drew their pastel sweaters closer about themselves, but the breeze lasted briefly. The dust fell to earth in disordered piles, and the fire, reinvigorated, bathed the group in a ruddy, cherry glow. However, when their eyes had readjusted to the light, they noticed that two more had joined the group.

Then the killing began.

CHAPTER 5

Highway Low

B radan stopped dead. He tried to identify the feeling that had just wafted across his cerebral cortex. The sensation was akin to having each of his neurons immersed in cool, effervescent liquid, not unpleasant but startling. He looked about him and saw only cars in the San Francisco Airport's parking structure and a distant family laden with luggage waiting for an elevator. The tingling sensation lingered for a moment then faded, to be replaced by recognition: It was the signature of another magician's spell, something so remote in his memory he didn't place it at first. Excepting his own remembrances, the last vestiges of Celtic wisdom and magic had faded shortly after Merlin's demise fifteen centuries ago. Since then, he'd had the planet to himself. He was a lone hiker who'd just seen a distant campfire in a forest known to be deserted.

It was inconceivable that someone could have stumbled onto lost knowledge of this type. Probably it had just been some freakish reflection of one of his own spells.

He found his car jammed between two smaller vehicles. The Tesla Model S was wedged between a Mercedes and a Korean vehicle with bare millimeters to spare between them all. His neighbors were parked at angles forming a wedge too narrow to give him clearance to back out. Maybe their drivers had been rushing for flights. Maybe they'd been assholes.

"Crap." He'd never leave this incredibly cramped spot without damaging the Tesla's paint. He could try to locate the other cars' owners by using plate numbers to have them paged. However, surely they were already in London or Delhi. Now Bradan cursed in Celtic. Modern English simply didn't have the right cadences for true invective. One row over, a car windshield shattered.

Calming himself with an effort, Bradan pondered for a moment then quietly spoke several rhyming stanzas. A frigid breeze cut through the structure, momentarily swirling his hair. The Mercedes on his Tesla's left rolled forward slowly before crunching against a concrete pillar, crumpling its grill and scratching its front body panels. The Korean import to the Tesla's right shoved itself with equal deliberation into a steel structural support. The support crushed a front headlight. Plastic and glass splattered to the pavement.

"Merry Christmas," Bradan said.

He climbed in and leaned against the steering wheel for a moment, recovering gradually. The Tesla's autopilot had already started his car. He'd let it do the driving on the tedious commute over to Oakland; better than magic. The car backed easily out onto the structure's main drive toward the exit. He almost put on a pair of Ray-Ban sunglasses sitting on the dashboard. This was habit; driving the Model S demanded appropriate attire. However, it was too dark today for shades.

Leaving the airport's ensnaring grip, the autopilot began the delicate process of merging onto Highway 101 heading north toward San Francisco and the Bay Bridge to Oakland. Traffic was intense and rain cascaded from the sky, complicating driving further. The rituals involved in commuting about the

Bay Area were every bit as complex as the most esoteric of Celtic magic practiced in lonely forest groves. Now, with a balance of diplomacy and bluff, the autopilot inserted the car between a tractor-trailer emblazoned with the logo of a consumer electronics supplier and a Toyota hybrid. He watched the truck's taillights centimeters from the Tesla's grill and braced himself for the upcoming drive to the East Bay. Visibility in the slate-gray netherworld was limited and surrounding vehicles swam past as half-seen objects in a blurred haze of rain.

Bradan stared ahead and grunted in surprise. Two seagulls flew in formation looking down at the traffic with a raptor's focus. The creatures were huge, with an albatross's wingspan, and seemed oblivious to the downpour. Indeed, they were an integral part of the storm. Given traffic's modest speed, the birds had no trouble keeping up with its flow. The truck's brake lights flared blood-red as traffic slowed to a walking pace. When Bradan looked upward again, he didn't see the birds.

Just behind him, a dented gray van jammed itself in front of the hybrid to sit on Bradan's tail. The hybrid's horn blared, but the rain reduced this to a small bleat. The van now filled the Model S's entire rearview mirror. It lacked both headlights, and the front bumper hung at angle. The vehicle's interior was too dark for Bradan to see the driver. Bradan frowned. He hated having some creep centimeters from his rear bumper, but short of shifting lanes—impossible at the moment—he seemed to be stuck with the son of a bitch.

Forget about it. Bradan consciously relaxed his shoulders and focused on the radio's public news station. While visiting his family, he'd intentionally paid no attention whatsoever to national happenings. Now it was back to a routine and time to catch up.

"Shit." One of the stories described events on Angel Island—some sort of serial murderer had slaughtered five people several weeks ago and the police were evidently making no progress, though the best official thinking had it that terrorism wasn't the motive. Evidently there had been one survivor, who wasn't able to provide usable descriptions of the attacker. The details were lurid but sketchy, just an outline of the butchery. Well, his North Beach neighborhood had always been safe enough. Definitely time to listen to something more relaxing.

"My classical music station," he told the car's autopilot. The Tesla had a reasonably sophisticated chip intelligence, which Bradan appreciated until the Tesla's resident ghost began competing with the autopilot for control of the car.

He drove for a few moments, serenaded by a Chopin piano concerto while 101's cacophony and the downpour beat uselessly against the sleek car's glass and aluminum. The deep upholstery created the perfect acoustics for the light, refined piece. Suddenly, Tammy Wynette's soprano replaced the delicate piano. The radio had spontaneously tuned itself to a country channel.

"Hello, Connie," Bradan said.

"Don't be mad, lover." The voice wasn't really Southern, wasn't quite Midwestern. Bradan guessed it might have originated in Kentucky or West Virginia. A smoky overtone softened the regionalisms; the speaker had loved cigarettes more than anything. Bradan glanced at the radio out of habit. The voice didn't really emanate from any particular location in his car. Just after buying the Model S, he'd suspected the sound system, but he didn't think so now. It just surrounded him, emanating from the vehicle's sheet metal. Odd that the phantom would choose to haunt a modern vehicle; something older, say a '59

Cadillac Coupe de Ville, would have seemed more fitting. He'd have to ask Connie about that.

"It could be worse," the disembodied voice continued. "I could play that modern country crap. That'll really drive you crazy. At least Tammy had something to say."

"Too much to say," Bradan said.

Well, it could *indeed* be worse. The ghost kept the volume down this morning. Also, she wasn't playing her other favorite genre, acid rock from the late '60s for the sheer joy of creating aural anarchy at 110 decibels. In musical matters, a haunted Tesla could be a problematic possession.

"Maybe I'll let you listen to Beethoven later," Connie said. "I just ain't in the mood now after settin' in that cold garage for a month."

"That was Chopin," Bradan corrected.

"Like I care."

Now, the country tune was replaced by Nico's cold vocals drifting over The Velvet Underground's lazy, decadent chords.

The autopilot maneuvered carefully as downtown San Francisco access ramps fed more and still more traffic onto the freeway heading east toward Berkeley and Oakland. It was 10:00 a.m. and vehicles packed the bridge's approaches, drivers staring fixedly ahead. The commute across the Bay Bridge coagulated like blood in a freshly dead corpse. Through it all, the gray van stayed locked to the Tesla's tail. Bradan still couldn't see anything of its driver through the opaque windshield.

"The vehicle behind the car is too close for this speed," the Tesla's autopilot told him in a woman's voice that matched the timbre of his condo's AI. Their tonal similarity made them cybernetic sisters.

Fuck this. "I'll drive," Bradan said.

He spotted a paper-thin gap between two cars in a neighboring lane and stepped on the accelerator. A billion electric horses kicked in sweeping him past the appliance truck, allowing the Model S to merge into the next lane. The surge of acceleration pushed him back into the seat and left the van trapped many cars back in slower traffic.

"What's with that son of a bitch?" Connie asked.

Bradan checked the rearview mirror. "Don't know, but he's gone."

"He was too goddamn persistent for my taste. By the way, the autopilot did a nice job gettin' us out from between those little econoboxes back in parking at the airport. Why would anyone be caught dead riding in one of those things?"

"If it's not a rhetorical question, you can answer that better than me," Bradan said.

"At least I had the sense to be killed in a half-decent car," Connie said. Bradan heard wistful sadness in her tone.

Originally he didn't think he wanted a vehicle. The right spell was all he needed when he had to go somewhere. However, this modern world forced a lot of moving about and he found it taxing to use his arts for routine travel. Perhaps a car was in order after all. It had to be the right vehicle, though. Something high-tech but with soul. He'd found that in spades with the Tesla.

Bradan decided that Merlin would have approved of his choice. That was before the radio spontaneously started playing dated country tunes alternating with reverb- and feedback-drenched psychedelic music.

On the Bay Bridge, he rode along still listening to Connie's selections. Bradan smiled. He reflected that his haunted car didn't really fit into ultra-urban, congested San Francisco.

However, neither did an ancient Briton. He visualized himself in the electric vehicle flying down some deserted, rural two-lane in southern Indiana with an open bottle of Jack Daniel's within easy reach and a loaded .357 in the glove compartment, looking for someone who'd done him wrong. Bradan laughed. The image was so absurd. Instead of handguns, he packed his Rollerblades in the trunk in case he had a spare moment to go skating in Golden Gate Park. Right now, despite obnoxious Bay Area drivers, the tranquility engendered by his vacation still permeated his psyche. Violence was the last thing in the air.

"It must have been nice not having to drive these last few weeks," he said. "With all this rain."

"That parking garage was chilly and there wasn't anyone to talk with while I was recharging. The autopilot is too dumb to have a meaningful conversation. It was cramped, too. I only really feel alive when I'm out driving." Connie chuckled. "Know that must sound crazy, considering what happened to me, gettin' killed in an accident. How was the family in Miami?"

"They're doing well, very well." Bradan thought about the brood he'd sired with Trini Alvarez. Their three children had married within South Florida's burgeoning Cuban-American community. He'd seen them all during his visit, including two days fishing in the Keys.

"Don't it seem strange to any of your kids that you look so young?"

"Nothing gray hair dye and a bit of makeup around the eyes can't fix, but you have a point. That won't work for too many more years."

"What then?" Connie asked.

"I arrange my death and go on with life. My children and grandchildren miss me for a while, then they go on with their lives. I've done it before over the years—many times. There are more bureaucratic details to handle these days, but even the IRS and social security computers can be fooled."

"You must lose count of your families."

"Memory's a funny thing, Connie. I remember them all."

"Memory ain't my friend, either," she agreed. "Where're we goin', anyway?"

"To get my suitcases. I made it to San Francisco, but the bags went to Oakland. If I left it to the airline to get them to me, I wouldn't see my stuff till next summer."

"Service ain't what it used to be," Connie agreed.

"Time to destination is about forty-five minutes given current traffic and weather conditions," the car's autopilot informed him.

"Ah, shut up, computer," Connie told the autopilot. "We'll get there when we get there. Modern technology is crap."

At times Bradan felt that he refereed an argument between Connie and the Tesla's autopilot, though Connie was the real soul of the vehicle.

The Tesla lapsed into silence except for Hank Williams's tenor singing a sardonic counterpoint to his drive. The choice of singers would be deliberate, he thought, cautioning him about life's folly.

He stared through the windshield. They were on the bridge now. The tunnel-like lower deck reminded him of the bowels of an enormous serpent with the bolt-studded heavy girders and I-beams forming the ribs. Rain seeping through from the upper deck perfectly mimicked digestive bile; he and the other cars were the python's latest meal. Unlike the open deck above, there was no sight of the Bay's vistas.

A quartet of bikers blasted past in a burst of dirty thunder, tires slithering on the wet pavement as they zigzagged through the cars. Their noise reverberated gigantically against the bridge's steel superstructure. They were Hells Angels or some other East Bay gang, Bradan guessed. Leather, insignias, and metal bikes, they reminded him of outlaw knights from the Dark Ages.

On the lower deck, everyone, bikers included, was monochromatic. Periodically the wind drove rain between the girders to wash over the vehicles. The predominant color was gray. Even the occasional maintenance worker laboring in the wretched weather had acquired the same hue. The image evoked H. G. Wells' description of a future in which he and the other drivers were Morlocks trudging along through underground caverns.

"What's it like, being dead?" Bradan asked.

"You'd know, too," the ghost responded. "Didn't that Dark Ages witch kill you?"

"Cynbel brought me back in minutes. You've been dead for, what, years?"

For several moments there was silence in the Tesla.

"Being dead's like nothing, nothing at all," Connie said.

Hank Williams broke in again quietly to sing about wounded love accompanied by the warm, antique rhythm of a stand-up bass.

"Sorry I asked," he said.

"It's okay, lover. I'd wonder, too, if I were still alive. By the way, what's it like living fifteen hundred years?"

"Touché," Bradan muttered. "We make a good pair. You died too soon and I've lived rather too long."

"Did I say something wrong? You don't look a day over thirty. I wasn't trying to get back at you. Just curious."

"It's poison. Sometimes you remember much more than you'd want. Especially the parts I wish I could redo."

"Feel the same way," she said. "At least *you* can make amends."

"No I can't," he said. They were about midspan now and passed a station wagon full of kids dressed up for a holiday party as the spirits of Christmas long past. He carefully inspected surrounding traffic looking for the gray van, but didn't see it. Bradan was relieved. *The bastard must be sitting on someone else's tail.*

"Where's Julie?" the ghost asked.

"She moved out before I went to Miami," Bradan said. "Her belongings went with her, so I don't think I'll see her again."

"Small loss," Connie said. "I never liked that gal. Cute, but no sense of humor. Impulsive, too. Who am I to talk, though? That was the story of my life." The voice was a husky, wistful chuckle. "If you want, I'll tell the autopilot to turn the station back to your classical music. It might be a comfort."

"Leave it where it is," Bradan said. "Crying and whining songs are fine right now."

Connie didn't respond. Maybe she held her peace out of respect for his extinct relationship with Julie. Bradan smiled. That would be in character. Whoever she'd been in life, the woman appeared to have seen enough men come and go to feel that even the most worthless fling deserved a few moments of reflection. They drove on with only the radio quietly playing Patsy Cline's "Walkin' After Midnight."

"Want me to drive for a spell?" she asked.

"Kind of you," Bradan said. "You're better than the autopilot, but let's leave it to the Tesla today." Indeed, when he let her, Connie could expertly maneuver through the worst congestion, allowing him to sleep in the back seat. Ironic that the technology of autonomous vehicles had converged with Connie's ghostly, supernatural control over the Tesla.

The Bay Bridge's traffic speed picked up, a massive beast assembled from myriad components, sensing prey ahead. No one could accuse Bay Area commuters of a complacent, relaxed approach toward their sacred highway drives. Bradan reflected that if the atomized, California lifestyle had a collective experience, driving was it. He'd never lived in a time when so many people were so detached from one another. He missed the sense of community from days gone by. Other things he didn't miss.

"I think we're in for a bad patch ahead," the phantom said. The radio turned itself down to allow Bradan to better hear.

"Julie left," Bradan snapped. "I'll get over it."

"That's not what I meant," Connie said. "I can't tell you what to expect, but something bad is coming this way. Just a feelin'."

"You're full of good news today," Bradan said. "I remember too much once in a while. But aside from that and the occasional mild earthquake, life has been pretty uneventful recently. I get along with my grandkids and I'm making money with this ridiculous business of mine."

"Maybe it's nothing, but if I was you, I'd dust off some heavy spells."

The gray van materialized in Bradan's lane, then swept past him and muscled its way back into his lane bare millimeters in front of him, close enough to almost tear the Model S's bumper off. The van's back end loomed as large as a barn door before him. Bradan clearly saw its many dents and scratches, indicating the driver customarily commuted this way.

"Shit," Bradan snarled.

"You are too close to the vehicle ahead of you for this speed," the Tesla's autopilot noted. Connie snickered at this prudent guidance.

He tightened his grip on the wheel and momentarily considered leaning on his horn. The Tesla, whatever its flaws, could sound a massive, blaring honk, which usually bullied even the stupidest motorist into submission. This time he decided against it.

A sticker on the back of the van notified the world that Smith & Wesson insured the vehicle's possessions. Its driver must pack a 9mm in the glove compartment. During yesterday evening's commute, someone over in Oakland blew a man away with a shotgun during a traffic altercation. Driving on the Bay Area's massive freeway system bore a remarkable resemblance to travel along the muddy dirt paths in the forests near Glastonbury. In his youth, Bradan knew of men who'd had their heads chopped through to their chins over a few simple belongings. To hell with the van. He slowed to let the distance grow between the vehicles.

"What's the matter, lover?" Connie asked. "You gonna let him get away with that? How much of a magician are you?"

"Connie, I'm too old, much too old, to have my masculinity challenged over some traffic squabble."

"But it did make you mad, right? That's why you held the wheel tighter."

"I can't slip anything past you," Bradan said.

Suddenly, the van ahead braked hard. Bradan stomped on his own brakes and yanked the electric car to the right while jerking his head about to see if the neighboring lane was clear. The Tesla skidded on the wet asphalt and the rear slewed sideways for a second before regaining traction. The seat belt kept him from being hurled about. Adrenaline hit Bradan's brain and his

66 PETER W. BLAISDELL

breath shortened. Barely in control, he shot past the van on its right, just missing a red Mustang convertible, top up in the rain, and a tractor-trailer. Bradan had an ephemeral sensation of the trucker leaning out his window to swear at him.

Now ahead and two lanes to the right of the van, Bradan watched in the rearview mirror as it surged after him, crossing intervening lanes and accelerating to close the distance, a great white shark zooming in on a seal. Bradan floored the accelerator only to find this escape route blocked by the befuddled Mustang driver who, paralyzed with fear, had dropped his speed to forty miles per hour.

Bradan put the Tesla in Ludicrous Mode, which meant that he had crazy speed on tap and could outrun the van easily, but the gaps in traffic weren't large enough for him to break into the open where he'd have the advantage.

"Get the fuck out of the way!" Bradan yelled.

"You are too close to the vehicle ahead of you for this speed."

"Shut up. Autopilot, set your volume to zero."

He still hadn't seen anything of the van's driver.

"That guy's trying to hit us," Connie screamed.

Bradan now had enough clearance to pass the Mustang on the left. Angling sharply to avoid two other cars, he raced the Model S up to ninety miles per hour trying to outrun his attacker while zigzagging through traffic. He leaned on the horn. The van zipped after him, grazing a white sedan that spun out of control to collide with a pickup, sending both vehicles into the guardrail, all that separated them from a sixty-meter fall to the Bay below.

"Let's see if we can distract the fucker!" Bradan shouted. He was doing over one hundred now, tires maintaining cat's grip even in the rain, but then he had to slow, confronted by a wall of cars dead ahead.

The quartet of bikers he'd seen a few minutes before, evocative of ancient knights, gave him an idea. Traffic on the bridge was dense, but nothing was immediately behind him as other vehicles scrambled to stay away from the maniacs in the Tesla and the van. Excellent. Bradan didn't want to involve any more bystanders than he could help. He spoke several verses in Celtic as the van veered sharply toward him again.

"Goddamn—look out!" the Tesla yelled. "Can't you do something?"

Bradan accelerated then hammered the brakes to avoid his careening attacker, who had managed to close the distance between them to a few meters. Wasn't his spell going to work? At first nothing happened and he wondered if he'd bungled the enchantment's meter. However, some instinct made him check his rearview mirror. Far back, almost hidden among massed traffic in the bridge's gloom, a faint object appeared, rapidly closing on him and the van. The object resolved itself into a figure on horseback looking almost as metallic as the girders and riding like Death pursued him. Cars and a tractor-trailer swerved aside to avoid the rider. The tractor-trailer's driver braked hard to avoid the horseman, and the whole rig slewed sideways. The normally ultra-aggressive Bay Area drivers didn't honk at the apparition as it galloped past, the horse's hooves striking sparks on the asphalt and metal of the bridge's roadway. Amazingly, the knight had no trouble overtaking traffic speeding at sixty-five miles an hour.

Bradan saw that the rider was a mounted warrior with a circular shield emblazoned with abstract Celtic symbols. However, it wasn't a purely decorative element of the rider's gear, as gouges and several deep dents marred its metallic surface. The warrior himself was large, covered to the knees with a chain-mail hauberk and wearing a Roman helmet with hinged guards extending down to his chin. His eyes were visible and focused on the van. The knight leveled his lance.

The warrior deftly skirted Bradan's interposed car and pulled up beside the driver's window of the van. The knight raised the lance to ram his weapon's steel tip through the window. The van driver must have seen the apparition, because his vehicle jerked away from the horseman and instantly lost control, swerving sideways to slam into the bridge's side railing with a crash. Bradan yanked the Tesla's wheel hard left to avoid the rebounding wreck. The horseman also nimbly skipped past the careening van, which executed a 180-degree turn before hitting the railing again and coming to a grinding halt pointing backward amid a shower of sparks.

"Ah, Gawain, ever the courteous knight to a man in need; I apologize for calling you forth for such a modest deed," Bradan said.

Now riding in front of the Tesla, effortlessly pacing Bradan at seventy miles an hour, the warrior turned in his saddle and saluted Bradan with his lance, then galloped ahead through traffic, gradually becoming more diaphanous until he vanished.

Bradan paused a moment in respect. "Rest easy," he breathed.

Connie let out a rebel yell of glee. "All right, sugar, you showed that asshole in the van. He's got a *long* fuckin' way to walk."

Bradan inhaled deeply several times to catch his breath. He held on to the steering wheel for support, trying to keep the electric car in its lane. The Tesla's interior had become hot and he lowered the window, ignoring the spray of rain that splashed inside the car. The silence following the collision was stunning.

"Parlor games," he whispered.

"Was the horse guy real?" Connie asked.

"No. It was a trick of the light. The image couldn't have thrown a real lance at the van."

"Well, it worked," she said.

"The van didn't realize it was all bluff. I'm just a conjurer. The really heavy stuff is beyond me."

But he felt the old exultation of magic when he used it for vengeance. That was always best.

"That shit seemed after us personally," Connie said.

"That he did," Bradan answered. The bastard had been on his tail since he'd left the airport. So who was he? Bradan couldn't remember doing anything to provoke such intensely vengeful ire from anyone. Occasionally, a client argued over a bill, but violence was beyond what most of them were capable of. Anyone truly angry with him usually resorted to lawsuits, not murder. Besides, he'd been out of town for almost six weeks—surely long enough for hard feelings, if any existed, to cool.

"You gonna tell the cops?" Connie asked.

Bradan thought for a moment. His breathing began to return to normal.

"They'll get him, assuming he survived the crash." More pragmatic thoughts seeped into his considerations. He'd just been a party, albeit entirely innocent, to a potential vehicular manslaughter charge. Several cars had crashed because of his evasive maneuvers. All things considered, he'd be lucky to stay out of prison and avoid expensive court fights, let alone keep his driver's license, unless he could clearly establish what had happened.

He was across the Bay now and the bridge's five lanes debouched into the rain and leaden sky with some cars swinging north toward Berkeley and others south toward Oakland, San Leandro, and Fremont.

"Someone must have reported our plate number to the highway patrol," Bradan said. "We don't have a choice about calling this in."

Besides, as sick as the son of a bitch who had just tried to kill him no doubt was, he didn't deserve to lie untended in the middle of the rainy bridge. Bradan reached into his sport coat pocket for the phone, then realized it was dead and he'd left the charger with the rest of his lost baggage.

"There's an emergency phone just over there on the right side," Connie said helpfully. "See that antique-looking yellow box at the side of the road?"

"Do you want me to call 9-1-1 on your car phone?" the Tesla's autopilot piped in.

_____

A police car pulled up close behind the Tesla, its blue, orange, and red lights flashing surreally in the storm. Bradan watched rain bounce off the vehicle, enveloping it in dense mist as the rebounding drops met the falling ones. The cop inside must have debated hard about whether to undergo the soaking that a brief dash between the two cars would subject him to. Finally his door whipped open and a rain-coated figure emerged to bolt over to the passenger side window. Bradan already had it half lowered.

"You're Bradan? I'm Officer Lopez."

"Yeah. I called in about fifteen minutes ago. Here's my license."

The tall policeman looked him over, clearly trying to judge what sort of risk Bradan might pose. Bradan guessed that what had just transpired on the bridge must have been sketchy to the cop; who had done what to whom? Other drivers must have phoned in confused versions of two vehicles playing high-speed bumper car on the lower deck and wild references to an armored horseman glimpsed in the downpour. Was Bradan the perpetrator?

"Why don't you come on over to my car so I get out of the rain? I need some information about what happened back there." He nodded toward the bridge. The lower deck yawned like a dark maw.

Bradan spent the next half hour describing the chase. He didn't mention Gawain. Periodically, other cops pulled up to check out Bradan and the Tesla, confer with Lopez, and then roll off into the storm. One took several pictures of his car.

"Who was driving the van?" Bradan asked.

"Don't know. It was empty when we got to it."

"Self-driver?" Bradan asked.

"Don't think so. The van's too old to be set up for that. Had to be someone at the wheel, a person. They'll see who it's registered to and check up and down the bridge. Maybe the driver wandered off. It happens when people are stunned after an accident. It's also possible some Good Samaritan picked him up and took him in for medical treatment and we just haven't heard about it yet. Somebody'll check local hospitals and clinics. Miracle of miracles, it seems no one else was hurt."

"Could the van driver have been thrown over the edge?"

Lopez shrugged. "Sure. I saw the van and it was pretty crunched. It must have been doing eighty when it hit the railing. Lucky the gas tank didn't go up. Maybe the guy went through the windshield."

"Long way down," Bradan said.

"Long way down," the cop agreed. He picked up his radio and talked for a minute with someone Bradan guessed was a dispatcher, who relayed his question to other cops back on the bridge with the van's wreckage.

"The windshield was partially crushed, but intact—no holes big enough for someone to have been thrown through." Lopez laughed. "Maybe they just got out and walked away. We'll check your theory, though. They'll have the Coast Guard— or maybe it's SFPD's Marine Unit, or Oakland's, whoever has jurisdiction—take a look."

"Any blood inside?" Bradan asked. He listened to rain on the car's roof like someone was at work on it with a jackhammer.

"Find out on the news. I don't know myself." It was plainly time to reestablish who was questioning whom here. "Did you see a horse?"

Bradan was expecting this one, but played dumb. "Horse?"

"Yeah. At least a dozen people thought they saw some guy maybe carrying a spear, on a horse, running around when the van bought it."

Bradan laughed with as much genuine mirth as he could muster. "No. I was trying to avoid the van. I saw lots of cars, but no knights."

"Knights? Did I say that?" the cop asked.

Come on. Bradan looked at the policeman. What was Sherlock trying to probe for?

"A man on a horse with a spear," Bradan said. "Isn't that a knight from a bedtime story? Why? What did people on the bridge think they saw?"

"Who the fuck knows? Yeah, some said it was a knight. A trucker thought it was like Robin Hood or *Game of Thrones*. Most of them didn't know what they saw in all the rain. You just filled in the blank pretty quickly."

Bradan shrugged. "You mentioned the spear." He patted his

wet hair. He needed to get his suitcases and go home to a warm shower.

"Officer, how else can I help you today? That nutcase in the van tried to kill me. You said the other witnesses agreed with my version of what happened. Here's my phone number on the business card. I've lived in the city for years, so I'm not running off if you need more questions answered. I'm already bracing myself if insurance investigators from the other drivers contact me. I'd be happy to help insurance, the police, whoever—though if it gets really hot and heavy, I'll ask my lawyer to sit in, but right now I've got lost bags coming into Oakland Airport and then I want to get back to my condo, dry off, and recuperate with a vodka tonic or maybe just vodka and no tonic."

"Sure. We can find you if we need to. Don't speed and keep a weather eye out."

CHAPTER 6

Voices from Past Futures

Near the surf's edge, eight kids sat on beach towels in the sand around a driftwood bonfire that barely kept Ocean Beach's dense nighttime fog—almost a falling mist—from freezing them all. The sun had set hours back. A bottle of tequila made the rounds, supplementing the fire's warmth. Someone smoked a joint. A few other fires, orange pinpoints of light kilometers down the seashore, provided far distant company for the kids on the empty stretch of sand.

"Look," said a girl in a sand-smudged UC Berkeley sweatshirt.

"Why?" asked the guy sitting beside her. He took a long pull on the bottle.

"In the water, right there."

"Son of a bitch. They must be cold. And stupid."

Now everyone saw them. With hardly a splash, two figures emerged from among the breakers moving directly toward the little group.

"Fucking cold night for swimming . . ." The boy's taunt locked in his throat as the intruders moved right on into their circle, no sense of personal space here. One of the visitors spoke a few rhyming words that immobilized the kids like they'd all been injected with a paralytic. There was a precise choreography to what came next: hacking ax blows to the base of the skull, followed by garroting, which crushed the windpipe and snapped the spinal cord. Finally, a knife slash across the neck facilitated maximal bleeding.

Before leaving, one of the two visitors, maybe as an afterthought, casually scrawled a few symbols in the sand.

———

A cathedral of California redwoods filtered the morning's sunshine down to the forest floor, where a huge, sawed-through stump made a perfect altar amid the pine needles. The man screamed as he watched his wife cut up and screamed louder still as the kids met the same fate. He had little voice left when his own turn came. Muir Woods' gothic-scale trunks distorted and deadened sounds and the needles and dirt soaked up the blood.

———

"Bradan, they murdered them all. They're after me, too." The words poured out of the answering machine in a torrent. "Dylan's dead. I saw them pull a rope tight around his neck. He has to be. I looked back as I ran. Leah, maybe Robert, too—all of them. Leah had her throat cut open. I saw her vertebrae. They had a bowl underneath to catch the blood. I think they threw someone in the fire alive—I heard screams as I ran. They did it, I couldn't believe it." The speaker paused, breathing hard.

Bradan stood next to his answering machine, stunned. He'd just gotten out of the shower and stood with only a towel on, listening to the dozens of messages accumulated during his long holiday. He hadn't checked once during his vacation, hadn't answered his cell phone. His home was a frozen meat locker. The condo knew his travel schedule and had turned the heat on hours before he arrived, but this hadn't yet driven away six weeks of damp cold and it appeared that it never would. The living room's icy hardwood floor chilled his bare feet.

Bradan looked out the windows. It was nighttime and rain still cascaded down, running in thick rivers on the glass, driven by surges of wind. A bright desk lamp poured white light onto the answering machine, interrogating it for more details. Aside from this pool of cold brilliance, the room was dark. Shadows hid Bradan's clothing lying in a sodden pile in the middle of the floor where he'd left them before rushing to the shower. His luggage sat in an unopened heap beside the clothing. The room's sole festive element was Claire's gold-and-red-wrapped early Christmas present that she'd thoughtfully left on Bradan's kitchen counter awaiting his return. He'd open this later.

"Call me! Get over here, for God's sake, if you haven't left town already," the answering machine resumed. Then a brief dial tone sounded before his answering machine cut that off like a guillotine.

Tintagel scrambled to his feet and made a sound between a growl and a howl.

"Quiet," Bradan whispered to the animal. The call was no prank. Something truly bad must have happened, based on the wolf's reaction to the caller's tone. Was it Danielle? He hardly recognized her voice; she'd tried to whisper and scream at the same time. Wherever she had called from seemed to echo her voice from the inside of some cavernous bunker.

Tintagel stood shivering near Bradan's leg. Absently he patted the animal. He'd never seen him so clingy.

"You must be flying." The second message floated through his condo. "I've tried calling the police and the park rangers. I

pray to God that they'll get to me before those crazies do."
The line went dead again.

Bradan replayed the two messages. The caller was Danielle. Her terror came through even more palpably on a second listening. Bradan also noted that she'd abandoned her agnosticism. Her repeated petitions for the Christian God's intervention sounded strange from a woman who'd professed devotion to a natural, New Age theology without a single paternalistic god. Whatever she'd seen had shaken her faith to its core.

Bradan looked at the calls' times and dates dutifully logged in by the machine. They'd both been received on November 1, the first at 12:40 p.m., the second a few minutes later. Was she still alive? He tried to remember what he'd last talked about with Danielle, some sort of plans for a Samhain ceremony on Angel Island delving into folklore, in search of their inner pagan.

He fast-forwarded through the rest of the calls, nonemergency client issues, an overdue bill, and a call from Claire checking in. Nothing else from Danielle until he got to a message from a male caller.

"Mr. Badon? My name is Jack LaPlante. I'm an attorney and we have a mutual client, Danielle Pomeroy. I gather from your message you won't be back in the Bay Area until December 12, but in case you're checking communications while you're gone, please give me a call. Danielle is in some serious trouble and has asked me to represent her."

Bradan called Danielle's number but got no response, not even voice mail. The phone just rang and rang. He'd ignore the lawyer until Monday morning. What the fuck was happening?

"Claire, it's me, Bradan." He knocked softly again. The hall outside her place was dark. Bradan looked up to check that the light fixtures functioned. They did, but their illuminations seemed vitiated by the cold, dank air that filtered into the building from the deluge outside.

Indistinctly, he heard steps padding closer. Then the door was opened exactly the length of its short security chain and Claire peered cautiously out. She looked him over carefully before softening slightly in recognition.

"Hi, Bradan. Glad you're back. You want your mail."

"I'm not waking you?" Through the slit, he saw the collar of her bathrobe. Her black hair brushed it.

"It's okay. I was about to go to bed, but come on in for a second." Claire smiled briefly, the corners of her mouth twisting in self-deprecation upon realizing that the door created an impregnable barrier to any such invitation.

"With all this crazy shit happening, it's good having you back in the building," she said. "I was in your place a few times for the dog. Everything seemed fine. Did you get my present?"

He nodded. The door closed briefly to allow her to disengage the chain, then swung wide open. Claire stood with the robe pulled tightly around her body against the hallway's chill.

Had she just stepped out of the shower after washing away the day? He inhaled soap and felt moisture in the air. Her hair was damp.

"How are you doing?" he asked, thinking Claire looked in control but tense. "I guess there have been problems while I've been gone."

"Out in Miami, you didn't hear about any of the killings here?"

"It was a vacation. I didn't watch the news, didn't check any messages, answered no calls. I spent time down in the Keys with my relatives." Damn, he'd almost slipped and said "grandson." What would Claire say to that? No gray hair, no wrinkles, but he had a twenty-two-year-old grandson.

"We caught a marlin, almost trophy size, off Key Largo."

"You schedule your vacations well," she said. "We've had crappy weather here in the city." Claire crossed the room and peeked out between the curtains. "The window is leaking around the edges." She touched the pane. "It's been coming down hard for days. With all this weird stuff going on and the weather, my nerves are shot. I'm installing another deadbolt." She walked toward her kitchen. "Listen, what can I get you? Tea? Something stronger?"

"Tea would be good."

A little apartment-sized Christmas tree stood in the corner beside the window. Claire had scattered a few wrapped presents beneath it. However, despite pretty decorations and candy canes, the pine wasn't a pleasant, seasonal tradition tonight. Instead it intruded into the living room as a reminder of a time when Christmas was a patina devised by the early Christian church attempting to co-opt and pacify a hostile wilderness with its deep-rooted, midwinter, barbarian rituals.

As Claire moved into the kitchen, Bradan looked around. Quaint old habits, books, she'd put them almost everywhere in the stylish but cramped little living room with bamboo hardwood floors. Though they'd been neighbors for a long time, he'd never seen the inside of Claire's place. There were plants and pictures here, too, most apparently of her relatives, a large Chinese family with brothers and sisters, aunts and sour-looking uncles all clustered about the mother and father, the center of this little universe. Bradan had seen many boring mementos of domestic bliss. However, these were shot with a clear artistic sensibility that individualized each person while capturing the group's changing circumstances over time. The same aesthetics guided her choice of plum-colored, lacquered-wood picture frames.

"I took them all," Claire remarked, now back in the living room with two cups. She set them down on a low Danish modern coffee table strewn with accounting texts and, incongruously, a massive Russian novel. He couldn't quite see the author's name, Turgenev? Claire watched him look over her home, then sat down opposite him on a charcoal-black couch that contrasted with her frost-white bathrobe. The robe wasn't quite thick enough to cover her nipples' impressions in the soft fabric. Embarrassed at his wandering attention, Bradan picked up the tea.

"Do you have a gun?" she asked.

"Do I need one?"

"Maybe. I've thought about buying one the last few weeks. Crazy. I'd always thought they were for right-wingers."

Claire handed him a tablet. "Check this CNN story. It started with some killings on Angel Island last Halloween, but that just got things going."

Bradan scanned the news summary.

"Who's Cynbel?" Claire said. "Am I saying the word right? Is it a name?"

"What?" Bradan was startled by the suggestive effect the network's news accounts had produced in him. Intuition and memory had filled in missing details and saturated the images with gory color. He put the tablet on the coffee table.

Danielle's phone message had a context now. The priests would need ritual killings to fuel their powers for whatever grander purposes they intended. He stopped this train of thought in its tracks. Why did it have to be Cynbel and Aennati? Danielle had mentioned two people in her hysterical phone messages. She hadn't described them. How could his client and her bunch of friends have brought back the priests? His parchment was the only source for a resurrection ritual, and he was almost certain that he'd put the case in his safe before traveling. For added security, the Lucite covering was bulletproof; no one could get at it. He'd never even transcribed the parchment's wording into his computer's library of spells.

"You said 'Cynbel,'" Claire repeated. "Or something close to it, and then you said another name, 'Aennati'?"

Bradan collected himself. "Just mumbling. I don't watch enough media to be hardened to this kind of shit. Whoever this killer is, they really seem to be into ceremony."

"He—or they—sound completely psycho."

"I take it stories on the Net or TV haven't been very informative?"

Claire nodded. "My guess is the cops don't want copycats." She sipped her tea. "They killed twelve people in just a few weeks."

"Seventeen, if you count what happened on Angel Island." Bradan stared at the curtained window for a minute, hearing the rain batter it. It was all hideous, but it wasn't Cynbel and Aennati.

"Other stupid crap has happened, too. A whole family died in the Marina on Halloween night, but that was because a gas main ruptured in the quake and blew up near a townhouse. No connection to the killings. Please, let's talk about something else."

"Thanks for the present," he said. "Haven't opened it yet." The murders made exchanging silly little gifts seem a mindless holiday banality. However, Claire brightened noticeably.

"That's okay," she said. "It's before Christmas."

"I got distracted listening to my phone messages, but if this is a good time for you, I'll bring it down now. In fact, we'll trade. I picked up something for you in Florida." He was gratified to see that Claire looked intrigued.

"I'll get Tintagel. He doesn't want to be alone."

"Bring him. He's the kind of friend we need right now."

Back up in his room, Bradan entered his office. The parchment sat in its case on his desk. He hadn't returned it to the wall safe before leaving for Florida. He'd been in a rush to pack. So what? Danielle and her husband had possibly seen the text when they visited him on Halloween, but they wouldn't have known what it was or how to use it. The text was mostly Latin with some Celtic symbols. Even assuming that one of them read Latin, the Celtic would have baffled them. He locked the case in his safe.

However, his world was now more uncertain.

"Was anyone in the office between the first of November and the twelfth of December besides me or Tintagel?" he asked the condo.

"No."

"How about on Halloween?"

"Several individuals. Julie and two of your clients."

Bradan sat on the edge of his desk thinking. Julie had only been in the office for moments as she gathered her stuff. He'd been with her and she hadn't evidenced the slightest interest in the parchment. On the other hand, Danielle and her husband were fascinated by folklore and the occult. They could have examined the parchment, but even armed with the spell, they would have had to butcher people to make the words effective. No, it seemed certain that a pair of modern serial killers knowledgeable about pagan rites stalked the Bay Area. Maybe they got off on leaving obscure symbols scattered about the killing grounds. That was horrible but believable. Modern times spawned monsters. Danielle and her friends had had the ghastly misfortune to run into some of them during their excursion to Angel Island.

Bradan rummaged around in his suitcases for Claire's gift. He remembered that picking it out hadn't been easy. Choosing a present meant making judgments about her preferences and also deciding how he felt about her. Did he really know her well enough to get her perfume? Besides, maybe she didn't wear it. Clothing was a rather personal selection, too. He'd ultimately settled on a delicate sketch of the Everglades by a local Cuban-American artist. This choice, too, seemed to be a gamble, though he liked the picture a lot himself. However, after seeing Claire's home, defined by its books and framed photographs, he decided he'd guessed well.

"Bradan, it's wonderful! It'll go right there." She pointed over the couch. "That's about the last spot where I've got wall space left. Tell me how you got it."

Bradan described the Boca Raton gallery where he'd purchased it with more enjoyment than he expected, and the next hour passed pleasantly. He worked consciously to push aside thoughts of slaughter.

"Let's have a look at what you've gotten me. I love presents. Guess I'm a perpetual kid." He tried to repress the irony.

He pulled the wrapping paper off her gift to reveal a small tin of tea and an hourglass.

"It's a special blend my father created," Claire explained. "It's kept him and my mom healthy just about forever."

"And the hourglass?" Was time running out?

"It's for creating the perfect cup of tea. Brewing has to be timed to the microsecond. There's exactly the right amount of sand and no more in the chambers."

"What kind of tea?"

"It's part of the oolong family. This one translates to the Iron Goddess of Mercy. I can ask Dad for more if you enjoy it. My mother and father owned a store on Stockton Street in Chinatown. The two of them sold herbs and traditional medicines until they retired last year. I think half the old folks in the neighborhood use the tea blends my father imported. That's why there are so many old Chinese still running around the city. Better than the fountain of youth."

"I could use a slug of that tea—and the more rejuvenating, the better." Bradan collapsed into a kitchen chair. "God, it's good to sit down."

His phone rang.

"Yeah," he said, willing it to be harmless, a marketing call or Julie gloating about her new condo.

"Bradan? Am I speaking to Bradan? Bradan, it's Danielle. I needed to talk to you. Didn't you get my calls? You dropped off the earth when I needed you. You won't believe what happened. I wanted that night on Angel Island to be good, but it wasn't. Not at all."

CHAPTER 7

Finding Fault

The earth heaved under the Druids, a bull goaded by an electric prod. The nascent quake beneath San Francisco produced a deep, subliminal rumbling that made the air itself vibrate. In harmony, Cynbel and Aennati chanted the rhymes required to coax the rocks beneath San Francisco to release the grinding tectonic tension that had built along the region's several major and countless minor faults. In the city, people struggled to keep their footing as the ground bucked. Balance unaffected, the priests stood atop the north hill of Twin Peaks Park that overlooked Market Street and the dense clusters of glass towers three hundred meters below. Low clouds whose color matched Cynbel's robe filled the sky. In the city center, tall palaces swayed with the tremor's force and sheets of glass popped out of their frames to plummet like meat cleavers to the streets. Older buildings fared worse as the mortar gluing bricks together crumbled. In the Marina district, with unmatched views of the Bay but built on sand and landfill, foundations gave way. One posh three-story row house collapsed into itself with an explosion of dust, stucco, and plywood. The whole city would splinter if the quake continued.

Rhythmic Celtic phrases followed one another inexorably

with the emphasis precisely on certain syllables. The contrapuntal pattern was as complicated as the most elaborate Baroque fugue with the rumbling earth playing the basso profundo. The priests' enchantment irritated seismic forces in the same way that a nettle deeply buried in a silvertip grizzly bear's hide would provoke it to explode. Heat built up as titanic, impacted masses of stone grated together.

Over the Druids, hawks, gulls, ravens, and other birds swirled in giant circles, wings fluttering, but otherwise they didn't utter a sound. The flock seemed to hold its collective breath waiting for disaster on the ground below. However, the momentum toward a rupture in the Earth's crust slowed, then stalled completely as the tremor quieted. The quake was stillborn. Status quo ante.

Cynbel and Aennati collapsed into the grass on the hill overlooking the city they'd almost dismembered. Above them the birds dispersed, a puff of dandelion-down blown by a child. Paying no attention to the priests a little way away, sightseers enjoyed the vistas from an overlook on the park's south peak and laughed at calamity averted and resumed buying souvenirs from vendors and posing for pictures with the city and Bay in the background. Directly below the peaks, there was a hushed moment, then San Francisco noisily set about picking up after the quake. A lone siren floated over the commotion, but shortly many others joined it. Several converged on a darkening column of smoke rising above the Mission District's packed housing, where a punctured gas line had ignited.

"We have to be stronger to make this happen," Aennati said. She dabbed sweat off her forehead with the edge of a sleeve blotched with blood from killings. The stains hardly showed against the garment's earthen hue.

"Obviously," Cynbel said sarcastically. He reclined full length against the hillside. Brilliant yellow buttercups grew around him.

"The city should have splintered—it's sitting on top of a dragon's spine," he said. "We called out the spell and we sacrificed to make it potent. We'll kill more to give it the force it needs."

"People to sacrifice are easy to find," the priestess said. "It's a crowded age. We only have to take care not to be noticed. Before sacrificing her, I talked to the girl on the beach in her own language to understand a little of this strange place that we've come to. Merlin and Arthur are fairy tales and we're less than that—no one remembers us."

"We were leaders past and we will be again," Cynbel said.

A breeze deferentially stroked Aennati's hair, long, slightly wavy, and the color of obsidian. The priestess looked down at the city seeing a landscape already barren of humanity.

A family of tourists on a nearby hill waved at the priests. Cynbel waved back.

"All this metal and glass, so vastly larger than Londinium," he said.

"It's too big to be understood," she said.

"They don't understand what they've made themselves. You could think of it as magic, but it's not. They've only left tame, civilized patches of green. Where are the trees and rivers? Is there any room for animals? Even the rainwater we drink is brackish. They've put buildings and roads on top of places that should be shrines to the wild. How do people stay close to their souls?"

The hill shuddered in an aftershock. The ground was still nauseous from the priests' ministrations.

"There is no place for sacred moments." Cynbel pointed at the buildings. "After the Earth shakes all this away, there will be."

He picked a single buttercup and whispered a few words. Now he held a small circle of yellow flowers in his hands with their long stems interwoven to form a tiara. He placed it on Aennati's head.

"Queen of the Bay," he said.

The priestess inclined her head to acknowledge the honor. "It's a dirty realm."

On the water near the Bay Bridge, five ships floated, fat ducks surrounded by smaller vessels. Oil leaked from one of them, creating a spreading black pool. A lighter, iridescent sheen covered the water beyond the main body of oil. Cynbel and Aennati stared at the mess.

"That boat has fouled the water for days," Cynbel said. "There are smells in the air that are wholly unnatural. If we don't create a big quake soon, there won't be anything to save." He heaved himself to his feet and stretched. His cloak streamed out behind him in the wind.

He looked to the south. In the far distance, a pall of smoke rose from the horizon to the sky.

"Is that us? No, we didn't do it. It started before we created the quakes."

"Their forests are burning," Aennati said. "Rains haven't stopped the fires; the drought lasted too long."

"They've changed the very weather."

"Bradan?" Aennati asked.

"We should thank him for inadvertently having his followers bring us back," Cynbel said. "That was not his intention."

"He wrecked *our* plans once. He can do it again."

"He has no Merlin to help him. Murdering him will be easy. We found him effortlessly yesterday when he used a spell. We almost got him on the big bridge. It was inventive to revive

Gawain's shade to divert the attack, but luck won't help him again. All he can do is small magic."

"Do you think he's realized that we tried to kill him?"

Cynbel shrugged. "We disguised the attack to fit this modern realm, but he may suspect. It wasn't hard to find a tool for the purpose. Angry people fighting the world are as common now as they were in our time. All we had to do was manipulate the mind of the man in the vehicle to hate Bradan."

"There were several quakes recently that we had nothing to do with," she said. "But Bradan will notice that the biggest happen coincident with magic. He'll realize that enchanters are culpable. We should remove him."

"You detest him," the priest said.

Aennati wound a strand of her hair around one finger and pulled hard enough to make the hair almost disappear into her flesh.

"However we do it, save your energy," Cynbel said imperturbably. "We waste sacrificial bloodletting when we deploy magic frivolously. Use the local setting for tools and inspiration; it saves effort. Our strength is for vital things. This place could be perfect, but it will take everything from us to purify it. That's the big victory. Bradan is a fly."

"He was the reason we died once and it's urgent to execute him now," Aennati said. "This place has forgotten magic and there are no Druids to teach them. They can't imagine a threat like us, but Bradan can. It's an organized kingdom. They resemble Romans. Soldiers or authorities visited each of our killing grounds not long after we left. They stayed for days inspecting the remnants. Once Bradan realizes for certain that we're here, he'll alert them and they can impede our plans. In his mind he'll redeem himself for betraying Merlin by stopping us."

Cynbel nodded. "He has a conscience so he's predictable. There is another reason to find him: he has the incantation that brought us back. His followers must have gotten the spell and used it on Samhain."

"Why would they have access to it?" Aennati said.

"Maybe they transcribed it from my scribe's parchment. Why Bradan kept it, I don't know—perhaps to reanimate his family or Merlin—but it animated us instead, as I foretold."

"It did its job. Why think of it further?"

"It's an unusual spell. I created it to be supple. For one thing, I could perform the blood sacrifice needed to power the spell after someone else had brought me back; in a way, I was repaying a debt by killing the individuals on the island. Other potent magic must have sacrifice before the incantation is read. My spell is also unusual in that it can be reversed if it's rearranged. That's well beyond what that novice Bradan is capable of. Nonetheless, it is a risk, so we'll take it from him."

The priest picked up a stray coin from the grass and tossed it far out over the panorama, a tiny copper comet flashing toward San Francisco's center.

"For luck," he said.

CHAPTER 8

New Age Piety

"Did anyone follow you?"

Bradan spun around and checked. The street high up in the Berkeley Hills looked safe, almost somnolent, excepting a downed power line from the quake. A utility truck ministered to the damage. Porsches and Mercedes sat in front of five- and six-bedroom homes with brilliant views of the Bay and the redwoods. A forest encircled the whole neighborhood. However, to Bradan it looked to be just a rather tame, arranged collection of trees.

"Did you see anyone?" he asked. Was Danielle's anxiety grounded in a tangible threat or was she still too traumatized by what had happened on Angel Island to separate real danger from paranoia?

He wanted to learn more about her ceremony and find out if the intricate knowledge capable of reviving Cynbel and Aennati had floated across the centuries, swept along like a black leaf on the river Styx.

She shook her head. "I don't think so, but I'm not sure."

His client looked completely beaten. Bluish smudges under her eyes showed that she hadn't slept much. She'd lost weight, too, but the thinning wasn't healthy; a floral skirt hung loosely about her waist.

A Bentley was parked haphazardly in the driveway dappled with bird shit.

"No one's out there," he said. Raindrops began to fall on the brick path leading to the house.

"Can I come in?"

"Oh, of course." She looked searchingly past his shoulder down Grizzly Peak Boulevard to confirm his guarantee of safety then stepped aside, leaving one hand on the doorknob and closing it the instant he stepped across the threshold.

"I hear things at night," she said. "Maybe it's just the trees."

This wasn't the woman he'd known before he left for his vacation. That person had been boisterous and certain of what she wanted, however silly the goal. Now Danielle was tentative in her own home.

They walked into the expansive, high-ceilinged living room that Bradan recalled had an incredible view of the East Bay, San Francisco, and the Golden Gate. Danielle lived way up in the Berkeley Hills. On summer evenings at twilight, the panorama of the surrounding cities planted amid water, hills, and islands made it hard to discern the interface between God and man's handiwork. Hardwood floors throughout Danielle's home and a basket of pinecones sitting on a teak side table reinforced the setting's natural flavor. Today, however, the windows were all curtained, making the room a hermetically sealed mausoleum. Bradan suspected that this was to block any vista that included Angel Island.

"Feel the quake?" she asked. Her tone indicated she was only making conversation. The Hayward fault ran directly beneath these hills. Even earthquakes didn't penetrate her other anxieties.

"It woke me this morning," he said.

In truth, the effervescent sensation of a spell had pulled him from sleep, blending seamlessly with his troubled dreams of other times and places. The sensation felt similar to what had hit him at the airport the day before. For several moments he'd lain half awake, too tired to identify what he experienced. Then the old building's shudders yanked him fully awake. This one was big; the tremors continued. He heard a plate hit the kitchen floor. The floor under him shifted and creaked. Fleetingly, he recalled that it wasn't just intensity but also duration that determined an earthquake's destructiveness. He threw off the covers and jumped up from the futon to stand in center of his bedroom. Now what? Rush out of the building? Get underneath a table in case more things fell over and the windows shattered? The magical emanations continued in synchrony with the quake. Then both stopped.

Bradan sat down on the edge of his futon. He picked up his pillow and used it to wipe his face and neck. The spell and the quake were linked. He threw the pillow aside. Tintagel trotted into the bedroom and snuggled up to him. Bradan knew of no natural process, including an earthquake, that on its own could generate a spell's signature. Maybe a modern amateur steeped in Celtic lore and ritual could have attempted to re-create such magic, but the effort would have been clumsy and ineffectual. Aside from Bradan, the arcane knowledge no longer existed to couple human sacrifice with enchantment. So had Cynbel and Aennati indeed been resurrected? He dressed quickly. He needed to get over to talk to Danielle and hear her story firsthand.

"Was this one bigger than the Halloween quake?" he asked Danielle. "I was already in the air heading for Miami that evening." The instant he asked the question, Bradan realized that any reference to Halloween would force his client to recollect events that horrified her. Let Danielle bring the topic up when she was ready—if she ever could discuss it.

"I don't know," Danielle said flatly.

Bradan nodded.

The living room's illumination came from a single floor lamp, sitting in its own little pool of light, transforming the room into harsh lunar zones of black and bright white light. Bradan shivered. The room was as frozen as his home had been after weeks without heat when he'd returned to it yesterday evening. A stone fireplace with the remnants of a long-dead blaze sat just beyond the lamp's glow. It was an animal's lair. He tried not to breathe deeply. The house needed to have the windows thrown open to the sky to let the smell of pine and open air wash through.

"How are you feeling, Danielle?" Bradan touched her shoulder gently. "Is there anything I can do to help?"

"Thanks for coming over. I'm all right. Just listening to me would be good. My friends stay away. I've talked to mainly police, lawyers, and my psychiatrist these last few weeks."

"You're no criminal and you're also not crazy," Bradan said. "Can I sit down?"

"Wherever."

She collapsed into a wicker chair suspended from the ceiling. It creaked as she arranged herself. The stark light deepened her face's wrinkles. Bradan settled himself in a Danish modern sofa opposite her with a glass coffee table in between. He'd been here last summer as a reluctant guest at a party honoring an au courant author of children's cookbooks. The place looked much the same as he remembered it, packed with artifacts chosen with sincerity if not good taste representing half a dozen indigenous cultures around the world. Today the pieces all seemed to have faces. A copy of a sixth-century Peruvian portrait jar with a grave countenance rested on top of a bookcase. The jar kept Shiva, Lord of the Dance and waster of worlds, company as he flailed a dozen arms about himself. Above the fireplace, several Nepalese prayer wheels had been arranged in a circular pattern while, next to Bradan, a vividly painted Pacific Northwest Indian mask affixed to the wall leered down at him with long tongue lolling out of its mouth. None of these totems had warded off the evil that had befallen his client.

After a moment spent staring at her hands, Danielle recollected herself. "Want a drink?"

"If you're having something."

With an effort that made Bradan regret accepting her pro forma hospitality, she pulled herself out of the chair and wandered into the dimly lit kitchen. He watched her pass a large rack of caffeine-free herbal teas, stop for a moment to consider the selection, then reach behind them into a cupboard and pulled out a bottle of Tanqueray.

"We had Dylan's funeral early in November," Danielle said. "A lot of people came. Even from work. You knew he was the art director at Thistle & Flower Press, didn't you? He did the graphics and artwork for their books, web stuff, too. They published a lot of cookbooks, vegetarian mostly. The whole place came to see him buried—even the company owner. That woman never even respected Dylan because he was always going over budget, but she came. Leah's funeral was a day later. I went to that, too, of course. And all the others."

She poured clear liquid into two tumblers. His client not only never drank, she wasted no opportunity to lecture anyone who'd listen about the health-enhancing value of caffeine-free, sugar-free, nonalcoholic beverages.

"Dylan was a good person," he said. "I wish I'd been here to pay last respects. I know how close you were." There didn't seem a lot else to say. Actually, Bradan had hardly met Danielle's husband except when their paths crossed by chance at Berkeley coffeehouses or when he occasionally accompanied his wife to one of Bradan's counseling sessions.

Back in the living room, she passed him a glass. He sniffed cautiously.

"Gin," she said.

"Straight?"

"Ran out of vermouth." She fell back into her chair with a sigh. "You'll want to know what happened."

Bradan did desperately want details about Angel Island, but looking at her, at her house, he didn't have the heart to push.

"It's okay. Talking is good for me. That's what my psychologist says. We were doing the ritual on Halloween. We were all feeling something good was happening. The whole island changed into a different place from another time. We had this big bonfire going. I threw in some wood figurines. Then there was a quake. There were fires in the Marina. We could see them in the distance. People came from somewhere, the trees near us, I think. Crazies. They attacked us and I ran."

Bradan hadn't noticed the little crucifix worn on a gold necklace around her neck before, but Danielle fingered it now. Christ glittered in the lamp's light.

"You read something to set the mood?" he asked.

"Yeah." She looked uncomfortable. "It was probably wrong, but I took a picture of your parchment. It was in a clear case, not hidden. We talked about it a little when Dylan and I came over that morning. You said it was folklore from pre-Christian England. If you'd wanted it to be private, you would have put it away."

Bradan looked at the floor. Anger swept over him, not directed at Danielle, but at himself for not seeing the risk, however remote, that the incantation could be used. He was guilty of the worst sort of hubris in thinking that he alone could possess such knowledge and keep it—even in a concealed safe.

He'd taunted the gods.

All it had taken was his carelessness in leaving the parchment exposed one time and a commonplace bit of technology in the form of a phone to release this genie.

But Danielle and her crew couldn't have made the resurrection ritual work—not even on Samhain—without human sacrifice. He wondered if somehow accidental deaths in the quake could have created the energy needed to power the ritual. Or whatever entity had been resurrected had used the murder of Danielle's husband and friends immediately after their revival to pay back the magical debt incurred by their resurrection. If anyone could have designed a spell adaptable enough to facilitate this, it would have been Cynbel. Maybe an eldritch combination of death, the Samhain date, and the Angel Island setting had catalyzed the Druids' return to life. However, this was too far to stretch magical capability. Danielle and her group had run across modern psychopaths. Without resorting to ancient demons, recent history was full of perfectly human inhuman behavior including the Zodiac Killer and various cults.

"You read Latin?" he asked. "There were also a few Celtic symbols. Even academics don't agree on what those mean."

"I had Latin when I was a kid because my parents sent me to a Catholic grade school and junior high. It was hard going because I'd forgotten a lot, but I remembered more than I thought I would. I guess the nuns beat something into me. For sure, we didn't know how to pronounce ancient Celtic, but the Latin guided us about how to say stuff and where we couldn't figure out the pronunciation, we made guesses about the way it should sound."

"Your phone . . . ?"

"I lost it when I ran." She drained her gin in two gulps.

"How did they look, the people who attacked you?" Bradan tried to keep his voice interested but not reflect the intensity he felt. Danielle's lassitude had worn away like veneer abraded by coarse sandpaper as she'd told her story. Now he guessed she was barely under control.

She exhaled deeply. "Why do you care? They were just nuts. They must have seen our fire and come for us. In a weird way, I feel that I called them. Dr. Cannon—I see him pretty often these days—says that's survivor's guilt." She ran her hand through her gray hair. "Bradan, I can't believe Dylan's dead." She looked at her empty glass.

"I'll pour you another," he said. "Just a man and a woman did it?"

"Did I say that?"

Danielle's suspicious response made him think of the cop on the Bay Bridge.

"Well, you're right, best I can recall," she added. "Maybe there were more, but I didn't see them. The detectives found that hard to believe. They also thought the 'cult paraphernalia' at the crime scene was peculiar."

"What do you mean?"

"We burned some wooden animal figurines in wicker baskets, just to set the mood. It was supposed be symbolic. We didn't hurt anything living. The Celts did that kind of stuff, right?"

"We should talk about something else," Bradan said, thinking Danielle was too fragile to be pressed for more information now. He reached out and touched her arm. She smiled wanly.

"The detectives think I might have had a hand in it, you know, some kind of weird cult thing where I'd slaughter people I loved." She ran her hand through her hair again. "I hired a lawyer. He thinks he has some ideas about how to prove I had nothing to do with the killing."

"Anyone who knows you would realize how absurd it is that you would hurt people," Bradan said. "Besides, how could you, a single individual, kill five other people so quickly?"

"It's stupid, all right, but for the time being, I'm not supposed to leave the county without telling them."

"The police just want to make sure that they have a witness when they catch the people who did this."

"They'll never get them," Danielle said flatly. "Anyone who could butcher all my friends as quickly as they did isn't going to let some homicide detective catch them. Leah especially, I just can't understand how she could have been killed. She seemed so capable of handling any situation. I didn't hear any guns. How else could it have been done so fast? She was so full of power and certainty. You knew she was a white witch, didn't you?"

"She met a real witch," Bradan said quietly as he walked back into the living room with the gin. He'd poured some for himself, too.

"What?" Danielle looked at him.

"Nothing. Here's your glass."

"I'm there alone." Danielle started the story again so quickly it took him a second to realize that she was recalling the night on Angel Island again. "The man and woman had the deadest

100 PETER W. BLAISDELL

eyes I've ever seen. I think the man was there first. Then some moments later, the woman showed up. I ran away from our fire through a forest before I wound up in a building. I thought they were chasing me the whole time, but I never saw anyone, heard Dylan and my friends screaming as I ran. I hid in the building, had no idea where I was." She tossed off the second glass.

"In a building?" Bradan tried to remember Angel Island's layout. He'd been there last summer for a day trip, but he couldn't think of a structure she might have hidden in.

"There's an old immigration center and barracks," he finally said. "American authorities kept Chinese in it when they came to California in the '30s. I think the park service has rebuilt part of it as a museum."

"I guess that's what the ranger said when he found me the next morning. Honestly, I don't remember or care. Whatever it was, there was some construction going on and I climbed up the scaffolding to get in."

"Where'd you drop the phone?" Bradan wondered if the cops could have picked it up or some day-tourist visiting the park. Now the incantation could go viral depending on who had the phone. He reeled in his panicky thoughts. That risk seemed low; the intense rain in the intervening weeks would surely have destroyed the phone if it hadn't been found when the crime scene was examined. Even if the phone had been recovered, no one would know what the spell signified. Still, he needed to try to find the phone if it still existed, and destroy it.

"Maybe I lost it in the woods when I was running. I don't recall anything very well except the sounds of people dying. Do you think they're still after me?"

"No," he said with as much reassurance as he could muster. "After Angel Island, they've been killing people all over the Bay.

It seems to be random. They're just after numbers."

"Who could do these things?"

"I can't begin to guess," he said. "It's sad, but there are plenty of murderous nuts around. One of them might have been inspired by misreading ancient Celtic ritual."

Danielle's doorbell rang. They both jumped at the sound. She eased herself out of the chair.

"Bradan, can you come along with me to the door?"

"If somebody's after you, they wouldn't ring first," he said. "Is there a peephole in your door?"

Danielle nodded and together they crept down the hallway toward the house's front entrance, Bradan feeling foolish, but tense, too.

Danielle looked through the peephole, then threw the front door open with a sigh.

"Oh, Jack, thank God it's just you."

"Just me, just me," the visitor said with a breezy tone that implied he was pacifying an old but slightly addled acquaintance. "So, Danielle, how goes it?"

Bradan stared curiously at the man who moved through the entrance and into the living room as if he owned the home. This had to be the lawyer who'd left a message for him. In person his voice was the same mix of unctuous solicitude and condescension Bradan remembered. Bradan resisted an urge to kick him.

"Christ, open a window, will you? Smells like a cat died in here." Jack sank into the couch where Bradan had been sitting. The lawyer was of medium height and, Bradan guessed, about forty. He patted down sandy hair that was thinning at the top. He had dressed as casually as a senior executive going into the office on a Saturday, maybe a bit more ostentatiously than a regular company man. Bradan guessed Jack had to have a least one gold chain around his neck, perhaps more.

"Hello," Bradan said.

"Hi, you must be Bradan. What luck that I show up when you've dropped by. Danielle's mentioned you many times. I'm Jack LaPlante. I work with Fierstein and Marcotti in Oakland." Still sitting, the man stuck out his hand. "I left at least one message for you. Did you get it?"

Bradan looked him over. His accusatory tone irritated Bradan, but he masked the feeling. Danielle clearly needed all the help, legal and otherwise, she could get.

"I've just gotten back into town," Bradan said. "I meant to call Monday."

"Danielle mentioned that you were away. Bradan, you're an intelligent guy, I can tell that about you right away, so I'll cut to the chase. I think you know information that would help Danielle. Right now, the district attorney doesn't have enough to indict her, or they'd have her in prison with no bail set, but there isn't enough to absolve her of a role in those heinous killings, either. That's why she's under surveillance. I had my admin call all the people with the last name Badon in the Miami area—there aren't many—and none of them seemed to be related to you."

Bradan's throat tightened. The Indian mask laughed at his discomfort. This was just what he needed: some half-assed lawyer who bathed in a tub of sandalwood shampoo bumbling around among his relations. Would he ever connect the Alvarez clan with Bradan? The lawyer was clearly trying to shift blame away from Danielle any way he could. Dragging Bradan in would muddy the waters and divert police attention from Danielle. LaPlante was as subtle as a jackhammer.

"I'm trying to act on my client's behalf, and if you're half as fond of her as she seems to think, you'll help us out. I want to establish to myself once and for all that you were out of town on Halloween weekend–"

"–and not orchestrating the killing on Angel Island."

"You said it, not me, but now that's it out there on the table, yeah. Who else but you knew Danielle and her friends were at the park that night? And Danielle tells me you're unusually knowledgeable about some of this cult stuff, folklore and so on. In fact, it's your business, isn't it?" LaPlante pulled the wristband of his gold Rolex and let it snap back to emphasize the point.

"Jack, Bradan is very positive in his approach to rituals." Danielle seemed as surprised as Bradan by the aggressive tone LaPlante was taking. "What are you saying?"

"Sure, Danielle." LaPlante smiled broadly and threw an arm along the top of the sofa, showing off the line of his camel-hair sport coat. "I'm not accusing Bradan of anything. Did I say I was? I'm just asking for the name of one of his relatives in Florida, just one, who can confirm that he was there on Halloween night."

Bradan stared at the lawyer. LaPlante was becoming a major pain. Danielle must have been truly desperate to bring him onboard. Who wouldn't be with the police openly skeptical about her role in the killings? However, if LaPlante succeeded in finding the Florida branch of Bradan's family, the Alvarezes would indeed verify his presence in Miami on Halloween, raising a whole set of new questions about why he used two names and how he could look sixty in one city and thirty in another. The barrier between two closets in his life looked ready to dissolve.

"Jack." Bradan intentionally used the lawyer's first name, matching the lawyer's condescending overfamiliarity and hoping it would bug him. "I'm not involved no matter who you contact. A hundred people must have seen me in Florida while I was there. I've got credit card receipts from Palm Beach down to Key West. Forget about me. I'm no attorney, but if Danielle's prints aren't on any of the murder weapons and none of the victim's blood is on her clothing, the police can't have much of a case. Anyway, how is one person with no gun supposed to have killed four—no, five—people without leaving a single survivor?"

"I'm pursuing every angle, Bradan. So don't try telling me my job. You're part of it somehow. I can feel it."

"You can 'feel' my involvement? Jack, baby, I enjoy my privacy—a lot." Bradan felt anger crushing strategy. "If you try to drag me and my family into this, you'll hear from my lawyer."

LaPlante laughed expansively. "Bradan, Bradan, Bradan, can you imagine how often I've heard that kind of stuff? Am I supposed to be scared? I'm here to help Danielle and that's just what I'm going to do. By the way, what kind of name is Bradan? Can't I just call you Brad? No need to put on airs."

Bradan took two strides to stand over the sitting lawyer. "Jack, let me get this right. You think I'm a mass murderer who slashed open five people's throats on Angel Island after strangling them with enough force to crush their spines? Then I burned what was left in a fire as part of some ritual? I'm supposed to have done the same thing out on Ocean Beach and up in Muir Woods to another dozen people?"

Bradan moved closer until he touched LaPlante, forcing the lawyer to stare straight up at him. LaPlante reached into his sport coat pocket for a phone, but Bradan was faster and grabbed the lawyer's forearm.

"I've got only one question for you. If I did all that to people who didn't make me mad, what do you think I'd do to someone I despise?"

LaPlante's face flushed red then white. He didn't move a muscle. Abruptly Bradan released the attorney's arm, backed away and walked toward the door.

"Thanks for the drink, Danielle. Stay safe. If you want to talk, give me a call when this asshole is far out of the way. He'd throw me under the bus."

Danielle, looking a bit stunned, followed him into the hallway. "Jack had no call to antagonize you."

As Bradan walked down the front steps, he heard the two talking inside. "He didn't have anything to do with it, Jack. I've known Bradan since forever."

"In that case, we'll sue the park service for letting killers onto Angel Island to prey on you and your loved ones. Their response time was very slow and they're liable, as I see it. But how did Bradan know so much about how everyone died?"

CHAPTER 9

Dancing Off the Beat

Bradan didn't find a parking space for the Tesla any closer than five long, badly-lit blocks from the Paradise. A sporadic chilly breeze cut the humidity from the recent rains and signaled an imminent shift to winter weather, but it was still warmer than normal. Every year the weather seemed more unsettled. Crumpled pages from a newspaper—did anyone read those anymore?—blew along the sidewalk in front of him and, out on Folsom, traffic skirted a large pumpkin someone had smashed in the middle of the street. It was a crushed skull surrounded by brain matter. If Cynbel and Aennati had been resurrected, they'd do worse to him. Trying to set aside his disquiet, Bradan let the breeze refresh him as he walked toward the club; the wind carried a sense of exhilaration that comes when the night is just beginning and has potential.

He stayed clear of the alley mouths and checked other passersby as they approached him. There were more prosaic threats than ancient Celts. Gang graffiti on the walls staked out turf ownership block by block. Ahead, two street people, one in a rumpled army jacket, the other in a huge overcoat that stretched almost to the pavement, peed brazenly on a new, red pickup, its chrome still in showroom condition. As he passed the winos, Bradan reeled from the urine's stench. Whatever they'd consumed, it allowed them to baptize the truck with oceans of fluid. Bradan wondered what the vehicle owner's reaction would be upon discovering this commentary on San Francisco's class distinctions.

He jumped as a string of firecrackers went off in an alley he'd just passed. At night, the neighborhood of newly gentrified bars and clubs set amid warehouses south of the city center was mean and caution never hurt, especially on a Saturday when he shared the sidewalk with a variety of street life. Last weekend they'd found a German tourist robbed and shot to death one street down from the block where he now walked. Floodlit tips of San Francisco's downtown glass towers peeked over the warehouse roofs like nervous voyeurs anxious for a look at the night's decadence. He wished he'd brought the wolf along for company, but his pet was staying with Claire to give his neighbor some sense of security.

He'd brooded over Danielle's story. It still seemed impossible that her group of pacifistic neo-pagans could have re-created Cynbel and Aennati from dust with or without the text of the resurrection incantation. However, he'd resolved to locate her phone on Angel Island if it weren't lost or destroyed—very long odds, indeed. Besides his parchment, it was the only other place the resurrection spell existed, and, once on a phone, it could go viral with unpredictable effect. He'd burn the parchment and pulverize the phone. Now he needed a way to discreetly get out to the island late at night after day visitors left. Wally, one of the club's bartenders, had a boat.

The Paradise was a massive converted warehouse at the corner of Folsom and 8th. A long line of people stood outside, leaning lazily against the building's brick wall and chatting in the dark as the bouncers slowly filtered them into the club. In finding the end of the queue, Bradan passed in review of the assembled crowd, black clothing, short dresses, frozen smiles, vacant stares, lovely breasts; but the recent butchery in the city had penetrated even this supremely blasé crowd's armor of indifference. The shadows and the attitudes made the whole scene as ritualistic as nighttime ceremonies he'd witnessed at stone circles in pre-Christian Britain. Bits of overheard conversation in a dozen voices meshed together into a tapestry of anxiety.

One of the bouncers, bearded, hulking, with blue-black hair touching his shoulders and huge tattooed biceps exposed by a sleeveless T-shirt, nodded a sullen greeting at Bradan as he paid his way into the club. If he'd been issued a spear, the man could have doubled as a guard at Druid rites.

"Wally working tonight?" Bradan asked.

"Think so," the bouncer said. "Check at the bar. Where's Julie?"

"She's got the flu." Bradan pushed into the club. He wasn't going to explain the intricacies of his relationship's dissolution to this Neanderthal.

Though the Paradise's exterior was uninspired, the interior was elaborately planned and executed with rococo flair, another world entirely. It was dark enough to enhance appearance but not to hide it. Mirrors confronted Bradan inside the entrance, sending his reflection right back at him or off in a hundred directions to join thousands of other images in mirrors lining walls that encircled the dance floor. The images collided and merged with a pleasant conviviality Bradan didn't see among the club's louche patrons.

Small spotlights set into the ceiling sent intense, focused

columns of light downward, creating little islands of illumination. Dust swam in the light. Bradan noticed a tall Asian woman wearing black who paused, transfixed in one of the columns, to scrutinize herself in a mirror, displaying a dark mane of hair and sharp cheekbones. She exchanged a faint, cold smile with her reflection and moved off.

Bradan missed Julie. This was her favorite club and he arrived here tonight following the habits learned during his now dead relationship. They'd come to the Paradise often enough that Bradan knew most of the staff by name. Trying to push her from his mind, he continued on to the main floor, packed with dancers, their bodies meshed with the beat. They drifted past him insulated behind a wall of cool. He wondered if anyone here had the capacity for abstract thought.

In the room's center, on a pedestal high above the dance floor and almost as tangible as the real dancers, a holographic projection of a lithe young woman with dark hair down to the middle of her back moved to the music in the smoky air above the ensemble. She might have been South Asian or Middle Eastern, might have been Latin. To Bradan, the ambiguity of her ethnicity made her iconic of the city. The holograph was nude save for a G-string. Sweat dewed her skin as the image shifted in patterns as intricate as Arabic script. She licked the middle finger of her left hand and let it slide slowly over her breasts, moving concentrically around the areola before touching each nipple in turn, leaving the faintest moisture trail on her skin that evaporated almost as soon as it was drawn. Then the fingers slid downward across her belly and between her legs and began gentle circular motions. Everyone was a pagan tonight.

Bradan walked around the figure captured by lust, but also by a feeling of affinity for the holographic technology that rendered the woman so sensual and real. His own arts allowed him to create illusions, too. These days who could say where the border between enchantment and science was. She snapped her G-string against her hip, sending a spray of virtual sweat down at him. Excellent. He had better rapport with cyber women than real ones. He blew the projection a kiss.

The music swirled over everything, amplified to infinity, so loud Bradan felt his heart mimic its pulse. Broad washes of harmonized vocals overlaid with a chrome waterfall of synthesizers gave the songs an ethereal quality contrasting with the crushing bass and percussion that punctuated the melody and powered the music along surfing a wave of rhythm. The vocalist breathed out an orgasm at 120 decibels.

Bradan deliberately turned away from the cute dancers, all too evocative of Julie, toward the bar. Lost love wasn't the only thing he needed to forget tonight; he wanted something to wash away thoughts of the tricky crossroads where magic met reality. The rows of bottles behind the bar were banks of variegate gems in the shifting light. Whatever their color, they all contained elixirs he needed. He also needed Wally's boat.

Bradan tried to catch the attention of someone behind the counter to quench his Sahara-scale thirst. The closest bartender, a petite, redheaded woman with tattooed breasts wearing only khaki pants held up by paisley suspenders, stood besieged by people ordering some of the most complicated mixed drinks Bradan had ever heard of. Rye and Cointreau garnished with cilantro over shaved ice must be fashionable this Christmas.

"Cute art on your boobs," someone complimented the concentric circles surrounding the bartender's aureole. "Did the tattoo hurt?"

"Not much," the bartender said. "The tattoo guy used a topical anesthetic made from curare. That kind of numbed everything."

"Do you serve kale here as bar food?" a woman asked. "I don't actually like it, but I do eat it, ironically."

Bradan groaned to himself. It could take years to service this crew. Should he materialize a drink for himself and skip the wait?

"Hi, Bradan," someone screamed in his ear. "What can I get for you?"

Bradan recognized the accented voice, turned, and nodded a greeting at Whalid al-Ahmar. Along with a talent for making the best vodka tonics in San Francisco, Wally was a brilliant photographer. Bradan had several of his pictures, including a shot of Julie and himself at Half Moon Bay, scattered about his home amid his other artwork. The man had a gift for recognizing singularity in banal scenes. Vermeer could hardly have done better. Bradan had always enjoyed the company of artists. Maybe abnormally long life was conducive to developing an aesthete's taste.

He ordered a double Jack Daniel's—no ice, thank you very much—and then another. And another.

"A good day?" The bartender kept pouring.

"Excellent," Bradan said, floating on a sea of ethanol fumes. "When's your break? We need to talk."

"Certainly, my friend. I have fifteen minutes at midnight." Wally looked him over. "Where's Julie?"

"Shit," muttered Bradan. Louder he said, "She's decided to explore her options. Evidently I'm not one of them."

Even through the din, the bartender caught Bradan's sarcasm. "The day is over, my friend," he said, setting yet another whiskey down on the bar. Bradan tossed it off like a gunslinger.

Wally leaned his short, wiry frame against the bar and spoke close to Bradan's ear:

"Come, fill the Cup, and in the Fire of Spring
The winter Garment of Repentance fling:
the Bird of Time has but a little way
To fly—and Lo! the Bird is on the Wing."

Bradan laughed at the unexpected verses in this raucous setting. "You're quite the intellectual," he said.

"I admire poetry. You have so little of it here."

Bradan looked at Wally. "Who did you quote, or is it your own?"

Wally smiled. "From Omar Khayyam, I believe. He was a Persian and I'm an Arab. No matter, the sentiment is true."

Bradan felt the hot surge of Jack Daniel's warm his stomach. Carelessly, playing along with the outré turn the conversation had taken, he said, "Ah, he wrote after my time."

"Age is in the spirit only, my friend, not the flesh. For some reason, I think you understand that. You must pardon my overfamiliarity. I know you well, but not that well. Come, you've finished your drink. Have another."

Bradan nodded and watched Wally splash more of the amber liquor into his glass. He drained the glass in a microsecond. Maybe this was a night to let his car drive him home.

"Thanks for taking care of Tintagel while I was away in Florida," he said. The words had to be forced out through all the alcohol he'd taken onboard.

"Ah Bradan, you have it wrong. Your dog took care of me. A more independent animal I've never seen and good company with these crazy murders happening all over town. All I had to

do was toss him a raw steak every night, though it truly seemed
he would have been happier hunting for meals himself."

"He would have," Bradan said. "Did you take him out to the
boat? Tintagel loves water." Bradan tried to remember if he'd
ever seen Wally's boat. The photographer had recently acquired
an old vessel of some kind that he now used as a photographic
workshop and sometime living quarters.

"Yes, last weekend. I usually don't visit it much in the winter,
but I couldn't resist. Odd how I've come to enjoy the water. I
grew up far from the ocean. Anytime you wish to see the Bay
from my boat, you must come over."

"That's what we need to talk about during your break. It
would be a pretty big favor."

Wally leaned against the bar looking over the dance floor. "A
full house tonight. The women are lovelier than usual. They are
truly magical creatures, no?"

"Magical? I think it may be a while before anyone puts a spell
on me."

The bartender nodded philosophically and pulled a pack of
cigarettes from his T-shirt pocket. Then he grimaced disgustedly
and stuffed them back.

"Of course, one cannot smoke inside. A foolish rule. I'll have
to wait for my break and go out on the street. This city is a little
too concerned about health. Do they all want to live forever?"
He winked conspiratorially at Bradan.

Someone screaming for a gin and tonic called Wally down
to the other end of the bar. Bradan had no idea where he came
from; his heavy accent sounded Middle Eastern. This matched
his appearance, black curly hair ringing a small thinning patch
on top, and a dark complexion.

Excepting the small, bare-breasted redhead, Wally was

about half the size of the club's other staff who must double as bouncers if drinkers became violent. However, his dress blended right in with the Paradise's staff: well-worn jeans and a T-shirt emblazoned with the Grateful Dead's grinning death's-head.

Suddenly the whole club shook. Momentarily the lights dimmed, then strengthened, before going out completely coincident with a warble in the music followed by silence. The ground continued to move under Bradan's feet as several of the bottles behind the bar hit the floor with a densely spaced sequence of crashes. Seconds later, in the quiet, a few people laughed, but most didn't say anything. Bradan was aware of how hot the club was in the darkness. He felt no hint of a spell. Maybe this was just an aftershock from the morning temblor. Then the quake ended. He stood in pitch black for several moments. People started to talk around him. One of the bartenders snapped on a flashlight and played it over the broken liquor bottles. Then the lights came back and the music resumed with concussive volume.

Bradan looked down the bar and caught Wally's eye. The bartender shrugged resignedly, then reached down to pick up a split Johnnie Walker whisky bottle and toss its remnants into a plastic trash barrel.

"Sorry about that, folks," a DJ cut in over the music. "We spare no effort to keep things hopping for you. We're going to have a little trouble with the drinks for a while. We'll deal with it as quickly as we can. Bear with us, please. Half price on everything as soon as we get this fucking mess cleaned up. Happy holidays!"

The music resumed at full volume, barely drowning out the cheers.

Where was his drink? Bradan stared at the floor and saw his glass in a thousand pieces. Wally and every other staff member were throwing away debris, reshelving intact bottles, or mopping behind the counter. They'd be awhile. Other people sitting at the bar looked as bad-tempered and thirsty as he was.

"Shit." Bradan massaged his temples trying to restore clarity to his thinking and then intoned a brief series of metered rhymes. A delicate crystal goblet of clear liquid appeared before him on the counter. Bradan raised the glass and sipped.

Lighter fluid. Bradan slammed the glass down hard enough to crack the stem and rubbed the tip of his tongue with a shirtsleeve. Then he tried again. This time an amber-colored fluid filled a new glass. He sniffed cautiously. Jack Daniel's. He mopped some sweat off his forehead from the exertion and took a deep gulp.

"Can you do that for me?"

Bradan stared at a short black man in a leather jacket standing next to him who looked intently at him.

"Do what?" Bradan asked with as much innocence as he could muster.

"Get a drink for free," his neighbor said.

"I didn't get it free."

"I saw you," the black guy said stubbornly. "You were slick. That glass just showed up in front of you."

Bradan had to nip this one in the bud. "What do think I am, a fucking magician? Maybe you'd better warn the bartenders."

The man turned away from Bradan. Thank heavens this age was so rational. You could challenge anyone's reason and they'd invariably back down no matter what they'd seen. Three hundred years ago he'd have been burned at the stake. Tonight they only shrugged.

He turned his attention back to the dance floor again. Waves of lust mixed with eighty-six-proof spirits to heighten the scene's sensuality. Across the packed room, he spotted a tall dark-haired woman staring into one of the floor-to-ceiling mirrors with her back toward him. The lighting shifted continuously, rearranging patterns of shadow, and people got in the way, but she looked familiar. Bradan stared harder trying to pick out more details.

"Wally, do you recognize her?"

"Ah Bradan, without Julie, you already have your eyes open for other girls." He followed Bradan's stare. Bradan watched Wally's expression shift from mild, indulgent curiosity to admiration tinged with anxiety.

"You know her?" Bradan repeated.

The bartender continued to look at the woman whose profile was now visible. "I wish. She is beautiful. This isn't her kind of place." He poured tap beer for a couple further down the bar before returning. "I leave the mysterious ones to you. And here is another small puzzle."

Wally picked up Bradan's crystal goblet and examined it closely, holding it up to one of the lights above the bar. "Is this one of ours?" He raised his eyebrows. "Want another drink?"

"Always."

The woman Bradan watched now turned fully around and looked at the crowd. Wally was right; her figure was as pretty and supple as the most nubile of the young dancers. She wore a long black dress with loose sleeves and tight enough across the chest to emphasize her breasts. A thin gold headband resembling a tiara kept her hair out of her eyes. Two gold chains encircled her neck. Nothing about this was de rigueur for the Paradise's female patrons, but no one paid her more than casual attention. It was a weekend in San Francisco. The club's lighting suffused everything in crimson, dipping the dancers in a vat of blood.

Bradan's erotic interest dissipated, usurped by fear. He

brought the cold glass up to his forehead and pressed it against his skin, leaving a damp residue between his eyes. His gut felt like it was trying to digest a mass of lard. Aennati? It had been a day for phantoms. Why should the night be different?

Bradan stared at her. He remembered the priestess and he worked to pick out features that would distinguish this woman from the fifth-century priestess, some characteristic that would make her unfamiliar and harmless. She stood apart, separated not by distance—she observed the scene amid a surging sea of dancers—but by her expression of aloofness that seemed to Bradan to be rooted in an awareness of superiority far beyond that of even the coolest dancer to effect.

A tall young man moved purposefully up to her through the dense crowd and spoke into her ear. Bradan guessed he must be asking her to dance, maybe offering her a drink. She turned and stared directly into his face. As far as Bradan could see, she didn't say a thing, but the man's casual self-confidence shifted rapidly to mortification and he seemed to melt back into the crowd, diminishing physically as he retreated. Bradan had just seen a common little drama with an uncommon coda.

Now the woman stared directly at Bradan. Did she know he'd watched her all along? Stunned, he spilled his drink sloppily over the bar. It was Aennati, the sorceress reincarnate. Was her right arm splattered with blood? She lifted a cocktail glass to stir the liquor and ice with her forefinger, all the while regarding him. The sorceress hadn't forgotten that he'd once spat at her.

Bradan set his glass down with a bang and shoved through the crowd toward the exit. He looked over his shoulder. She wasn't where he'd seen her a moment before. Instead, he saw dancers, a moving school of fish in the ocean amid alternating multicolored patches of light. However, on the pedestal in the room's center where the holograph had swayed in her sensual dance just moments before, he now saw Aennati in a G-string, her movements flawlessly intertwined with the music's rhythm. She drew Celtic symbols in the smoky air above the ensemble, the signs lingering easily discernable even in the dim light.

Outside the Paradise, on Folsom, Bradan breathed deeply, flushing smells of perfume, drink, and sweat from his lungs. A stretch limousine pulled up and three Latino couples burst out of the vehicle amid a cloud of giggling, cigarette smoke, and chatter. They moved toward the club before the bored driver could even make a pretense of holding the car door open. Bradan looked around. There were plenty of people milling about on the sidewalk or standing in line waiting to get into the club, but no one remotely resembled the priestess.

It was foggy, but the only thing out of the ordinary was a couple of police cars by a club across the street. Blue and orange light splashed the surroundings. Two vehicles had crashed. Bradan guessed the quake had made someone lose control.

He almost ran back to the Tesla, feeling the liquor's effects. The sidewalk seemed to drift in front of him. Probably, Bradan had only seen a woman with Aennati's appearance and supernatural poise. In his intoxicated state he'd imagined the sorceress. That sounded logical, especially given his recent preoccupation with events long past. However, Aennati's manner couldn't be mimicked. Anxiously musing, he came abreast of the red pickup still reeking of the winos' urine.

"That's him—the woman described him." The statement came from one of three men standing beside a warehouse wall close to the truck.

Abstracted, Bradan at first didn't think the remark referred to him. Then one of the men lunged forward, grabbed Bradan's arm, and flung him to the sidewalk. As Bradan hit the concrete, he instinctively rolled, trying not to give his attackers a vulnerable, stationary target. As he moved, he had fleeting images of the men. They were big guys and looked drunk and mean. The man who'd thrown him was fat enough to bulge his shirt out of his pants. A bushy, badly shaved mustache too long on one side made his face look lopsided. Unevenly cut brown hair only made it worse. To Bradan, his expression was a blend of stupidity and self-sympathy for wrongs the world had done him. One of his two companions was bearded and bald. He might work out at a gym and wore a tank top even on this breezy night to show off his muscular arms. The third man incongruously wore a blazer and gripped a can of beer.

Bradan lurched to one side, still on the ground, just in time to avoid being kicked in the head by the same man who'd thrown him. The momentum of his attacker's kick sent him off balance and ricocheting into a parking meter. Peripherally, Bradan noted the bald man crowding in behind his first assailant, but they were more drunk than he was and weren't coordinating their attack effectively. This gave him the bare second he needed to scramble to his feet. They were young guys from Daly City or some other working-class suburb south of San Francisco, but why the hell were they attacking him? Maybe just for the fun of it.

"You're dead, asshole. You pissed on your last car!" the guy with the muscles shouted.

"I didn't piss on anyth—"

The rest of Bradan's answer was cut off as he ducked a punch. Bradan feinted a counterpunch and then kicked the fat man in the balls. The man's shirt popped several buttons and he doubled over and fell to his knees, retching. Bradan hadn't survived fifteen centuries without learning something of street brawls. And he watched mixed martial arts competitions on many a misspent weekend glued to his set. He picked up pointers on technique wherever he could get them. Nonetheless, these ugly bastards meant to fuck him up but good and he didn't know if he could fend them off forever.

"Shit, this is just like last Saturday, fights all the time down here," a woman said to her boyfriend.

"It's so cruel," another girl said. "But let's check it out." A little crowd had gathered to watch the fight, behind and around the cars parked along Folsom. Nobody was going to intervene, though. Too bad the lighting on the foggy nighttime street wasn't better.

With one of his attackers momentarily out of action, Bradan let out his breath in a rush. Without thinking—with thought might come hesitation—he lunged at the two remaining assailants. He had to do damage quickly before they could recover and coordinate an attack on him. Were any of them armed? His drink-fogged mind tried to clear itself and he jumped into a flying kick aimed at the midsection of the guy with the tank top. Bradan heard a crack on impact indicating that he might have snapped a rib. The hoarse shout of pain confirmed injury. The man's body spun backward crashing into the remaining attacker, sending them both backward into the brick warehouse wall. This third man dropped his beer can, but he didn't fall down.

Bradan expected him to run. He'd seemed to be the least belligerent of three and had hung back a step or two while his two friends did the fighting. But instead of fleeing, the bastard rummaged quickly through his jacket pocket and pulled out a pistol. In the fleeting instant it took Bradan to get his new situation, a series of ephemeral sensations rushed at him. He noted that the big, stainless steel automatic looked very clean. The guy pointing it at his throat must have just picked it up new. However, a sooty powder smudge rimmed the bore; this gun had been fired recently. The man's brown eyes were composed for killing and had narrowed slightly.

"Any cops around?" a spectator remarked disinterestedly. Bradan didn't hear any sirens.

"Cut it out!" an older, slightly built spectator yelled at the man with the gun. Among the bystanders, he seemed uniquely disturbed at the violence. "It isn't worth shooting him."

Distracted for a second, the man with the gun shouted, "You're next, cocksucker!"

Bradan turned and sprinted back toward the Paradise, conscious of how large a target his back made. No police, no help, could he work a spell? Fear paralyzed his mind like so long ago when Cynbel had threatened him with the hot iron. The crowd of people who'd watched the fight scattered behind cars or pressed against building walls to get out of the line of fire. A woman laughed loudly. The only person still standing in plain view was the dark-haired fellow playing Good Samaritan. He gestured with huge arm movements and screamed at something out on Folsom.

The Paradise's bouncers would be slow to break up an altercation outside the club. Why get involved in something that could get them sued if they won the fight or killed if they lost it?

A police car rolled to a stop just ahead of Bradan, one wheel pushing over the curb with a crunch. He heard a bursting pop amplified by the warehouse's walls, and a hole appeared in the police car's windshield sending little spider webs of cracks through the glass. The shot must have barely missed him. Bradan dived head first onto the sidewalk, almost landing atop a used condom and some half-eaten candy bars. His ears still ringing, he looked up to see a cop desperately push himself out the car door opposite the man with the gun. Had the policeman been hit? A second policeman Bradan hadn't seen originally tumbled out beside the first, keeping the car interposed between himself and the gunman.

Shit, he was sandwiched between the cops with guns now poking up from behind the hood of their cruiser and the man behind him with the cannon. All the guns in the world pointed at him. Among them there was enough firepower so that stray shots were sure to hit him as he lay sprawled on the filthy sidewalk. He wondered if he'd die. A hell of a lot of good his spells did him now. He couldn't begin to put together a coherent train of thought let alone the complicated rhymes needed to work magic.

Bradan waited for the firefight to start. Instead he heard a confused scramble behind him. In front of him, one of the cops steadied his pistol with a two-handed grip on his car hood. Only his eyes and the automatic were visible. The other policeman had dropped completely behind the car. Bradan listened as he shouted his location to a dispatcher.

Bradan heard someone behind him groan. Was it the thug he'd kicked? He watched both cops poke their heads over the hood, one older and white, the other a young, compact Latino with his hair in a short, military-style cut. Slowly they rose, their guns extended and pointing at him. Bradan rolled slightly to see what had happened to his assailants. He saw the fat man still crumpled on the ground, though he seemed to be trying to shift his legs. One of his shoes had come off. The other two were gone. They must have disappeared into one of the alleys off Folsom. Tonight wasn't the time to test one's mortality in a pitched fight.

"He's not the one who started it," the Good Samaritan yelled at the police. "They attacked him."

"Okay," the older cop said smoothly, keeping everything very reasonable. His gun remained pointed at Bradan's head. "Keep your hands in sight. Juan, keep your focus down the street in case the shooter comes back. I'll check this one."

He skirted the edge of his car and approached Bradan cautiously and reached forward to pat Bradan down. "Get up slowly," he said. "Show me your hands."

"Sure," Bradan said. The last thing he needed was to survive a gunfight only to be shot by this tense cop. Very gently, Bradan eased himself off the asphalt into a standing position.

"Your wallet. With one hand. Slowly, slowly."

Bradan extracted his wallet and passed it over to the cop who flipped it open and quickly examined its contents, flicking his eyes back and forth between Bradan and his wallet. The more the cop saw, the more he seemed to relax. The paraphernalia of some sort of New Age counselor might arouse amused contempt, but not suspicion.

A second police car muscled its way onto the sidewalk, rolling over the curb between two parked cars. Two policemen eased out of the vehicle, guns drawn. With reinforcements the two original cops relaxed further, but the younger cop kept looking down Folsom expecting the gunman to return.

"You almost got dusted," he said. "You weren't too far from that guy when he shot at you. Just the luck of the bullet that you're still here."

"The luck of the bullet," agreed Bradan.

"You know him?" The older cop nodded at Bradan's remaining

assailant still groaning on the pavement, who'd now levered himself into a sitting position with his back against a parking meter.

"No," Bradan said. "He seemed to know me. Thought I'd done something to his truck. I never saw him before, though."

"Juan, secure that man." The older cop gestured at the second pair of cops. "Also, get those guys to look over the alleys around here and take statements from anyone who thinks they saw what happened."

"No one will have seen anything," the younger cop said.

"Always the cynic, Juan. Where's your faith in the citizenry? There'll be more cavalry here soon."

The older the cop looked Bradan over. "Maybe you need medical attention, too?"

"I'm okay." He wanted to get home after first seeing someone who could have been Aennati's twin, then being jumped by a bunch of thugs in some absurd street altercation. One of the jerks had mentioned a woman.

The younger cop stooped beside the fat guy and began questioning him. Two more squad cars pulled up and began rerouting vehicular traffic to other streets. Pedestrians wandered past on the opposite side of the street paying little attention to the drama. A plainclothes policemen joined the older cop, who Bradan now noted wore a sergeant's stripes. Then everyone asked Bradan more questions. Another police car slowly cruised up Folsom, looking for the two men who'd fled, and a police drone swirled by overhead.

"Do you know anything about some woman with dark hair and wearing a black dress?"

Bradan stammered a reply. "No. Well, maybe. I saw a person at the Paradise about an hour ago. She reminded me of someone

I used to know." There was no way he was going to explain a 1,500-year-old pagan priestess to the San Francisco police. Why were they even asking about her?

"Did you know her well?"

"Officer, what's she got to do with me getting shot at?"

"That guy over there says that she told him and his buddies that you defaced his new truck. Actually, you're supposed to have peed on it." The cops didn't resist laughing. "So, who is this mystery lady?"

Bradan could see the sergeant's attitude was almost flip, but he wasn't going to let the point go.

"I knew her a long time ago, if she's who I think she is. I really didn't see her that well. It could have been anybody. The club isn't well-lit."

The younger cop nodded, perhaps a bit too agreeably. Bradan thought that he was being set up verbally.

"Then why would she sic those guys on you? Did you approach her in the club? Maybe try to talk to her?"

Bradan shuddered. He wished the cops hadn't fixated on Aennati. "I barely saw her. Ask the bartender, Wally. I spent most of my time talking to him." Bradan glanced over at the fat guy. One of the later-arriving cops had him in wrist restraints and was walking him over to a squad car.

"What happens to him?"

"We book him for assault. Other stuff too possibly, since they shot at us. Who knows in this city? Maybe the bail will be set low and he'll walk. First, hopefully he'll tell us who the guy with the gun is." The situation was plainly wrapping up. All the bystanders had left and the block of Folsom where they stood was quiet and the squad cars drifted off to other Saturday night felonies and misdemeanors. Fog crept over the neighborhood.

"All right, Bradan, that's about it for right now," the sergeant said. He looked at Bradan. "There is a report that I think is about you from yesterday. It came up when we ran your ID just now. You were involved in a pretty major wreck on the Bay Bridge. Another driver was trying to ram your car. I'm sure you can guess my next question: Is this just a string of bad luck, or have you made some enemies? Narcotics? Some bad business issues?"

Bradan shook his head.

"Nothing to say right now? Think it over. You're a witness to what happened tonight with officers taking fire, of course, so a detective may want to interview you. If you decide you have any more to tell us in the meantime, we're not hard to get hold of." He looked at the Latin cop. "You gave him our card, Juan? Bradan, you've got a collection of cards going. You got one yesterday, too, from the highway patrol."

"Are you okay to drive?" his partner asked.

Bradan nodded.

"Good," the sergeant said. "Get out of the neighborhood. We still haven't got that sucker with the gun. I don't think he'll be back. Who knows?"

The sergeant turned to his partner. "Get the plate number for that truck. One of the three must own it. Let's get it towed off, too."

Bradan left the two policemen talking and laughing—another night's work—and walked back to his Tesla, staring observantly about him as he went.

CHAPTER 10

Runes and Ruins of Other Times, Other Places

"What did Aennati do to you?" Connie asked with concern. "Use some kind of magic?"

Bradan massaged a bruise on his shoulder. "Not quite. She told some assholes that I'd pissed on their truck. They tried to jump me. When that didn't work, they shot at me."

There was a pause while the ghost digested this piece of intelligence. Finally, Connie asked, "If someone peed on me, would you shoot them?"

Bradan loosened his tense grip on the steering wheel. "You do put things in perspective," he said.

Talking to Connie was a comfort right now. The big car rolled along Folsom past clubs spilling raucous nightlife out onto the street. It was closing time. Fog had moved into the city, lending the revelers a spectral quality as they moved away from the swaths of lemon light emanating from the open doors. Bradan wanted out of this neighborhood fast. The electric vehicle passed through several blocks of deserted warehouses and decrepit hotels destined to be sacrificed shortly on the altar of urban beautification. He peered down side streets, dark corridors with no discernible terminus. Swirls of mist dimmed other vehicles' headlights and hazed the street lamps, otherworldly orbs floating above the damp pavement. It was foggier than usual even for San Francisco and he felt moisture on his skin.

"Do you think it was her? Aennati, I mean?" asked Connie.

"That's the question, isn't it?" Bradan said. "What I saw agrees with Danielle's story. It looked like Aennati even though she was across the club when I saw her, but it's impossible to believe. I'm so drunk. Aennati and Cynbel are so long dead, they're not legends anymore, even back in England. No one except a very experienced magician willing to kill people to facilitate their spell could even have tried to resurrect them after so much time."

"You're still here," Connie said.

Bradan lowered the windows on both sides of the car. Almost on its own, the big Tesla smoothly accelerated, heading for home. They must have been hitting fifty as he pushed it to beat the lights, and a cool blast of night air swept over him and began to eat away at the Jack Daniel's fumes in his brain. Clarity of thought amplified his apprehension.

"Your ethanol levels are above the legal limit for driving," the car's autopilot said.

"Turn the volume down," Bradan ordered.

"I'll get you home," Connie said. "Ignore that bitchy autopilot."

A trail of sweat traced its way from his armpit down his side. Maybe it was blood. He'd hit the sidewalk hard during the fight. He replayed the scene in the Paradise again, trying to recall the woman he'd seen.

His car sped north across Market Street through the banks and investment houses in the downtown financial district. The Tesla's sophisticated suspension absorbed the bumps and potholes. Here the avenues were completely deserted. Far above, faint in the dense mist, he saw a few solitary lights in the towers, tiny, gauzy pinpoints in a dark necropolis. He didn't know what time it was, but even very late at night, the city usually showed some life, an occasional sound, a few cabs at least. Not tonight. He traveled through a mammoth museum displaying lifeless exhibits of twenty-first-century architecture.

"What does she look like?" Connie asked.

"Like the coldest dream you've ever dreamt."

"You'll be sleeping with one eye open."

"Both eyes. If it was Aennati." He wasn't quite at the point of certainty.

"Why didn't she kill you? Why set some dumb punks on you?"

"I don't know. She looked tired." He glanced at the symbols encircling his wrist. "These are some slight protection against a spell. Maybe she'd spent herself doing something else and wanted to save energy. Maybe she was just playing with me."

"Well, those guys didn't get you. Could she will you dead now if she wanted?"

"Doesn't work that way," Bradan said. "Aennati has to see me to kill me." He tried to push the whiskey fog aside long enough to describe enchantment's constraints. "A spell is a drop of ink in water. The further you are from the place where the ink hits the water, the more diffuse it gets. Magic definitely can affect things over a long distance, but it's not specific unless you're able to see what you're doing. If she strengthened herself with human sacrifice, she could wipe out an entire neighborhood without being on the scene, but she could never be really sure she got me specifically."

"How'd she know to look for you at the Paradise?"

Bradan thought he had an explanation. "I worked a spell—a small one—in the bar so I could get a drink. She sensed it and came after me."

"So, what's the plan?" Connie asked.

"Stay out of sight," Bradan said. "Until I can find Danielle's phone—or get out of Dodge."

"I was you, I'd run."

"It might come to that. I'm no hero. I tried that once at Tintagel and it didn't work. Living a long life makes you a realist. If they've really come back, I can't take these bastards by myself."

He told the autopilot to get the local public radio station. "Before you switch it to Dwight Yoakam, I want to hear about the quake."

They caught the middle of a rundown on damage to various parts of the Bay Area and the surrounding region. Evidently, this temblor had been felt as far north as Mendocino up the coast about 240 kilometers. Most of San Francisco had fared pretty well, though a fire department official guessed that several older buildings might have to be condemned. Looters roamed several blocks around Union Square lined with classy boutiques, helping themselves to merchandise now vulnerable because of broken windows and disabled security systems. The Marina District, built on unstable landfill at the turn of the century, had suffered worse. The houses had collapsed including one in which an entire family had been crushed.

"Too bad about them," Bradan said quietly.

Shit. The Bay Area sat on shaky foundations. Would his building be standing? The Marina wasn't that far from the North Beach. Hopefully, Claire and his ground-floor neighbor, Tony, were okay. He raced through a yellow light changing to red.

"What do you see when we're driving?" Bradan asked as he zipped along.

"Just what's through the windshield or in the mirrors. Can't see that well tonight. Black as a witch's tit."

"An apt simile, considering who I think I just met."

Bradan stared about him. Connie had a point. This usually well-lit part of town looked dark enough tonight for someone to have thrown an enormous roll of charcoal-colored cotton over everything. It wasn't quake damage; the streetlights were all on, but they seemed to glow dimly, hazed by the nighttime fog amid the black and silver reflections on the office buildings. His car's image flashed past on the glass like an elongated hearse or a ceremonial chariot for the dead from his own archaic time.

Figures on Bush Street caught his eye and Bradan glanced to his left. Two men stood dangerously close to the street's edge. One held a can, the other a liquor bottle. Bradan winced, expecting a collision. Further ahead, a small Asian woman stood directly in his lane. She stared about her distractedly, running her hand through her hair, paying no attention to him. Connie murmured something sad and respectful and nimbly shifted lanes; Bradan hardly had to nudge the steering wheel to avoid the woman.

Now he saw that there were dozens of figures standing singly or in clusters scattered about the downtown streets. Sometimes they talked to one another. Those by themselves looked around, many with surprised expressions. Despite their diversity in clothing and grouping, all were similar in gray coloration with their pigmentation sucked away, leaving only a pale-blue jacket on one or a faded crimson skirt on another. If he looked hard enough, he could see the wounds that had killed them. He tried not to focus on the specters.

He knew they were impressions of past tragedy, without substance. Occasionally, when he was tired from a spell's exertions or late at night, he saw them in their hundreds arrayed across the freeways, overpasses, and streets, lasting remnants of a fleeting instant of battered metal and crushed bodies. Some of them were victims of other calamities, murders, diseases, from as far back as there had been humans in this region.

"Please, no," Bradan said. "At least let me be followed by my own phantoms. Just let me drive."

His request was answered and he was back in Cynbel's hall, bodies dangling from the rafters. The modern apparitions had flung his mind back to ancient horrors. Then it all disappeared, his unbidden past and the modern specters.

"Odd how they pop up," Connie's voice said. "One moment we're driving along and the next we've got to look sharp or we'd run into them. Maybe it's 'cause it's almost Christmas."

"You could go right through them," said Bradan.

"Could, but I won't. I'm one of them in a way. Going into the windshield at 110 miles per hour and no seat belt makes you sympathetic."

"I guess it would." He was recovering his poise after seeing the apparitions. Phantoms had been part of his life for fifteen hundred years, but he still felt uneasy in their presence. He was a magician, not a medium.

"Kinda creepy night," Connie said as they turned off Columbus onto Filbert with a squeal of tires.

"Like a Cocteau film."

"Don't watch foreign stuff. Anyway, can't barely see our place. Park me close to home, sugar."

"Sure. Some jerk has got our garage access almost blocked, but we can just barely squeeze past."

Bradan hustled up the building's front steps, which were swathed in eucalyptus leaves. The place seemed to be intact. Above him, heavy fog wreathed Coit Tower and the stand of pines and eucalyptus that clustered about its base. The tower was lit at night, but in the mist, it had a pallid, sickly appearance, a skeletal finger pointing at the sky as if to accuse the gods for unfairly cursing San Francisco.

He paused a moment before entering and looked up, smelling the damp pine. Memory transformed the scene into a fifth-century stone watchtower surrounded by a dark forest and fields. The crude blocks composing the tower were roughly cut and almost big enough to intimidate potential attackers with their bulk alone. Soldiers in mail shirts and metal helmets peered out at the hostile evergreens nearby as the mist condensed on their spear tips and iron shield bosses. One guard pulled his heavy plaid cloak more closely about him against the night's dampness.

The warrior's armor looked almost Roman, but, several generations ago, the last legions had been called back to the European continent during one of the interminable civil wars that racked the imperial remnants. More probing inspection of the guards showed long, wild, braided hair beneath the helmets and barbaric clothing no disciplined legionnaire would have worn.

The watchtower brooded above the surrounding trees and the dew-dampened grass. In the middle distance, amid the night mists rising from the ground, stood the ruins of a Roman-style villa, a sedate and pretty oddity better suited to a Mediterranean hillside overlooking olive groves than the cold, half-wild English countryside on which it sat. In fact, confirming the native land's reaction to this alien intrusion, the villa now appeared as a blackened pucker on the hilly green meadow. Soot smudged the building's walls and its roof had caved in, leaving dull red tiles strewn around like a giant had shaken the countryside to wring dust out of a rug. Stone mosaics, as blue as a southern sea, had once intricately decorated the structure's walls but were now defaced and smashed. Weeds overgrew the remnants of extensive cultivated fields surrounding the structure.

Counterbalancing the villa, almost two hundred meters off, a large burial mound sat near a stream, some Saxon or Pict war chief's final resting spot where the great man had been laid to rest amid his favored weapons and the plunder accumulated on raids along the British coast and up the vulnerable island's estuaries. As a final taunting commentary on the shifting ownership of the land, a large Roman ornamental urn with a barbarian war banner planted in it had been placed atop the burial mound. Perhaps the urn had once graced the neighboring villa; the banner had certainly witnessed the bloody defeats of Romanized Celtic defenders of the old order.

Bradan inhaled San Francisco's night air, shocking his lungs. The raw sensation yanked him back to the present. Some ancient remembrances were fresher than yesterday's thoughts. Aennati had been a figment of his overheated imagination, too. Certainly, remembering her had dredged memories to the surface that he'd thought had been silted over during intervening years. Usually, living in San Francisco stimulated him enough to keep recollections away, but tonight thoughts of times long past shouldered aside current sensations.

Bradan turned around and looked northwest. In the fog he couldn't see the Bay at all or even the expensive condos on Russian and Nob Hill not far away. The row houses lining his block loomed indistinctly. Normally, the city generated a raucous cacophony even in the dead of night; now Bradan had to listen closely to catch its thready pulse. San Francisco made muted noises enduring a troubled sleep. Shots, sirens, cries, and the almost subliminal rumble of heavy vehicles blended together seamlessly to create a softly anxious voice. Tonight it was easy to believe that the cheery Christmas season was only a veneer over a far older calendar of dark midwinter holidays.

He stared up. Only Claire seemed to be awake, judging by the light glowing through the curtains of her window. The woman must be working on a presentation or maybe she was picking up the latest temblor's residue from her floor. Down Filbert, he noticed dim light from inside a gray sedan. The vehicle was parked next to a hydrant. Inside the vehicle, Bradan thought that he perceived a figure staring into a tablet or screen. Bradan shrugged inwardly. He considered trying to get a better look, but there seemed no obvious threat.

Letting himself into the building quietly, he padded up the steep flights of stairs. There were six units besides his in the vintage 1930s structure, and his decorous neighbors would take great offense at a noisy disturbance this late at night. At last he got to the fifth-floor landing before his flat.

Burned into the door was a series of Celtic symbols, elaborate and sinister. Whoever inscribed them had done it with such force that the thick, old oak panels were scarred with deep gouges. He smelled ozone.

"Welcome back," he snarled—his home, his belongings.

Bradan looked down the staircase, but saw no danger there. Could they be waiting inside? Had the wolf been hurt? What about Claire? He didn't feel the presence of an enchanter, but that guaranteed nothing. Aennati or Cynbel would try to mask their presence. Still, he trusted his instincts. At least one of the priests had been here but was now gone.

He considered the inscriptions. The symbols were pre-Roman. The Celt's elaborate stories and verses were meant to be sung or spoken and the tribes cultivated memory to detail their feats. However, they'd been practical enough to see that depicting some concepts symbolically made sense. Curses, for example.

Bradan deciphered the message. It had been many years since he'd last used this sort of iconography, but their meaning was clear. He was to be murdered soon. His gut rocked with anger and fright. He knew certainly now that the woman he'd seen at the Paradise was Aennati. Cynbel must have returned, too. Bradan suspected that the symbols on his door were meant to frighten him. Terrified victims were easier to dispense with. Bradan felt a headache stretching from temple to temple; a needle-sharp icicle had been rammed through his frontal lobes.

The priestess hadn't succeeded in killing him at the club and must have decided to ambush him at his condo later in the evening. Magic was a funny thing. Though one became habituated to the signature of one's own enchantments like the smells of a familiar kitchen that went unnoticed, he could sense someone else's work. Similarly, if she focused, Aennati would feel residual emanations of Bradan's past spells akin to spider webs ever so light and faintly adhesive. She must have used these to find his dwelling. To an adept, his home was a lighthouse on a dark shore. He'd worked countless spells there over the years. They'd all been minor-league magic, but their effect was cumulative and they'd left an indelible stain.

The condo recognized him and unlocked the front door. He pushed it open with the toe of his shoe, trying not to touch the portal in any other way.

"Is anyone inside?" he asked his condo.

"No, but I have an update . . ."

"Later." Bradan walked very cautiously into his apartment. In his office, the wall safe containing the parchment was smashed open, fragments of hardened-steel confetti scattered on the floor. The parchment was gone. He stood for a moment feeling nothing.

Behind him, scratching claws bounding up the stairs gave him enough warning to begin turning around. Tintagel sprang at his throat. The wolf's jaws were open, baring its canines.

"It's me," Bradan managed to hiss before crashing to the floor. His breath whooshed out of his lungs. The wolf stood on him and extended its nose carefully until it touched Bradan's chin. Tintagel weighed a ton. The animal sniffed then recoiled in distaste. Bradan guessed he didn't like whiskey.

"Get off. It's me."

Mollified, the wolf lessened its weight on him.

"Bradan?" Claire's hesitant voice came up from the stairwell. He pushed Tintagel off and struggled to his feet. He felt bruised everywhere. First, thugs ambushed him and now his own pet had tackled him.

She moved tentatively up the stairs to join him. "God, I saw your door earlier. Who did that? That's why your dog went crazy a while ago. Tintagel howled loudly enough to wake up the whole neighborhood. Even Tony. You know how soundly he sleeps. I tried to quiet Tintagel by talking to him, but he kept on. I didn't want to get too close to those engravings."

"Shit," Bradan mumbled. He should leave. His residence would never be a safe haven again. Whatever he faced, he needed several hours of sleep to compose himself for the effort. His carefully arranged life had just fragmented like a porcelain vase dropped from a high shelf. If he stayed, he and his neighbors would be endangered.

"What does it say?" Claire asked. She glanced at his door and turned away from it deliberately. "Is it Linear B from the

Yucatan or Egyptian hieroglyphics?"

"Who knows?" He didn't want to pique her curiosity more than it already was. He still hoped to keep the lid on a situation spinning out of his control. Blabbering to Claire wouldn't help. Tintagel nuzzled Bradan's leg. Bradan guessed he was trying to make amends for his earlier hostility. Absently, Bradan patted the animal.

"Any guesses about who did it? There any way this has anything to do with the murders? The news reports mentioned strange symbols at the crime scenes." The woman's intuition was excellent.

"When did you see it first?"

"About 1:30, when the dog went crazy," Claire said. "It spooked me pretty bad." She ran her fingers through her hair.

"I think that was sometime after the quake, judging by when Tintagel started howling. The lights went out here for a while. I came up to check on you, see if you were back. The peculiar thing was, the letters were smoking. Somebody burned them into your door with an etching tool or acid." She paused then asked, "What's going on?"

"I don't know. Random city shit, a joke of some kind, a client. In my business, you run into a creep sooner or later. I'll fix the door with putty and wood stain in the morning. No reason to let the homeowners association know."

"They know already because of all the commotion," Claire said. "Your condo alerted the security service. They came pretty quick. I also called the cops, and two uniforms with a homicide detective showed up almost immediately. I think when I described the symbols, they figured that there was a connection to things they'd seen at the serial killing sites. For sure they want to talk to you and they gave me a card to pass along."

Bradan groaned inwardly. He didn't need any more cops this weekend. "You did the right thing. I'll talk to them if and when they show again."

"The detective took pictures and said that they're going to try to get an FBI forensics team over tomorrow along with local lab guys from the SFPD. They also want a folklore professor from UC Berkeley to come by and examine your door. I guess they already had her look at the various sites of all these murders."

"They'll try to get a warrant before coming back," he said. "But I won't insist that they have one. They can come into my condo anytime and I'll cooperate as best I can." He reflected that he must by now be a person of considerable interest to the authorities, given the bridge incident yesterday, tonight's shooting, and now the evocative carvings on his door.

"I think they're watching the building—the police, that is," Claire said. "After checking out your door, they must see a link with the killings."

"I saw one in a parked car outside," Bradan said. "Don't think he saw me. The fog was super thick. He didn't try to stop me or ask questions."

Cops hanging around might discourage the priests from returning tonight. Cynbel and Aennati would find much of modern San Francisco utterly strange, but they'd understand the role of authorities and would view contending with them as a complication they didn't need at the moment.

"For Christ's sake, shut up!" Tony shouted up the stairs. "Haven't we all had enough tonight?"

"Sorry. We'll keep it down," Bradan said, directing his voice over the banister. A door slammed loudly below them.

Claire surveyed him with apparent concern. The poor woman looked upset herself. She wore the same white robe he'd seen her in last night, but it looked disheveled and her usually neatly combed black hair stood out at odd angles as though she'd slept on it right after a shower.

"I didn't know you wore glasses," Bradan said.

"I don't. Usually contacts, but it's late and my eyes are dry."

Outside, a foghorn sounded faintly.

"The building's front door hadn't been tampered with," Claire said. "But they got in. The police and Union Security looked it over after we saw what had happened up here. Thank God no one tried to force the door to my place."

"Tintagel would have taken them out if they'd tried." He had to continue the façade that whoever had desecrated his door was just a troubled client. The wolf was deadly, but Aennati or Cynbel would have destroyed the animal as easily as blowing out a candle.

"Back in a sec," she said and bounded down the stairs.

Bradan stood in his living room, listening. Even with the building under police watch, would the priests move on him again tonight? Bradan didn't think that Aennati would bother to set a trap for him. She was too direct. However, if they didn't come tonight, they'd be back soon. If the priests used magic to arrive, he might be able to detect them in time to escape.

If he had an advantage, it was his familiarity with modernity. He was acclimated to the possibilities of this age while they'd had only six weeks to acquire current knowledge. However, Bradan remembered Cynbel and Aennati as being adaptable during chaotic fifth-century Britain undergoing epochal dislocations.

His rooms lit themselves as he cautiously walked about and, with visibility, the potential threat receded. Tintagel peeked around his legs. Aside from the theft of the parchment, Bradan's instinctive first impression was that his domicile was as he'd left it when he'd gone to the Paradise—give or take dozens of books the quake had deposited on the floor. Cash from the safe lay scattered in bundles on the office floor. The Druids wouldn't care about it.

"Give me an update," he told the condo.

"A female intruder came into your living room at 1:26 a.m. She entered without coming through the front door. However, her movements inside your home activated the motion detector. I don't know that person's identity. I urgently notified Union Security of an unlawful entry. The intruder examined the premises carefully, then destroyed the safe containing your papers and defaced your front door before she left at 1:49 a.m. Union Security arrived at 1:51 a.m., entered, and checked all rooms. They asked me for an update and locked the front door when they left. The police and neighbors also came to look at the damaged door. The police entered and examined all rooms, but the neighbors did not come in."

Now the only extant copy of the resurrection spell was on Danielle's phone, assuming that it survived. He'd planned to destroy the parchment. Why would the priests bother with it? Probably to burn it. It had already served its purpose in allowing their revival. Bradan doubted that they planned to reanimate other dead. Instead it must threaten them. Rearranging selected phrases might return them to the grave. He was very familiar with it, though it was too long and intricate to completely memorize.

"Set the motion detector in the outside hall and inside every room to highest sensitivity," Bradan said. This might or might not give him some additional slight margin of warning if the Druids evaded police surveillance of his building and returned to finish the job.

"Sure," his home responded with modulated insouciance.

He kicked the text he'd authored, *Rituals of Healing*, hard enough to send it across the room. More sinister rituals were in the offing. He walked through the condo, a dead man come back as a spirit to inspect his worldly possessions one last time.

"Time to run," he told Tintagel.

The wolf had wandered into his bedroom and sniffed desultorily at roses in a broken vase by his bed. In his long, deracinated life, Bradan remembered fleeing a dozen other comfortable homes, Baghdad when a Mongol army sacked it, Florence when the French marched in, Paris when the guillotine was in vogue. Then he'd fled the tides of human history; now he faced his own kind.

"Or should we try to put this genie back in a bottle? The question is where we find a suitable fucking bottle."

He pulled some Glenlivet from a cupboard and set it on the kitchen table and reached for a glass then decided against it. He needed his wits—such as they were after a half dozen shots of Jack Daniel's. He was already drunk and too angry and terrified to appreciate fine liquor.

The oriental screen's cranes preening along the edge of a forest weren't bothered by Dark Ages sorcerers. Tintagel's nails clicked on the wood floor as he padded over to a water bowl in the kitchen. The wolf slurped noisily. Bradan relaxed. His pet now seemed untroubled and he'd learned to trust the animal's instincts.

Claire materialized in his doorway holding something in her hand.

Bradan touched her shoulder. "It's all right. I checked the place out. So did the security service. And the police. Even Tintagel is relaxed."

Claire looked over at the Correggio. "Looks like it's been cut out of its original frame with a butcher knife."

"Close. I used a bayonet. I was in a hurry to leave one of my former homes and I didn't have much space to pack things. Troubles with the landlord." He smiled faintly. Troubles with the firing squad, actually. He remembered leaving Madrid racing for the French border with only the valises he could carry. Franco's soldiers had claimed the rest of his possessions. At least he'd survived in 1939. Tintagel watched him with lambent eyes. Maybe he remembered, too. The wolf had torn the arm off a Spanish soldier holding a pistol to Bradan's chest.

Bradan looked about his comfortable North Beach dwelling. "New Age assistance for age-old problems. Discretion assured." He repeated the logo on his business cards with more self-mockery than he'd intended.

"I can loan you my gun," Claire said. Gingerly, she handed him a small semiautomatic. "Got it two weeks ago after the background check. I'm still not used to it even with the course they gave me. I guess I should learn how to shoot it safely, but you need a weapon more than me."

"Beretta 92 Compact," Bradan said. He ejected the clip and racked the slide back, which popped a bullet out of the chamber.

"You know guns?" she asked.

He nodded. "A little. You keep it loaded. Make sure that the safety is on unless you need to fire it."

"I can't believe that I'm having this conversation," she said. "I'm a Stanford MBA. My friends and family would choke if they knew that I owned a pistol. They'd disown me, but it seems prudent with the shit happening now. Are we safe? I'm tired, but I can't go to bed. I'm afraid they'll come back and hit my place."

"What happened tonight was for me."

"You sound pretty definite."

He put the bullet back in the clip, palmed the clip into the Beretta's grip, and gave her the gun back. "Keep it. I'll be fine."

Claire's gun was sleek and compact, but he needed heavier artillery to counter the Druids. His friend Rod might be able to help him get something unregistered.

"You know who did it?" Claire said. "Any chance that Julie would have been involved? Sometimes when a relationship goes sour, people do funny things. My ex-husband tried to pull all my savings out of our joint bank account, liquidate all of my stocks, too. Maybe Julie wanted to take one of the paintings."

"She preferred wind chimes."

Claire looked at him skeptically. "This affects me, too. I almost ran into whoever pulled this stunt. If it wasn't Julie, then who?"

"Stay away from my condo no matter what. Call the police if you even think something funny is happening. I believe that they're already watching the building, anyway, so things should be okay. I'm leaving for a little while. With me gone, I think whoever did this will have no interest in the building."

"Want me to watch your place?" she said. "I'm now armed."

"Fuck no. Stay away. Don't let the gun make you brave."

"You look scared."

He shrugged. "Okay, I'm terrified. Tired, too. And terminally angry. I'd tell the police if I had something definite that they could act on, but I don't."

"How can a person who seems to have such a history claim to be a man without a past? And have no enemies?"

Christ. More evasions required. In his lengthy existence, Bradan felt he'd developed the tactics of deception. How old was he? Where did he come by his belongings? Why did he speak of so much history from firsthand experience? It was all a game. The lies usually kicked in automatically. Tonight he was slow because of the liquor, or maybe because it seemed pointless. He wouldn't be able to explain Cynbel and Aennati away.

"Did I say that I had no past?" Another time he would have used her interest in him as an invitation to flirt. Why not? Julie was gone, probably already living with some corporate guy who leased a Porsche. Claire looked sensually appealing even in her rumpled robe. One of her small, tanned breasts was almost completely exposed by an open fold in the bathrobe. However, try as he might, there was no lust in him tonight. Rage and fear didn't leave room for it.

Bradan stiffened. He felt the whispery touch of enchantment caress his psyche. The source was some distance away and didn't seem to threaten him directly, but it was in the city. Cynbel and Aennati were back at work.

"What's going on?" Claire asked.

Bradan stood up. What deceits should he use now? He was so drunk that he couldn't be creative.

"God, Claire, I'm exhausted and I'm going to fall into bed. I'll worry about my door tomorrow."

He felt the magic again, the sensation stronger than before. The effect of the faraway spell rushed over his consciousness as a wave submerging a stretch of dry sand. The enchantment seemed to emanate from Golden Gate Park. Direction was never precise until one got quite close to the source. He also wasn't certain just what sort of spell was being cast. However, Bradan's intuition screamed at his conscious mind that he felt the magic of ceremonial killing. He couldn't mask the emotions crossing his face—terror, anger, and shock.

146 PETER W. BLAISDELL

The scene would be a duplicate of the Angel Island, Ocean Beach, or Muir Woods massacres where innocents fell into the priests' hands in a suitable natural setting. They'd be slaughtered with appropriate rite and recharge Cynbel and Aennati's power.

Everyone would assume that modern serial killers were at work, conscienceless and vicious, but ultimately bound by human frailties that would leave them vulnerable to inexorable police procedure. Should he flee now while he had the chance? They'd tried to murder him twice with minimal expenditure of energy. For now, they were husbanding their resources for grander targets. If he ran, he could set himself up elsewhere with his paintings and comforts. Maybe he could move back to Miami.

The Druids were here in the Bay Area because of him.

The other option: try to locate Cynbel and Aennati, catch them by surprise, and kill them. In any direct contest with the priests, he'd be crushed just like Arthur, who, knowing that the odds were impossible at the battle of Camlann, had led the remnants of his cavalry into the maw of a Saxon army tenfold larger than his little band. Arthur's knights had attacked, weapons swinging and honor intact, but in the end they'd utterly lost.

Arthur's knights didn't have modern technology. He wondered if Rod could get him an AR-15 or an Uzi.

Tonight there must be a third way, something between cowardice and bold idiocy. If the urgent goal was not to defeat the priests but just to rescue their victims, then perhaps distracting Cynbel and Aennati would offer the victims a chance to escape. That begged the question of how he'd create a diversion, but maybe circumstances would suggest a means once he got to the park. He'd also have to evade whatever police watched the building, but the mist was so dense that he thought he could use a basement exit without being noticed. He was really too drunk to drive, but Connie would see him to the park. What then? He'd just turned down Claire's offer of a gun.

CHAPTER 11

A Walk in the Park

Bradan smelled the corpses as he stood in the nighttime shadows amid pine trees overlooking the Stow Lake Boathouse. The structure and the lake whose edge it sat on were located dead center in Golden Gate Park. On a pleasant weekend afternoon, the place would be packed with people waiting for a boat rental to circumnavigate the little island in the center of the lake—really the body of water was no more than a duck pond—while bicyclists and skaters in skintight outfits zipped past along nearby paths.

Tonight, however, Bradan stared at the half dozen bodies strewn around the boathouse, so many candy wrappers, two draped over pilings, three others on a little jetty, the wooden planks soaking up their blood, a blonde woman lying face up, half in the pond with her hair forming a halo in the water around her head. Fog oozed over everything, including death, in the pretty park.

Bradan had tracked the enchantment's source, but he was too late to intervene. He couldn't immediately absorb the rapacity of Cynbel and Aennati's handiwork; some vivisectionist had labored with mad abandon. Modern violence, though endemic, was antiseptic by comparison, men and women shot leaving neat little holes that hardly bled. Here the entire area was permeated with gore and entrails and magic. He struggled to keep from being overwhelmed by memories of dangling bodies in Tintagel. Bradan stepped behind a tree trunk and stared about the lake. The fog hanging over the water's surface made it a boiling, black cauldron. He didn't try to resist a series of shivers, almost convulsions, that shook his body. He looked at the figure hanging over the piling; the killing had all happened moments before. The priests had to be near. Hardly breathing, he scanned the scene and did his best to register the macabre details without allowing his consciousness to dwell on what they meant. Tintagel stood by his side, quivering with fear. Bradan guessed the animal only stayed with him now out of blind loyalty.

On Stow Lake Drive, a small service road leading up to the pond, headlight beams probed toward him as a vehicle approached. Bradan couldn't begin to guess who this might be—late-shift park maintenance workers, kids seeking privacy for sex or drugs, a really lost tourist—but whoever, the new arrival complicated an already horrific situation.

The sound of branches being pushed aside yanked his attention back to the pond. Two elk, with light from the headlights dappling their backs, leaped with gigantic bounds over the woman lying in the pond, their hooves splashing in the shallow water. The corpses gaped upward at the animals. The deer paused briefly to survey the lake's environs. Bradan held his breath. Instinctively he knew that the elk were the killers. Following the butchery, the priests had changed into forms capable of moving through the park's dense vegetation with animal ease.

The huge beasts looked otherworldly, the male with an oversized rack of needle-sharp antlers. Both animals had hooves that could crush his backbone effortlessly. Faint phosphorescence enveloped the creatures and swirled out of their nostrils with each breath they blew into the night. Bradan recognized them as the Irish elk he'd seen during his youth in fifth-century England. Modern paleontologists maintained that the last of the enormous deer had died off in Neolithic times, but Bradan knew that a few pockets had survived in the least-traveled bogs and primitive forests of old Britain until his childhood. The park's soft patterns and manicured expanses meant nothing; the wild creatures' presence transformed the arboretum into a demon-sheltering wilderness.

One of the beasts, just twenty meters away, advanced slowly along the pond's edge toward him, sniffing the air as it came. Bradan did nothing, didn't breathe, didn't think. The pine he hid behind should conceal him, but the animals stayed focused on where he stood, big ears twitching and rotating like radar homing in on a target's position. Then their muscles bunched and both elk bounded toward him, rushing through the trees and underbrush effortlessly. Tintagel's ears flattened against his skull and the wolf bared its teeth at the onslaught, but this was an empty challenge.

Fleetingly, Bradan wondered why the Druids didn't simply kill him. He was now in their direct sight; all that was needed to work lethal and specific enchantment. Maybe it was simply the joy of clothing themselves in wild forms and racing after a fresh victim coupled with a visceral anticipation of goring and trampling him to death.

On foot, Bradan knew he'd lost this race. He couldn't stay ahead of Cynbel and Aennati for more than seconds. Suddenly, he was inspired by a memory of skating through Golden Gate last summer, snaking in and out of packs of other in-line skaters at breakneck velocity with Julie. His blades were still in the Tesla's trunk. Transportation spells were simple and almost foolproof over short distances. The priests knew he was here so he wasn't giving away anything by using magic. He concentrated on his skates and said the required enchantment. The Rollerblades materialized at his feet. Fighting nausea and fatigue, Bradan ripped his tennis shoes off and grabbed the blades, jammed his feet in, tightened the boots by yanking on the straps, and lumbered awkwardly a few meters across the grass toward Stow Lake Drive, then vaulted over the curb, almost falling headlong in the process as the blades spun out of control.

Trying to remember what skating technique he knew, Bradan half ran, half glided to accelerate quickly, and then lengthened his strides, tucking to reduce wind resistance and leaning way forward over the blades. A heavy clatter behind him indicated that the creatures, almost on top of him, had leaped onto Stow Lake Drive, too. He didn't turn around. Thank God these blades were meant for speed, with Mogema alloy frames and Kopp wheels rolling on almost frictionless bearings. Bradan felt like he moved on ice. He arced around a curve and down a hill, picking up velocity as he headed toward the main road through the park, John F. Kennedy Drive, crossing his legs over and swinging his arms in rhythm with long glides. He didn't see Tintagel but guessed the wolf was ranging behind trying to distract Cynbel and Aennati. He felt vibrations from heavy hooves pounding the pavement.

If he could make it across the park and into the Haight, about two and a half kilometers away, he might find safety amid neighborhood streets unfamiliar to Cynbel and Aennati. Even at this late hour, the Haight's street life would also complicate the chase for his pursuers, but he had a hideously long run toward whatever security civilization offered. He fled, a soul chased by hell's demons.

He swept onto JFK Drive, blanketed with fog, legs driving, racing as fast as the loose skates and his inexperience allowed. Air blasted past him and lacerated his lungs with every gulped breath. His hair streamed behind him. The wind sucked tears out of his eyeballs. He was out of shape. Through trees, he saw the Japanese Tea Garden and the de Young art museum sweep past on his right, indistinct in the mist. They might have been part of Tintagel's ramparts. A glance over his shoulder showed the elk close behind and bounding effortlessly after him with the male's heavy antlers tilted back for better balance. He had ultra-fast blades, but the elk gained on him. One of them veered off the road to the right into a stand of trees to be momentarily lost from his sight, trying to flank him, Bradan guessed. When would he reach the park's edge?

Bradan hit a speed bump and teetered wildly from one foot to the other, bending forward and back, before sprawling to the asphalt, hitting his shoulder painfully and scraping the palms of both hands raw. Miraculously, the skates stayed on. The sound of hoof-beats deafened Bradan and he rolled aside barely ahead of a goring thrust. He kicked wildly upward, aiming at its belly, and hit nothing. Bradan saw that both animals were on top of him, the smaller of the two without antlers—this must be Aennati—stamped downward just as Bradan rolled sideways while the larger lowered its head to impale him. Tintagel howled and snapped at the larger brute's haunches. With more adrenaline than he realized that he still had, Bradan lurched clumsily to his feet, almost falling back down. He hopped sideways, barely eluding yet another sweep of the antlers. The sheer size of the rack made it awkward to manipulate even for an animal with neck muscles as powerful as the elk. The other monster, now fully occupied, tried to stamp the life out of the wolf, but Tintagel was a phantom shifting about the deer's legs. Bradan dodged left, then sharp right, almost losing one of the skates in evasive maneuvering, but he regained momentum as he plowed down JFK. He saw lights ahead in the mist that might be the Haight. The fog was no longer something endemic to San Francisco, a quaint curiosity to tourists and a nuisance to the city's residents. It had become a dense mist that emanated from the ground in swirling gusts rather than falling as a gentle, diffuse moisture from the heavens.

A police radio chirped behind him and he heard an engine race. So the car on Stow Lake Drive had been the cops. Maybe the priests' victims had made enough noise before succumbing to bring John Law to the scene. The first officers would be stunned for a few moments by the number of dead and the circumstances of their killing, but would quickly organize themselves to scour the park and surrounding neighborhoods. They'd also note that the victims hadn't been dead long and that the manner in which they'd been butchered fit the pattern of other recent killings. A siren sounded behind them near the lake and then another from somewhere south of the park. The sounds cut dully through the mist.

His right thigh muscles were going to explode. Bradan risked a look back and saw both elk slow then stop with ears cocked to stare back in the direction of the police sounds. Their reaction was so natural that for a second he believed they were animals startled by human intrusion. Whatever the distraction, Bradan didn't miss a beat as he continued to skate away. He didn't have a good explanation about why he was here in the middle of the night near a half dozen bodies. The police weren't going to believe a few deer did the killing. Still, at the moment, running headlong into the cops would be the least of his worries.

In the distance, but getting closer quickly, Bradan now heard a helicopter and a couple of drones. He spared a glance upward but couldn't see anything for several moments. Finally, he discerned a sleek, white helicopter. It seemed to slow a bit as it approached the lake before moving higher and circling toward him as it tracked along JFK. The mist was diffuse directly above him, providing poor cover. *More police?* he wondered. Bradan now made out details on the helicopter and recognized that it was a television crew courtesy of Channel 7. Bradan snarled to himself. No carnage could be real without being ratified by the media.

Maybe the cops had been careless in their communications and a night news editor had picked up a lead. Ritual slaughter by Stow Lake over the holiday season. Bradan suspected it would play better than the Zodiac killings years back. The story would get national coverage, another quintessentially Californian tale. Anchorpeople would pontificate about declining morals and increasing violence all the while showing graphic pictures of the bodies being carted off.

An oval pool of bright, diffuse light materialized on the asphalt ahead of him connected to a cone of light probing downward into the fog.

"We're prime-time," Bradan shouted angrily at the wolf.

He watched a clean, white, little chopper lower itself directly above him then swing its tail around to align itself for a better camera angle. A man with headphones leaned out a window and centered a handheld camera on them. A soundman angled a mike down at them. Stupid! What did they expect to hear over the racket their own chopper was making? Was he supposed to shout a confession up at them? Was the damned thing going to land on him? Beyond the road, the grass prostrated itself before the news crew as the helicopter dropped ever lower. Tintagel snarled and snapped at them.

Bradan looked back down JFK. The elk were gone. The priests were still avoiding attention. Bradan wondered how well the concept of mass media translated for a fifth-century mentality.

Through the helicopter's windshield, Bradan saw the well-fed face of an anchorman he recognized from a nightly news program staring as a god down at them while talking into a microphone. The cameraman piped the whole scene live and real-time into the homes of any early-rising television watchers. How well could they see him in the mist and shifting light? What he was doing could only be construed as a culprit fleeing the crime scene.

A second, brightly-lit chopper came in much higher than the first one and angled toward him, spotlights probing downward. A rival station muscling in on the kill. Several drones from the news channels circled around the human-piloted choppers to provide extra camera angles on the action below.

Bradan laughed. Even in his exhausted, numbed state, the image of vultures closing in was too much to push away. Bradan recited several verses. The first time through, he missed some of the delicate rhymes and alliterations as he skated along. The second time he managed to force the spell out between pants. Tintagel's fur bristled. Instantly, there were a dozen identical copies of Bradan and the wolf all streaking along the drive heading toward the Haight on in-line skates. He now moved in the middle of a bunch of racers. The illusion was perfect; his mirror images, gliding along, stared back at him impassively. The real Bradan made a small motion with his hand and the formation scattered, fanning out to disperse like spokes on a wagon wheel.

The two choppers overhead jerked upward as if the pilots' fingers had been jammed into electric outlets. The Druids wouldn't be fooled.

"Put that on TV," Bradan shouted upward, gasping for breath. He could hardly force his thighs to move. He rolled erratically along Kezar Drive. As always, making the magic drained him. He was also completely winded from the sprint across the park.

He couldn't juggle this many illusions for long, but he didn't have to. The two choppers flew much higher now and circled erratically with their searchlights playing over the fog, trees, and grass, now tracking one skater, now another. Bradan flinched. They almost collided. The drones swirled chaotically, adding to the aerial disorder.

Now neither chopper followed them; the news crews pursued fakes. These would turn to shadows in a few moments, but by that time he would be among the Haight's streets and hard to find from the air.

Bradan's expelled his breath. The Haight's lights were straight ahead. Cautiously, he rolled the last few hundred meters hunched over and leaning on his knees, totally spent with exhaustion and fear. The skates had rubbed his feet raw. He swung wheezing onto Stanyan Street that separated Golden Gate Park from the neighborhood.

He'd returned to streetlights and soft civilization, but Cynbel and Aennati would finish the job when he was out of the media's focus. He looked up and down the street then back at the park's dark trees still oozing mist. There was no sign of his pursuers, but that wouldn't last. Time to make his way circuitously back to the Tesla. First, he'd ditch his phone. Best to assume someone would recognize him from the footage just shot as he'd fled through the park. With a phone he could be tracked. His magic identified him to the priests; his technology located him for the police. What a wonderful irony.

CHAPTER 12

House Call

"We'll kill Bradan at his home," Cynbel said. "He isn't nearby anymore. I don't feel him." The priest stood next to Aennati amid early-morning pedestrians on Haight Street. Both Cynbel and Aennati had shifted back to their human forms upon leaving the park.

"Gods, that felt good to chase him through the trees, but we wasted time," he continued. "We should have sacrificed him when we saw him. We'll have to find him when he next shows himself."

"If he doubted earlier, he knows we're here now," Aennati said. "He'll warn people."

"We don't understand them. They don't understand us. And it will take time to make them understand who we are. People think differently than in our day. They'll imagine other reasons for what's been happening. None of today's creeds use sacrifice."

Like a British morning, light nibbled fine mist that swaddled the neighborhood. Chaotic humanity, aging hippies, tourists, street people, and local residents meandered past upscale clothing boutiques and grubby little shops selling the paraphernalia of an age of incense, velvet, and ideals. The scene had a ritualized appearance; everyone acted a part in some time-hallowed pattern with a cosmic significance just a little beyond the observer's power to grasp. Even the obligatory narcotics sales taking place in the shelter of store awnings had a choreographed feel to them, where the players lived up to a neighborhood image.

"Wicked tattoos on that guy," a young man told his girlfriend as they passed Cynbel.

"A place on Ashbury Street does that stuff," the girl said. "Expensive ink."

"You've seen Bradan," Cynbel said to Aennati. "What can he do? Has he learned anything since our time?"

"Aside from a few illusions, very little."

"Then he can't defend himself. Still, he knows the city. Experience together with trickeries has kept him alive so far. Let's finish him."

"Kill him without ceremony?" Aennati asked. "We wouldn't become any stronger."

"Once we get him, you can slit his throat. Use whatever ritual you want. First we catch him. You've been to his home before—where was it, near the watchtower on the hill? By its look, it's not even a fort, it's purely decorative—symbolic of a whole era with its guard down."

The priestess intoned several lines and they both shifted in an eyeblink from Haight Street to stand in front of Bradan's scarred condo door, the process hardly eliciting a rustle from the priests' clothing, but both of them breathed hard for a few moments.

Cynbel inspected Bradan's door then spoke a few words. The door blew inward hard enough to pivot on its hinges and crash into the inside wall with an explosion of wood splinters around the doorjamb as the dead bolts ripped loose from the heavy wooden frame. Cynbel strode in looking about him at the residence illuminated with morning light coming through the big windows.

"Direct," Aennati said, sauntering in after him. She picked up a large sliver of wood from the ripped doorframe and tossed it on the sofa.

"There was no chance of surprise. Bradan's not here. If he'd been in, then we'd already have announced ourselves by your spell to get us here. We'll wait until he comes home."

"Intruders: Please identify yourselves within ten seconds or the San Francisco police and Union Security Services will be notified." A disembodied voice emanated from the all the rooms of Bradan's condo. "You will be prosecuted to the extent allowed by law for breaking and entering as well as trespassing and potentially burglary if you take anything."

The Druids looked startled. "He left a guard," Cynbel said.

They both walked quickly from room to room. The magician kicked at a wilted white rose lying on the floor in a bedroom.

"There is no one," the priestess said. "A similar thing happened when I first visited."

The condo's warning began to repeat itself. Cynbel uttered a spell and the security alert translated itself into Latin.

"A threat," the priest said.

He spoke another set of rhyming phrases and the alert halted mid-syllable.

"A protective spell?" he said. "I didn't feel anything. No matter, it won't bother us further whatever its origin."

Cynbel stared around at the living room. He randomly picked out a book from a shelf and looked it over before passing it to Aennati.

"They live as royals in this city. They have no right. Bradan's comfortable here. The room smells of flowers. It's decorated like a villa. That has made him reluctant to move." He looked at the symbols on Bradan's door. "Your greeting?"

"Intimidation," Aennati said.

"Too bad he didn't just run off. Though he has a young body, he has an old spirit that will resist uprooting."

"Bradan?" A woman's voice floated up the stairwell from below. "If it's Bradan, say so right now or I'll call the police."

"A complication . . ." Cynbel said.

". . . we don't need," Aennati answered.

They moved out of the condo, down the hall, over to the stairs, and glided down. Claire stood at the bottom of the stairs holding a pistol in one hand and a cell phone in the other. Catching sight of the descending priests, she raised the gun. Cynbel breathed out a couple of stanzas and Claire froze with her arm fully extended and the Beretta pointed at Aennati's forehead.

"What is it?" Arriving at the second floor, she circled Claire's motionless figure, looking curiously at the gun.

"A weapon, I'd say. We've seen city guards here carrying them. We'll fashion protection for ourselves if anyone decides to use them on us. She can keep this one for all the good that it will do her."

Aennati pulled a knife from her cloak.

"No," Cynbel said.

"We've had this argument before."

"She can help us."

"How?"

"She can explain about this time and place. We understand a little about it but not very much. Also, she must know Bradan. They're neighbors."

"That doesn't mean much in this era," Aennati said.

She yanked Claire's robe aside and regarded the captive now standing in emerald-green pajamas.

"She must understand what I'm saying," Cynbel said. "Even if she doesn't know Celtic or Latin, she suspects that we're arguing about what to do with her. Look. You can see it in her face."

"Does it matter?" Aennati said. "We're only disagreeing about when, not whether, she'll die."

"Maybe she knows where Bradan is. Or, if she doesn't, maybe we can use her as bait to bring him to us. You once trapped Merlin by using your quim."

The priestess ran her hand through Claire's hair. "It's not the same. Look at her features. She belongs to another tribe. She's no Celt. He won't care what we do to her."

"We lose nothing by trying."

Cynbel uttered a long spell, paused, waiting for effect, and then spoke in English. "Are you and Bradan friends?"

"Who are you?" the woman shouted. "Jesus, why can't I move?"

"The tall man who lives nearby, he has a wolf. Where is he?"

"You're the assholes that marked Bradan's door," she said. "Why can't I move? Tony, for God's sake, get up here."

"This is too much trouble," Aennati said. "I'll kill her." She didn't bother to switch back to Celtic.

Cynbel nodded. He saw that his captive understood because the fight left the woman. She was held immobile by the spell but nonetheless sagged as her muscles lost their rigidity from resisting his magic.

"Oh God, don't," she said. Tears started down her cheeks.

"Not here," Cynbel said. "Killing out of spite is worthless. We'll take her to the island. It's a better place." As an afterthought he added, "She knows him. You can see that. Maybe Bradan will try to find her."

"He'll suspect, but how will he be sure we've got her?" Aennati asked.

"Mark her door as you did his. Also, we can work some minor enchantment on the island so that he'll notice and come to us."

CHAPTER 13

Peep Show

"My cousin Manuel, he is so weird, he's turned on by lingerie on store dummies. What he'd do with a real woman, I cannot guess. Don't believe me? It's true. Every word is true. Besides, he never shows for work on time. It's his shift. Is the little shit here? No."

"Evening, Rod," Bradan called as he walked off Broadway into the sex shop sandwiched between a recently renovated architect's studio and a law office. In the ever-changing North Beach, Rod's storefront represented the residual sleaze factor from bygone days when every other building was a strip club or sold porn.

"Tintagel, get away from the door."

He saw Rod look up from his phone conversation as Bradan moved over to the glass counter trailed by the wolf. The big man leaned on it heavily looking at a tablet while he talked. A varied collection of dildos, whips, assorted love oils, and handcuffs had been artfully arranged under the glass. A big Christmas wreath hung on the wall behind him, partially covering an autographed poster of a nude adult film star staring down with a gaze so direct it turned the tables on the viewer, making them wonder who was naked.

"Hey, how you doing, Bradan? And there's Superdog."

Rod returned to his discussion with one tattooed forearm hanging loosely over the front of an antique cash register. The blue and red ink drawing showed the sun rising over a beautifully detailed desert scene. Hot morning light bled into starkly outlined cacti, mountains, and Indians against a horizon that receded into infinity. Though thick, Rod's forearm barely contained the panoramic piece of art etched with the linear precision of Ingres. Marring the intricate scene, "666" had been crudely scrawled on the skin just beneath the desert. Bradan knew this numbered Rod's days in prison.

If Bradan was going to retaliate against the Druids, he needed an equalizer, specifically an unregistered gun, preferably something that could go fully automatic. The only person Bradan knew who might have access to such a weapon was Rod. Would or could Rod help him?

"I'll fire his ass," Rod said. "He was supposed to help me clean up the quake mess, shit all over the floor. He comes here today, I am going to can him. I don't care what Mitch says. It's my store."

Bradan moved further away from the shop's open door, down the counter containing leather and mechanical accouterments of pleasure and pain. Greenish lighting from several ancient fluorescent tubes suspended by chains from the ceiling gave everything a phosphorescent quality and cast odd shadows in the shop. Bradan suspected that the floor of a tropical rainforest beneath a hundred meters of vegetation must have the same qualities of peculiar chiaroscuro. The Rubber Ducky certainly had a jungle aroma. Bradan sneezed. He'd tell Rod to back off on the jasmine and sandalwood incense. Bradan had told Rod that herbal fragrances would turn even the most parsimonious voyeur into a spendthrift consumer. Bradan had also said the aromas would add class and sophistication to the shop.

He glanced out the front door and saw a police car roll slowly by on Broadway washed in shifting neon light from the street's clubs. A cop in the passenger seat scanned the store's interior. Bradan held the countertop hard enough to break a thumbnail, then released his death grip and moved nonchalantly further inside. The cruiser didn't stop. Bradan felt his shoulder muscles lose some of their tension. He'd now interposed several stands packed with erotic videos—hadn't the Net taken this niche over?—between himself and the Ducky's entrance, wide open to the busy street's pedestrian traffic and possible police attention.

Bradan looked about the shop trying to size up the customers. A few people browsed among the paraphernalia, but in an era of Internet porn, crowds didn't patronize the Rubber Ducky except for the occasional San Francisco hipster who trolled the aisles more as an mocking commentary on neighborhood gentrification than out of genuine prurience. Outside, urban professionals hustled about en route to pick up kids or eat at new chichi restaurants. At the few remaining strip clubs, clusters of men hung around looking at barkers extolling their club's dancers using half-mocking tones that challenged the onlookers' masculinity to spend just a little money, come inside and see the action. More persuasive than the barkers, dancers periodically sauntered out onto the street, catching a breath of fresh air between performances. The women didn't seem too particular about covering themselves with the loose shifts that, aside from thongs, were all that they wore. The men would retreat before these visions of carnality, but then, often as not, would follow the women into the clubs in a ritualized interaction as old as the hills.

Bradan felt ridiculous here. The police couldn't have

connected him with the murders in the park yet; they never would. He'd been too far away for the television cameras to get a good shot of him, but caution was still in order. If he were already being sought, this crazy store had to be the last place in the North Beach anyone would look; the store's owner, Rodrigo Santiago, would be the last person to turn him in. The proprietor proudly wore tattoos acquired during a two-year stint for armed robbery. For Rod, running a sex shop was a big step toward bourgeois respectability. Presumably, Cynbel and Aennati would also search elsewhere, though Bradan was just three blocks from his home.

A meter away from him, a bearded biker stood in a denim jacket bearing a South Bay club insignia and Harley-Davidson logo. A motorcycle chain served as the belt for his oil-stained jeans—an appropriate stylistic accessory that could be used for chain whippings. The man had a simian quality suggesting that his ancestors had struggled halfway up the evolutionary ladder before growing tired and deciding to rest on a rung well below the top. Some Asian kids stood nearby looking out the front door frequently, expecting a parent to barge in and haul them back to homework and propriety. Bradan noted that everyone carefully avoided eye contact, at once self-conscious and lost in their lustful fantasies. Perfect. If questioned, nobody would remember him.

Earlier, exhausted after the previous night's activities and his mad flight through Golden Gate, he'd parked on a quiet street in the Sunset neighborhood near Ocean Beach and napped. Bradan had awakened suddenly, feeling potent spells. They weren't directed against him, but he sensed them as surf pounding a distant shore. The Druids were clearly manipulating their new environment.

Though he wasn't as adept as Cynbel and Aennati at using a spell's origin to locate its author, Bradan sensed that the priests had transported themselves from the Haight. Had the bastards moved to his home again? If they checked his entire building, how could he warn Claire, Tony, and his other neighbors without having to explain what his pursuers were?

"Time to shake them up," he had told Tintagel. "We've played their game, but it's our city. That's got to count."

Bradan heard Rod put his phone down on the glass case with a bang, pulling him out the unsettling memory.

"Merry Christmas," the owner shouted over at him in accented English. "It feels way too hot for December."

"Global warming," Bradan said.

"Didn't use to believe in it, but I do now. Want some porn? That will take your mind off the climate." Rod scratched his mustache reflectively, sizing Bradan up. "Hey, what happened? You been in a fight? You win?"

"No." Bradan touched a bruise on his chin. He hurt everywhere. He hoped he didn't see his reflection until he had a chance to clean up.

"No you were not in a fight, or no you did not win?" Rod sometimes used contractions, but, in Bradan's experience, the store owner seemed to sprinkle them into his sentences arbitrarily. It gave the owner an oddly deliberate and thoughtful phrasing out of character with his tough appearance.

"Long story," Bradan said. "Tell you another time."

Rod shrugged. Bradan thanked heaven that Rod could be the least inquisitive of souls when the occasion demanded. Sticking up liquor stores and surviving San Quentin schooled a man in keeping his own council.

"Hey, that aroma stuff worked," the store owner said. "It used to smell like mustard gas in here."

A late-model white sedan rolled past the Ducky's entrance. Was that another cop car, unmarked?

"How's Kristina?" Bradan asked. His voice must have sounded tense.

"She is doing great. UC Berkeley agrees with her. She wants to major in art history." Rod laughed. "Must be taking after her dad." He waved about him, encompassing the entire store. "This is art, right? But she has more style. Thanks for the recommendation you wrote for her. It helped get her in. You're kind of well-known as being an author on religions and faith. Berkeley don't admit too many poor Mexicans if their dad has a record."

"Kristina had strong grades."

Rod nodded. "Smart kid. So, what can I do for you? You want your money, right? Eleven hundred fifty I still owe you."

"Let's cancel that debt. I need a gun, unregistered, large caliber. Maybe a couple of guns. Also, let me use your phone."

"Fuck, what have you gotten into?"

"I need to hurt some people before they hurt other people. Before we talk about the gun, I need a phone."

"Local call?"

"Yep."

Rod handed him the phone and moved away, ostentatiously minding his own business. He walked into a back office. Bradan punched in Claire's number. No response. He then tried Tony. It was 11:00 p.m. His neighbor might be in bed already.

"Bradan, what's going on?" Tony sounded wide awake and scared.

"Lots," Bradan murmured into the phone. "Listen, I need a favor."

"You're a popular guy today," Tony cut him off. "First, the police came by. I thought it was to check your vandalized door, but instead they wanted to find out where you'd been last night, asked if I'd seen you. They wanted to know the exact times. I think they had a warrant to check out your place. Your door had been kicked in, anyway. Also, someone had tripped your condo's security system and alerted the cops—don't think your condo got any pictures of the intruders, though, kind of strange. The cops tried to talk to Claire too, because her front door was open and a bathrobe was in the hallway by the stairs. They thought it was hers. Whoever hit your door decided to do hers too because it's all marked up with those voodoo symbols. Our building's front door lock doesn't seem to keep out whoever's doing this. Plus, the police think Claire's gone, maybe kidnapped. Anyway, she's not in her condo."

Bradan froze. His stomach dropped a hundred meters, turning to ice during the free fall. He inhaled deeply.

"White?" Bradan asked.

"What?" Tony said.

"The robe, it was white?"

"I don't know. I didn't see it. Yeah, one of the detectives described it that way when they were interviewing me, I think."

"Crap," Bradan muttered.

"They asked me a whole bunch of questions. Strange that she left her door wide open with all this shit going on around town. You knew she's been thinking about buying a gun? The detectives were still there when the homeowners association head, Chou, came over—I don't know how he knew something was up. He saw your and Claire's doors and started screaming. He said the other residents need to meet to consider a lawsuit, you're a risk to your neighbors. Then a bloody news crew from

Channel 7 drops by. They're still here. I can see their van from my front window. I think another channel is here now too plus some bloggers representing witches. There also seems to be an unmarked cop about halfway down the block. He isn't going anywhere soon."

Bradan leaned heavily on Rod's counter right over the handcuffs. He scratched an itchy stubble of a beard. What he wouldn't give for a hot shower. Not in his home, though. Druids and detectives. Good thing he'd called ahead.

Cynbel and Aennati had Claire. The symbols on her door showed that. It said something else, too, that they wanted him to know they had her. If the priests had Claire, was she already dead, one more sop thrown before the gods to enhance their power? Killing a single person, excepting himself, wouldn't really help them much. Maybe she'd just gotten in the way when Cynbel and Aennati had dropped in this morning after playing cat and mouse with him in the park. His neighbor sure didn't deserve to have her neck crushed just for living one floor beneath him.

"There's more," Tony said.

"Do tell."

"I couldn't get back to sleep after all this shit. So, I turned on the TV. There was some kind of mass killing in Golden Gate Park last night. It even preempted earthquake coverage. Then there was a shot of you and some big animal that might have been Tintagel running across the park—he's a fucking werewolf. It made for some dramatic footage when your dog jumped up in the air and snapped at the news crew. Now I understand the attention. You're a suspect. Want my advice on who to get as an attorney?"

"You can see my face in the clip?" Bradan asked. He drummed

his fingers on the counter. It sounded like bones dancing.

"Look yourself. It's on all the channels. Nothing else on the news this evening. They're even running a special segment about all these killings lately on that dumb news program, *Soft Target*. You're a star."

"I'm a soft target. Tony, can you bring me my computer? It's in the dishwasher."

"Not a bad hiding place."

"My home knows you so the door will unlock, you can just walk right in, but if you get the sense that someone is still there, don't go in. Get out of the building, in fact." Cynbel and Aennati must have left when the police, Chou, and the news guys arrived, but who knew for sure?

"Bradan, I don't need to be let in. Maybe I wasn't clear. Whoever left the symbols on Claire's door also came back this morning and kicked yours in totally. You've hardly got a doorframe left, let alone a lockable door. I think a detective kind of propped it shut before she left."

"Can you get in and bring me the damned computer? That is, assuming the cops didn't seize it as evidence. I don't care what shape the door's in."

"Where are you?"

"The Rubber Ducky."

"The Ducky? Bradan, what the hell's gotten into you? You've become a real mystery."

"Not mysterious, just private, but my privacy's history at this point."

Bradan set the phone down next to the register working very hard not to smash it through the glass. What could he do to the priests to return the favor?

He looked upward at a screen running a continuous loop of

sex. At the moment, a woman sat astride a man rising way up then dropping slowly back down to impale herself with almost sincere moans of pleasure. Her breasts bounced in rhythm to the movements. The camera closed in for a better view. The Rubber Ducky's spectators gathered nearer, raptly attentive, waiting for the actress's synthetic climax. The act looked as stylized as a scene on a 480 BCE Greek amphora or a sixteenth-century French erotic folio.

"Rod, is that just a monitor or is it a TV, too?" Bradan asked. The proprietor had returned from his office carrying a backpack.

"It's also a TV. Do you care? TV do not show nothing as hot as this. That's Pussy Sweat up there. I think the guy is John Buck. Nah, maybe not. He ain't big enough."

"No, you were right the first time," the biker said. "It's Buck. The angle's bad so can't see all of him."

Rod looked at the screen and shrugged. "Maybe. They must be using a medium lens for that shot. Should use a close-up on the girl's face with a smash cut to his cock. Did you see Buck's other picture? Can't think of the name, but it's got Debi Garcia in it. Classic."

"Yeah, I saw it, but the lighting was bad in that one. They must have skimped on production costs."

"Gentlemen," Bradan interrupted glancing out the door again. "If it's not too much trouble, can we watch the news?"

Dead silence reigned in the Ducky.

"Please," Bradan added. An old man holding a pink dildo turned away from the screen to stare at him; he meant to bludgeon Bradan with the toy.

"What?" Rod said.

The biker rumbled something inarticulately menacing and fingered the chain around his waist. Even the Asian kids looked aghast. Bradan might as well have asked to see a Walt Disney feature, something with lots of cute animals but no actual bestiality.

"There was a murder," Bradan said. "Actually, a lot of murders in the park last night. The news is showing it all."

"How many killed?" the biker asked.

"Six, maybe more. Ritual slaughter. Those kind of things."

The biker looked at Rod for a moment. They both nodded. Using a remote, Rod stopped the couple in mid-orgasm and the news exploded onto the screen like a cum shot.

"We'll get to yesterday's 6.0 magnitude quake that shook the Bay Area in just a minute, but first we'll fill you in on the latest in a series of what must be San Francisco's bloodiest string of mass murders in this century, maybe in recorded history. Lisa, what can you tell us about what the media is already calling the Stow Lake Massacre?" The blond, well-groomed, slightly puffy-faced newscaster turned to his stunning Asian co-anchor.

"Dan, it's the worst I've ever seen," the co-anchor said, facing the camera directly. Absently, Bradan wondered just how many other mass murders the woman had seen.

"This whole situation definitely has elements of bizarre violence to it. Some of the victims were stabbed—decapitated, really—and then burned. We haven't been told this officially, but it seems similar to what happened out on Angel Island and Ocean Beach. And Muir Woods. Because of the bodies' condition, only two have been identified so far. Police are working to get names for the others. I'm speculating here, but the fact that it happened just before Christmas may be significant."

"Jesus, another one. I thought that shit only happened in L.A.," Rod said.

"Worse than the North Koreans," the old guy with the dildo said.

"Worse than Charlie Manson," the biker said. He pulled on his beard. "When I was a tiny kid, I met Manson on Santa Monica Beach once. Always wanted to be Charlie. But this stuff makes him look chickenshit."

"Welcome to the big leagues," Bradan murmured, staring at the images. "And the fun has just started. *Guerre à outrance.*"

"What?" the old man asked.

"Total war," Bradan said.

The co-anchor said breathlessly, "Lisa, we'll break away because the mayor's office scheduled a news conference shortly to talk about this situation and the quake, too. With the mayor newly elected, he'll want to show he's on top of things. Also, Channel 7 has exclusive pictures of what may be two of the assailants escaping from the murder scene through last night's fog heading toward the Haight neighborhood. We'll show that right now."

"Let's see it," the old man said.

Bradan held his breath. The screen filled with distant objects, indistinct and amorphous in the fog and darkness, but becoming visible in the center of the screen as they moved toward the camera. Bradan stifled a groan. Rod shot him a quick glance, then looked back at the screen.

Everyone in the store, including the old man, now clustered directly beneath the TV, following the developing drama. The anchor's voice-over described how the news chopper and drones had spotted the fleeing figures out in the open while heading to Stow Lake with a camera crew after getting a tip that another attack had occurred. The crew, suspecting that the fugitives must be connected to the horrors by the lake, had decided to delay investigating the crime scene and give chase instead. On screen, the copter rapidly overtook its prey. Now a tall figure and an animal were clearly visible. The image improved as spotlights hit them. Bradan hurtled along with the wolf beside him racing across the fog-shrouded avenue. Stark, giant shadows cast by the lights followed them as they fled and the mist reflected the glare pallidly. The camera zoomed in just as Bradan looked up.

Bradan noticed Rod stiffen, but the store owner didn't say anything.

"Fuck," Bradan breathed. Anyone seeing this gothic tableau would have to conclude that the man on the screen was the killer.

"Ugly-looking son of a bitch," biker said.

Bradan hoped he referred to the wolf.

"They'll shoot on sight," the biker continued.

Despite the fog, the picture's clarity and definition were pristine because of the drone's proximity to its quarry. Even the color was wonderful. Tintagel lunged upward at the news camera, canines bared. Now the picture froze with both of them in guilty poses. Bradan could guess why they didn't show the rest of the footage. It would be hard to explain to befuddled viewers the sudden appearance of a dozen mass murderers.

". . . and using facial recognition technology, sources have relayed to this station's reporters that the man may and, I repeat this, may be Bradan Badon, a Bay Area psychology counselor, author and noted New Age therapist. We're working to confirm that. Later in tonight's program, we'll have home security expert Merle Bernstein explain how you can protect your property and loved ones from this sort of violence."

Bradan turned away as San Francisco's mayor replaced the image of Bradan and the wolf. Bradan caught Rod's eye and they moved down the counter away from the others. Bradan knew what question would come first and braced himself.

"Did you do it?" Rod asked, keeping his voice low.

"No. I couldn't kill one person, let alone six." Bradan hoped he sounded convincing. The thing was, he was innocent as driven snow, but he have must appeared to be the killer. The question was, how would Rod react? Would he think Bradan was psycho enough to do it? Butchering six people wouldn't look good even to this ex-felon.

"What were you doin' out in the park in the middle of the night?"

"Rod, one day soon I'm going to tell you," Bradan said. "No time now. I was trying to help. If I'd gotten there a little earlier things might have gone differently. Maybe not."

"Your alibi doesn't sound good to me."

"I was talking to a neighbor when the killings were happening."

"Has your neighbor told this to the police?"

"I don't think so. She disappeared."

Rod just let his statement hang in the air as a big, fat birthday balloon.

Doing his best not to sound like a desperate murderer, Bradan added, "I tried to help people last night. You know me. Am I a killer?"

Bradan couldn't tell what Rod thought. The sex shop owner simply stared at him.

"I know who did kill those poor bastards," Bradan said. He was talking to himself.

Finally Rod said, "So tell the police. They don't believe you, the worst that'll happen is you sit in the county lockup until your lawyer bails you out. Can you prove you were somewhere else when all that happened? None of your prints are at the scene?" He waved at the screen that now showed Stow Lake, where forensics experts and coroners hauled away plastic-covered bodies.

"Maybe, if I can find my neighbor. If the police determine the exact time of death, it'll help, too. God knows how long that'll take."

Rod looked exasperated. "Spend a few days behind bars, then. The food ain't that bad. I survived. Watch out in the showers. When you get out, sue the city. Hell, sue the fuckin' network, too. They just associated your name with a mass killing. You just happened to be out for a stroll in the park at the wrong time. You got a good attorney, no? Do not use mine. The moron didn't know the first thing about evidentiary hearings."

Someone tapped Bradan's arm. Bradan whirled around.

"Tony," he said. It came out as a shout. His neighbor's hair seemed grayer and more unruly than usual. He looked fatigued.

"It's all right, Bradan. Just me."

"Who are you?" Rod asked. He stared at Tony. Bradan noticed the store owner's hand drift under the counter. Probably looking for a shotgun.

"My neighbor," Bradan said quickly. "Not the one I was with last night. This is the guy I called a minute ago." Tony passed him the laptop.

"I had to cross police tape to get into your place, but no detectives were around, so no problem finding it. The dishwasher was a good place to hide it. I used a ski mask so that your home's security cams won't have footage of me. I left the building by the back door and went down the Filbert Steps. I don't think anybody saw me."

"You should do this for a living," Bradan said. Damn, he'd

forgotten to warn his neighbor to be cautious. Thankfully, Tony had used his head.

"Bradan, you need a lawyer." Tony said it as a flat statement. "Here's a card. Talk to Nancy. I only do tax stuff, but when our firm needs criminal expertise, she's one of the best."

"Thanks," Bradan said, pocketing the card. He might use it. Eventually. When he could afford to worry about lethal injections and executions and other mundane issues. Right now the last thing he needed was to be caged, a sitting duck for Cynbel and Aennati.

"You know, you could just turn yourself in," Tony said. "Why wait for them to track you down? It'll just make you resemble the real perpetrator, whoever that was. A SWAT team might just shoot you by accident."

"That's what I say," Rod added.

"I know," Bradan said. "I'm not running from the police, just avoiding them for a couple of days. If I'm locked up, the people that did the Stow Lake thing and all the other stuff will know where to get me."

"In county lockup?" Rod asked. "Who we talking about here? Some kind of gang with connections inside the jail?"

"In a way," Bradan said.

"What have you gotten yourself into?" Tony asked. "Your biggest problem used to be getting paid on time for spiritual counseling. That and sneaking a hamburger when your foodie girlfriend wasn't looking."

Rod looked over at the customers still watching the screen, fascinated as a newscaster described the wound patterns with a surgeon's zest for anatomical detail. Deftly, Rod pulled a large, black steel semiautomatic from the backpack he'd retrieved from his office. He dropped three spare clips by the pistol.

"It's a Magnum Research Desert Eagle. It's chambered for .50. The thing on the barrel is a laser sight. Put the red dot on your target and pull the trigger. I've tried it myself. It works. Your troubles will vanish before your eyes."

"I know how use a laser sight," Bradan said.

"If you want to borrow it, it is yours, but if you use it, throw it in the Bay. I don't want to see it again. So, you fired a gun before?"

"Yes," Bradan said. "Miami, years ago." He hefted the pistol discreetly, shielding it from the other customers with his body.

"Cocaine?" Rod asked.

Bradan nodded. "Another life."

"Man, wouldn't have expected that from you. Ever shoot anyone?"

Bradan shook his head. "It never came to that."

"I don't know about this," Tony said. He stared at the gun with repugnance. "Getting caught with that, under the circumstances, they'll throw away the key." He eyed Rod. "It's not registered, is it?"

Rod looked at Tony as if he were a cretin.

"Thanks," Bradan said. The gun was heavy, but fit into his hand surprisingly easily. Rod had evidently modified the grip for better comfort and accuracy. Bradan popped the clip out. The storeowner kept it loaded. Bradan had seen more weapons in the last twenty-four hours than he had in the previous decade. He looked at the spare clips crammed with bullets.

"How many shots have I got in the clip? I'm not going to hold off an army."

"You never know," Rod said, jabbing a finger into Bradan's chest. "Better to have it and not need it than the other way 'round. I found that out when I was younger. Keep it for the time being. That weapon is state of the art."

Holding the .50 made Bradan feel distinctly uncomfortable; he enjoyed the intellectual challenge of applying the right spell to a situation. Nonetheless, the weapon would be essential to taking on the Druids. Technology could help him. Any spell he knew would threaten the priests about as much as blowing bubbles at them. Moreover, Cynbel and Aennati were still new to this world, leaving them unfamiliar with guns. Rod's cannon might be the edge he needed if he could ambush the Druids. The question then became how to lure them into range. He shoved the .50 and ammo into the backpack along with the laptop and slung it over his shoulder. The weapon was heavy. Carrying and concealing this thing would be a problem. Back in the day, he'd preferred 9mm's.

Tony shrugged. "Your funeral."

"Thanks," Bradan said. "This will help. Anything with more range? AR-15? Uzi? H&K MP5? I've fired all of them at one time or another."

Rod nodded encouragingly. "Not playing games. You got style, bro. I can get an M-16 with a grenade launcher, ex-military, but it will take time."

"No time," Bradan said. "I'll make do with the your canon."

"You're ready to take down a bank now," the shop owner said. "The pistol has self-stabilizing technology, keeps the barrel from climbing when you shoot. You stay on target. The sight can shift between laser and infrared. You can hit something in the dark if you have to. Plus, in the laser mode, the sight can blind your target."

"It's almost from a sci-fi movie."

"Whoever pulled that number in the park will look a lot better with a big hole in them," Rod said.

"What about you? This leaves you with nothing. You get some pretty rough customers at night. Kristina wants you around for her graduation."

"I have a sawed-off Remington pump behind the interactive computer games rack here."

"No shit." Tony looked at Rod and Bradan like they had a virus. "I gotta go. I'm so tired, I can hardly stand up."

To Bradan, his neighbor seemed more scared than exhausted.

"One thing, though, this is weird, but when I got your computer, I think someone else was in your condo. I didn't see anyone, but I had that feeling. Do you suppose the cops could have bugged your place or maybe one of the news crews planted someone up there, hiding in the closet or bathroom?"

Bradan was aware that both Tony and Rod watched him. "It was nothing," he said. "You got up too early this morning. Get some sleep."

Tony nodded. "Take care of yourself. I'll help any way I can. Call whenever. You want me to check out your room more thoroughly?"

"No. Don't worry about it. It's public property now. The police will be back again. It could have been the police, in which case they followed you to the Ducky."

Tony strolled over to the door and out onto Broadway. After a second he walked back in to the store, trying to look relaxed, but moving quickly. He was no actor.

"Bradan, you might talk to Rod here about using the back door out. There's two guys, they've gotta be cops, walking in and out of shops with some pictures. They're about one store away at Big Al's."

"Crap," Bradan said.

"This way," Rod hissed. He grabbed Bradan's shoulder.

182 PETER W. BLAISDELL

"Through my office in here."

"Tony, can you stall them?" Bradan called over his shoulder as he rushed around the counter. "Play tourist. Ask for directions to the Golden Gate."

"I'll try," Tony said.

Rod pulled a huge key ring from his pocket and hurriedly opened the office door. Tintagel scooted in after him, with the animal's tail barely clearing the door before Rod slammed it shut. Bradan heard an indistinct conversation between Tony and another man with an affable but insistent voice. He also heard Rod quickly lock the door behind him. That would buy him a few moments. The cop would have to get Rod to let him in to search his office. Of course, the detective would need a warrant for that. Then again, those Chinese kids couldn't be eighteen years old and that might be excuse enough to search the entire shop if Rod appeared to be hiding someone. Had any of the customers studied his face and connected him with the fleeing mass murderer? The biker had noted something. Maybe he'd keep shut. Maybe.

Bradan faced a window. Good. It was tiny and set high in the wall. Bad. This minuscule aperture would be a squeeze. He'd also have to pick Tintagel up and shove the wolf through and count himself lucky if the animal didn't take his head off in the process.

Quietly, he put his backpack down on Rod's desk, which was cluttered with spreadsheets showing the store's financial condition, and pushed a chair over beneath the window. The desk lamp was turned off, leaving the cramped room lit only by dim crepuscular light from neon signs coming through the little window's frosted glass. Voices came through the office door. A low rumble emanated from Tintagel's throat. Bradan made frantic hushing motions. Then he pulled on the window's handle. With a dull snap, it broke off. He stared at the rusted piece of metal in his hand. Didn't that son of a bitch Rod ever open this thing? Resisting the urge to hurl the broken handle at the wall, he gently laid it on the desk and gripped the window's lower edge, sliding his fingernails under the lip. Wrenching, he pulled upward. Unoiled, it grated halfway open. Not enough. With all his strength, he heaved again. A shrieking, scraping noise filled the office. The window now stood open.

"Tintagel," he whispered. He tried to pick the wolf up. With a snarl, the animal backed away from him. Bradan swore silently. Ancient Celtic wolves could be finicky. Someone outside tried the door handle. Tintagel looked at the open window, shifted position slightly, and then in a blur of fur, leaped directly from the floor partway through the aperture. Briefly, the big animal was half in, half out, a big furry stopper in the mouth of a bottle. Then, hind legs scrabbling noisily on wall and glass, he pushed himself through.

Bradan lunged at the window backpack in hand and stuck his head outside, then forced his shoulders through. Spells would be no help with the priests perhaps only three blocks away. The police, he might evade; Cynbel and Aennati, never. His sweater and shirt shredded on the crumbling metal sill as he pushed himself further out. Now his center of balance was outside the building and, both hands holding the backpack, unable to stop himself, he pivoted sharply downward, whacking his chin on the building's outer wall. Somehow he managed to keep the pack from smashing into the wall, too.

"Damn this shit."

Wriggling his legs to free them from the window's rusty grip, Bradan broke free and fell headfirst outward and down into an alley. As he dropped, he tucked and landed with a bruising crunch on his shoulders. Sprawled on the ground, he saw that he'd just missed several broken bottles and an old oil drum. Hell, he was a wizard par excellence, scrambling out of a pornographic toy store into a filthy little alley chased by detectives. Cynbel and Aennati needn't have to lift a finger to be rid of him. The SFPD would do that for them.

Bradan lurched upward, off balance, and looked around. There was a blank brick wall across from him. He turned around and stumbled into the oil drum, which responded with a melodious, echoing clang. Several meters down the alley, Tintagel sat on its haunches staring at him. Seeing that he stood upright, the animal turned and bounded toward Broadway. Bradan slung the pack over his shoulder and sprinted after the wolf.

"Stop! Stop right there!" The voice echoed after him. Bradan didn't need to turn around to know a cop must be poking his head out the window.

"Yo, sucker, I'll shoot!"

He knew the cop wouldn't pull the trigger because now Bradan barreled out onto Broadway's sidewalk amid four billion tourists, businesspeople, and a Chinese funeral entourage crawling down Broadway before turning onto Stockton, Chinatown's main drag. Bradan elbowed aside someone from the Peruvian navy and lunged onto Broadway, narrowly missing being pulverized by the hearse bearing a large and unflattering picture of the recently deceased. The car's horn deafened him as he pivoted off its front fender. As he spun away from the vehicle, he had a kaleidoscopic glimpse of a long entourage of black vehicles filled with startled faces. Then the funeral's escorting police car made a tight U-turn to come fishtailing up Broadway toward him as the cop floored it. Tintagel agilely skirted a family before leaping over a parked cab. The cabby, Plato's twin, never looked up from his book.

"Is that a wolf?" a woman shouted at her companion.

"Mommy, what do they sell in that store, ducks?" a kid asked his parent. Bradan missed the answer.

He prayed that the Tesla was parked, hopefully still unnoticed, a block down Kearny. Bradan, hurtling flat out, turned the corner, passed the biker he'd just seen in the Rubber Ducky, and ran straight down the middle of the street paced by the wolf who hardly seemed to be panting. Bradan gasped like an old steam engine. The neighborhood smelled of exotic spices and rotting fish guts. He saw his car ahead and looked over his shoulder. Hellfire, one of the tourists was waving his arms wildly, motioning the squad car to turn down Kearny. What a citizen. Then the biker grabbed the tourist by the arm and threw a crushing roundhouse punch that decked the fink. Bradan almost ran back to kiss the outlaw.

"Remember Charlie Manson," the gorilla shouted after him.

"My hero," Bradan gasped. He glanced back up toward Broadway. The cop had missed everything and plowed obliviously straight down the street, siren echoing off the brick walls.

Bradan yanked open the Tesla's door and threw the pack in the back seat. The wolf flew past him and landed on the passenger's side. Bradan jumped in and the engine came to life and the Tesla burned rubber as it surged out onto Kearny, gaining speed down the entire length of the block. An earsplitting rebel yell screamed out of the vehicle. Bradan didn't so much drive as hold on to the steering wheel as the car took an insane left turn onto Columbus, just missing a van emblazoned with lettering identifying it as the property of a Korean Baptist church. It was

Connie driving. The autopilot never took such risks. The Tesla's turn threw both Bradan and the wolf against the car's side. They zigzagged through traffic for another two blocks before turning onto Washington, quiet on a Sunday evening. He backed off on the juice, trying to blend with light traffic. He was safe for a moment.

"Put your shades on, sugar," the ghost said. "You'll look gangster."

"Image is important," Bradan said adjusting his Ray-Bans in the mirror. "Also, I'll be harder to recognize."

CHAPTER 14

Blinded by Science

The ruby-colored pinpoint of light danced around the rotunda's nighttime domed interior like a panicked firefly. Bradan switched off the gun's laser sight and the dot vanished. Where were the priests? Did they sense a trap? Bradan saw himself stand, arms folded in an attitude of unnatural calm and detachment, in the center of the Palace of Fine Art's outdoor rotunda. His laptop sat on the ground a short distance away concealed by masonry. Its screen emitted a bluish glow that illuminated the massive structure's twenty-meter-high Roman-style pillars and the rose-orange-hued dome these columns supported. Odd shadows created by the computer's light capered beyond the dome among dense vegetation as the plants surrounding the structure shifted in the wind coming off the Bay.

Bradan watched his image. The bait looked amazingly good, identical to himself, in fact. There was no hint of transparency; the figure had the substance and solidity of a flesh-and-blood person. The faux Bradan's long dark-brown hair even shifted slightly in the breeze. The real Bradan had the eerie sense that the image might become as impatient as he was at the Druids' tardiness and stroll off into the night. However, his doppelgänger was a passive figment of a microchip imagination generated

from the computer's large reference repository of spells. A half
hour before, he'd typed instructions and then taken cover as
the laptop's tinny speaker recited the selected enchantment. His
double materialized close to the laptop. Because the computer
generated the magic, his image would be almost coincident with
the spell's source, a decoy to catch two predators who would
home in unerringly on the magic's origin. Once Cynbel and
Aennati arrived, the image wouldn't fool them for a nanosecond,
but Bradan didn't need long, just enough time to pull the trigger.

Moreover, when the priests transported themselves to the
rotunda with a spell, maybe he could detect their point of origin.
That might be where the Cynbel and Aennati had imprisoned
Claire—if she was alive.

If the priests didn't use a spell, but arrived at the rotunda
by simply walking or came in the form of animals, then
Bradan wouldn't know where they'd come from. If he killed
both Cynbel and Aennati, he might never locate Claire. Under
the circumstances, his plan was to murder one of them and
hopefully panic the survivor into fleeing back to where they
were keeping her.

In any event, Cynbel and Aennati had better show soon
because the computer's battery wouldn't last forever. Though
fully charged, its battery would suffer the same energy depletion
Bradan's psyche experienced when he worked a spell.

He'd designed the gambit. Now he needed to master his
emotions. It wasn't cold, but he couldn't stop shaking. Sweat
soaked his armpits and back. If the priests arrived, he'd face the
individuals who'd turned him into a craven traitor in the fifth
century. He'd betrayed everyone he loved and precipitated the
end of a refined age in Britain. Could he hold the gun steady
when he saw them?

He crouched in the darkness just beyond the rotunda's periphery and close to a lagoon that bordered one side of the structure. The Palace of Fine Art's fluted columns enclosed the other side, forming a huge, block-long colonnade that mimicked the rotunda's Roman-style architecture. The museum and neighboring lagoon sat in the middle of trees, paths, and grass. The entire ensemble had been constructed for a trade fair at the turn of the twentieth century with the rotunda serving as its centerpiece, inspired by an eighteenth century Parisian museum that in turn was inspired by the Pantheon. Floodlights brilliantly illuminated the top of the dome and the columns but left vast puddles of blackness at ground level. Bradan had chosen the site because it seemed ideal for ambush, deserted at night and with a patchwork of lit and dark areas to highlight his pursuers while concealing himself. Ironically, the museum had once housed modern technology displays. How appropriate that he intended to dispose of the ancient magicians in a setting that mashed together archaic and contemporary themes, steampunk redux.

Everywhere Bradan looked, Roman gods, soldiers, chariot drivers, and maidens draped in diaphanous gowns warred or loved in jostling clusters on the edifice's stone reliefs. Other figures stood or leaned against the structure as freestanding statuary. The artist had rendered them in amazingly realistic poses with muscles clearly shown and their stony weapons sharp. They were similar to Arthur's soldiers, and Bradan could almost hear the echoes of the horses' exhalations and the stamp of sandaled feet. The affected Roman-style architecture lent the whole rotunda and old Exploratorium a classical look. Cynbel and Aennati would be stepping back into antiquity to meet their deaths. Tonight the Roman figures seemed to forget their own affairs to leer expectantly downward at him, their features animated by the computer's lighting.

He shifted cramped muscles and checked his digital watch. 1:05 a.m. Bradan glanced up at the heavens. No fog tonight. The stars blazed razor-sharp in the indigo-black sky. He had the galaxy to himself. Aside from the rotunda's spotlights and his computer, no human light competed with the Milky Way. It was as if the city had turned itself off to better view the coming contest.

Elegant townhouses in the distance with dark picture windows fronted the park as the city slept uneasily, perhaps dreaming of immutable futures. Bradan imagined the good burghers safely tucked into bed under high-thread-count comforters after being traumatized by earthquakes and the savagery on Angel Island and in Golden Gate Park.

He shivered as a breeze, stronger than the rest, pushed through the columns and trees touching his skin with cold satin. A rustling noise off to his right made Bradan whirl around. Two white swans landed in the pond a little distance away with soft splashes. They drifted over to the water's edge near the rotunda, serene as water birds in an oriental ink sketch. The moon's reflection bathed next to the swans. The stately creatures took no notice of his image within the rotunda. Then they vanished amid marshes.

"Hello, Bradan." The words were British Celtic.

Bradan yanked his attention back to the rotunda. Cynbel and Aennati stood regarding his image. From his hiding place, Bradan watched, so tense he felt his body vibrate. He gripped the weapon. They had not changed. Cynbel carried himself with the same gravitas and Aennati radiated the lethal focus he recollected so well. His image faced the two Druids with a resoluteness Bradan himself couldn't have mustered.

Bradan raised the Magnum smoothly, trying not to let adrenaline turn his arm into warm candle wax. The wizards would detect the ruse if for no other reason than the image's inability to talk back.

"As always, paralyzed with fear?" Cynbel's voice resonated, expanding to fill the rotunda. The lilting cadences of an old language found affinity in the pre-Christian architecture. It wasn't Latin, yet the antique figures on the stone reliefs understood and leaned closer, anticipating murder; Bradan's virtual twin was a martyr standing before them in the Coliseum.

But whose murder? Bradan steadied the heavy .50 with both hands, aiming at Cynbel's chest and preparing to activate the laser sight. It was damned hard to hold his arms still.

"Get it over with," Aennati said.

Cynbel spread his arms palms upward as if to say, there you are, the matter is out of my hands. He spoke four rhymed couplets. Bradan tried to ignore the words, but even twenty meters away and without being the direct target of the spell, he staggered, almost dropped the gun, and barely held himself upright. A blue-white flash lit the rotunda and flared outward beyond the columns with solar intensity. Light from the soundless explosion washed the distant townhouses with an incandescent splash.

Bradan had guessed what Cynbel planned and closed his eyes. Still, spots floated across his vision. After the killing in Golden Gate Park, the priests would be engorged with magical power. That strength allowed them to employ cataclysmic energies against objects they wanted to destroy. This was a small demonstration of their potency. They would easily overwhelm him in a direct confrontation. But this was an ambush. His vision clearing, Bradan flicked the laser sight on.

The priests stood unmoved and unaffected by the inferno Cynbel had just let loose, the sea breeze wafting away a residual haze of smoke. Bradan's image had vanished along with the computer, leaving an irregular blackened crater on the rotunda's floor and the nearest pillars cracked with huge sooty smudges stretching upward to the rotunda's dome.

Bradan stepped away from the concealing tree and centered the little red dot on Cynbel's chest, paused fleetingly to steady the cannon, and fired. The blast deafened him and, in the darkness, the muzzle flash seemed almost as searing as the wizard's spell. Cynbel staggered but didn't fall. Bradan snarled and fired again, the recoil jarring his arms all the way back to his shoulder sockets, but the pistol's stabilizing technology compensated and muted the recoil. It was surprisingly easy to fire. He swung the gun in a short arc to aim at Aennati. The Celtic headband made an ideal target. Careful. He couldn't kill them both without losing his chance to find Claire. He looked for Cynbel again and thought he saw the wizard moving behind a column. Bradan pulled the trigger. Adrenaline coursed through his veins and he barely heard the shots and lost count of the number of times he fired. Brass casings spun off into the night or clanged to the rotunda's stone floor. Where were they? Had he killed one or both?

Bradan lowered the weapon and moved cautiously to the edge of the rotunda to see its interior. A small war had occurred within. Several of the big columns were charred. The force of the priests' spells had pulverized the floor as if a giant fist had hammered it. A stone figurine of a Roman soldier had tumbled into the mess, shattered into fragments. Less spectacular, Bradan's .50 had deeply pockmarked several pillars. But the rotunda was empty, no bodies.

He'd failed. He had to get the hell out of here. Cynbel and Aennati would riposte as soon as they located him, but they had to see him to kill him. Behind Bradan, the lagoon began to boil. Bubbles roiled its surface, splattering his pants legs and burning through the fabric. Bradan leaped away. He watched a cluster of water reeds wither, blacken, and then bend into the now furiously foaming water. A live thing, the pond expanded beyond its original confines, sweeping after him. Bradan knew what Cynbel and Aennati were doing. Unsure of his exact location in the dark—he didn't intend to give away his location by using a spell—they were trying to flush him into the open. Laying waste to the park would be a crude but effective way of accomplishing this.

The pond water coagulated, transforming itself into pitch and sending great spouts of black goo upward. The heat intensified. Bradan reeled and staggered from the hot-asphalt stink. Through the steam and vapor, Bradan saw the rotunda. He didn't see the priests. Unsure of the nature of his gun or how many times he could fire at them, they had to be waiting for Bradan to show himself to create a more focused attack. Clearly, the Magnum hadn't destroyed them outright, but the heavy slugs' impact appeared to intimidate them.

Bradan couldn't wait longer by the tar's cooking heat. He saw an opening between the rotunda and the lagoon and sprinted toward it. If he could skirt the fouled water, he might make it back to Beach Street on the other side of the park where the Tesla waited. He was exposed, but it was dark—several of the rotunda's spotlights had been extinguished during Cynbel's blast—and the volcanic activity of the once placid little pond might cover his flight.

He noticed the two swans circling overhead untouched by the chaos below. They looked more like raptors now, blocking out the starlight, not tranquil park birds. To the Celts, a person's soul might as easily inhabit an animal's as a human's body. Nature was a continuum. The priests had needed no spell to transport themselves to his image. They'd simply flown.

Bradan dodged behind a shadowed column, moving closer to the water, trying to stay out of sight. However, the hot vapors through which he ran coalesced into forms as vivid as horrors from a nightmare. Improvising, he changed his intended path, which would have taken him too near the lagoon's inferno and whatever creatures the miasma brewed. Leaping over rubble, Bradan darted directly through the open rotunda, conscious with every step of how visible he was.

In the middle of the rotunda, Bradan stopped dead in his tracks. Ahead of him an armored figure pulled itself laboriously out of a stone panel carved with reliefs depicting brutal Roman warfare. Bradan watched, stunned, as the two-dimensional relief rapidly gained depth and substance and separated itself from the panel's embrace, first the head, now the shoulders, torso and legs in a mockery of birthing. Then the centurion dropped agilely to the rotunda's floor and turned to face Bradan squarely, drawing its short-sword and shrugging off the rictus of stone. It advanced toward Bradan, gaining fluidity with each step. Though it now moved with athletic vigor, the Roman and his armor retained the orange hue of the sandstone relief from which he'd originated.

"Shit," Bradan hissed.

Unable to keep him in sight long enough to utter a spell that would kill him outright, Cynbel and Aennati had called for assistance by giving life to the statues and reliefs, native beaters preceding the hunter to flush out prey. Unlike the incorporeal image his laptop had created, this warrior was real, moved with tactical craft, and was animated by purpose. The Druids had summoned a legionnaire fresh from battle, judging by the nicks on the weapon's edges and the warrior's blood-splattered armor. Gore was the one color on its otherwise monochromatic form.

In an instant, the centurion was almost on top of him. Bradan shouted in fear. He instinctively raised his gun and pulled the trigger in his attacker's face. The shot reverberated deafeningly and pulverized half the warrior's head, sending a cloud of stone fragments and dust in all directions. The impact knocked the soldier backward, but with unaffected vitality, it swung its sword downward in an arc that would have chopped Bradan's skull in two if it had landed. Banging his knee painfully, Bradan tumbled to the rotunda's floor, just avoiding the blow. He felt the rush of displaced air past his cheek.

He rolled sideways and regained his feet, frantically ducking a backhanded swipe and rushing toward the rotunda's nearest opening. Above him, on one of the massive stone blocks forming a base for a column, a second figure, this time a gladiator, arm muscles expertly chiseled, climbed nimbly off the perch from which it had provided symbolic support for the dome. He marveled at Cynbel's fine sense of irony in animating depictions of Roman life. Bradan's own tribe of Romanized Celts had been the heirs to civilized Latin rule on Britain before the barbarian incursions of Saxon, Pict, and Jute had crushed settled culture. Now Roman soldiers sought to destroy him.

Shouts and the staccato clattering of hooves behind Bradan told him that the centurion and gladiator had allies. He glanced back to see masses of legionnaires spilling into the rotunda armed with spears and swords. They raced after him across the stone floor, jumping agilely over debris. Bradan was too stunned to panic. His thoughts came in fragments. He registered sensations, but he couldn't develop a strategy to escape. A chariot drawn by two horses rolled through an arch, whipped on by a charioteer in a tunic. An armored soldier beside the driver cast a javelin directly at him. Bradan bent beneath the hurled missile, barely missed being impaled, and saw it catch the gladiator in the stomach with a shattering sound. The javelin disintegrated on impact, but gouged out a huge hole in the fighter's stomach.

Bradan sucked in his breath, leaped over the fallen combatant, fired another shot at the centurion, atomizing the rest of his head, and dashed for the rotunda's far side toward the one opening not crowded with uncanny killers. The horde speeding after him shouting oaths and carrying weapons Bradan hadn't heard or seen for fifteen centuries. Many of his pursuers wore plate armor, others were bare-chested to display jagged tattoos, perhaps auxiliaries. One bore aloft a legion's insignia mounted on a pole.

As Bradan flashed past a stone relief of an aristocratic Roman maiden reclining on a couch, the classical figure allowed her loosely draped gown to fall away entirely from her upper body as she leaned forward out of the stone to watch the hunt. The Roman nobility had seen their share of slaughter for sport.

Barely ahead of his pursuers, Bradan ran along a shadowed gravel path paralleling the museum. Two more javelins hissed by on either side of him. He didn't bother firing back. The gun's slide was racked open. It was ready for another clip. The .50's clip only held seven shots and he couldn't reload at a dead run. The cold air ripped into his lungs as he fled. He heard activity beyond the steaming lagoon and guessed that Cynbel must be directing legionnaires to circle around the water's far side to surround him. Terror and exertion soaked his clothing with sweat. A slashing sword stroke across his neck seemed inevitable. Bradan involuntarily groaned. He glanced back and was surprised to see he'd pulled ahead of the eldritch mass of soldiers. The weight of their weapons and armor must have given him the edge in speed. They'd stopped wasting energy shouting and settled into a grim chase.

He slowed ever so slightly to pull a spare clip from a pants pocket, almost dropping it in the process. He'd have to thank Rod for his foresight if he lived. As Bradan reduced his pace, the soldiers behind him shouted raucously, evidently believing their quarry had tired. If he could slot more bullets into the Magnum, he might conceivably blast his way out of the park, assuming the priests didn't create some new horror to pursue him through the city streets. Running awkwardly, he palmed the clip into the gun's grip and then accelerated back to full speed as he rounded the lagoon's corner almost crashing headlong into a legionnaire who held out his sword to impale Bradan. He spun away from the soldier and paused for a heartbeat to look about.

"Son of a bitch."

The entire field before him was covered with a hundred warriors deployed with military thoroughness to block any route no matter how agilely he dodged. The moon washed their stony ranks with white light, converting them all to alabaster chess pieces as they trotted toward him. No hurry now. With the museum blocking escape to his rear, they had him. The swans swooped low over the assembled troops.

Bradan bolted toward the nearest entrance for the Palace of Fine Arts, straight toward the building's doors. He'd shoot the heavy glass out, shift the chase inside the cavernous interior, and maybe lose himself amid the myriad of artwork and goofy science exhibits in its black interior. He thought most of the technology exhibits that had once been part of the collection had been relocated to the new Exploratorium on Pier 15/17, pristine and a bit soulless, but he believed that a few had been left at this original site pending disassembly or destruction. At the very least, the Druids might feel disoriented amid the various displays.

The Magnum bucked in his hand twice as he fired at the door. By now he barely flinched at the deafening reports. However, instead of shattering the pane as he'd expected, two neat holes appeared in the dark glass. Bradan knew something about ammunition and guessed that Rod must have loaded the gun with jacketed bullets that simply drilled through glass like air.

He heard a hiss as a sharp pain lanced across his shoulder before all the glass in the door ahead of him exploded with a crash. The hurled javelin continued its trajectory, skidding along the museum floor and smashing into a trashcan inside, which sent the container cartwheeling. Bradan leaped through the destroyed door, catching his foot on the frame. He fell to the floor, cutting the palms of both hands on the glass strewn about.

He tried to swear but hadn't the breath to utter a word. Another missile zipped overhead, ripping into an exhibit case directly in front of him and splintering its plastic and plywood. Barely able to discern his weapon in the crepuscular light, he picked up the pistol—his only equalizer—feeling its grip gum with his blood. He hauled himself upright and lurched forward into the museum's cavernous interior the size and shape of a commercial jet aircraft hangar. Small lamps suspended from the ceiling kilometers above provided dim illumination, like two dozen gibbous moons on an overcast night. On impulse and thanks to his rage, he whirled about to confront his pursuers. He had no plan. The first stony legionnaire forced itself through the shattered door. Others attacked the remaining entrances with short-swords, breaking the glass and metal. Beyond them, still outside, Bradan saw the swans hovering above the mayhem. Bradan sighted on the closest warrior, remembering to keep one eye closed to avoid losing his night vision in the muzzle flash. The little ruby bead danced erratically on the soldier's cuirass for an instant before Bradan pulled the trigger three times, his hand kicking up from the recoil. The lead legionnaire's upper chest fragmented into big blocks as the first bullet hit, then disintegrated into a cloud of flying stone chips and powdered rock under the second and third slugs' impact. Three other soldiers blew apart as the bullets plowed through the formation. However, undeterred, the rest of the cohort continued to hack at the doors. Bradan turned and ran toward the nearest exhibits, a score of legionnaires at his heels with their sandals clattering on the concrete floor. The only plan he could think of involved simply staying ahead of the pack and hoping there were exits at the far end of the hall that he could either shoot or kick his way through.

He'd been to the museum years ago, but he couldn't remember its layout. The place was huge and reminded him incongruously of Tintagel's hall. Deep patches of darkness alternated with only slightly grayer pools illuminated by light filtering through the broken entrance and lamps above. This seemed to be part of displays no longer intended for public viewing. Off to his right, massive engines seemingly left over from the early stages of the industrial revolution sat as if they had been left in a giant's machine shop waiting for someone to flip a switch and begin feeding human limbs into the contraptions' maws.

One of the swans swooped low overhead, making him raise his gun briefly before losing the bird in the darkness above. Bradan zigzagged to confuse Cynbel or Aennati or any soldier's aim who might be preparing to hurl yet another javelin into his spine as he dodged between exhibits explaining various meteorological phenomena. This included a cylindrical tank of still water twice his height, half illuminated and surreal. A briefly glimpsed sign indicated something about this exhibit demonstrating the principles of waterspouts and tornadoes. Another glass case nearby demonstrated weather conditions critical for cloud formation. All of the demonstrations were turned off, awaiting heuristic purpose tomorrow when school buses disgorged packs of bored kids or caravans of tourists from Iowa.

Bradan caromed into a tabletop display waist-high off the floor. His right hip felt like it had been smacked with a ball peen hammer. The impact activated the display and a booming voice rumbled through the hall.

"Desert winds shift sand grains from one dune to another in unique, never to be repeated patterns. In this display, fans simulate winds. Notice how they have created an intricate arrangement of small dunes. Now, push the red button to change the fan's direction and observe how new patterns appear."

Bradan pushed away from the exhibit to be enveloped in a cloud of sand. He shoved his hand before his mouth and eyes trying to keep out the choking grains driven by a roaring, howling wind. His throat felt abraded by coarse sandpaper as he sucked air into his lungs. He jammed the gun beneath the remnants of his sweater and the waistband of his pants, hoping to keep the flying grit from fouling its slide mechanism and laser sight. He'd be better off with a sword.

Bradan guessed the priests didn't know his exact location and, inspired by the setting, had expanded the exhibits in his general vicinity to gigantic proportions, intending that the drifting dunes either smother him or impede his flight, allowing the soldiers to catch him.

He tried to see through the wind-whipped sand grains. A dark figure loomed before him and struck at his stomach. Bradan barely managed to dodge the disemboweling thrust of a sword. He lurched away from the advancing figure, seeing other shapes converging on him less discomforted than he was by the sandstorm.

Bradan tripped and fell, sprawling into a growing, shifting dune and struggled upright, barely escaping being buried alive by the pile just as a dimly seen legionnaire attempted to impale him with a javelin. More by luck than skill, Bradan dodged this blow, wading backward in the sand, and grabbed the spear. For a moment, he struggled for possession of the weapon face to face with the animated stony figure who snarled but whose eyes were as dead and flat as flint. Other figures closed in amid the gale of flying grit.

Christ, the thing was strong, rock energized by titanic, unnatural forces. After a fleeting contest over the javelin, Bradan realized he'd lose this battle and pushed himself back to give his hand clearance while simultaneously pulling the gun out from beneath his sweater. Would it work after the sand bath? The muzzle flash created a searing orange afterimage on his retina. But he did see the soldier fall away from him, half its limestone guts blasted away. Bradan jerked the javelin out of the sand, the prize of this vicious little battle and, half blinded, sucking sand into his lungs, lurched away completely directionless.

Suddenly, he realized that he was running on the museum's floor with a sensation of equine fleetness after plowing through the sand and breathing air unclogged with grit. He stared about to regain a sense of direction. He saw one of the swans and fired at it, sending ringing echoes throughout the hall. Several exhibits lay directly ahead, organized into maze patterns by partitions and walls. Bradan ducked among these. Far off to his left, he saw a greenish glow and recognized an exit sign. He rushed toward it. Time to get out of this death trap. Cynbel and Aennati had acclimated too rapidly to the museum's technology.

"A capacitor stores charge in many ordinary household devices," a voice boomed above the exhibits.

"Help," Bradan breathed.

Was he near anything that conducted electricity? Even if the priests couldn't keep him in sight long enough to destroy him directly, one of the exhibits rendered monstrously large and malign would do the job for them—assuming the soldiers didn't get him first. He wasn't evading his pursuers here as much as wandering around in a large labyrinth laced with technological booby traps orchestrated by the Druids.

"Capacitors come in many varieties. The one in this exhibit is composed of two plates. Push the button to create a charge difference between the plates and then watch them move together. The charge is small, only one hundred volts at one-quarter amp." The voice paused slightly, correcting itself. "Only ten thousand volts at one thousand amps. As the plates draw nearer, a spark will jump from one plate to the other."

At either end of the science hall, two enormous plates began to move, ready to fry him as electricity shot across the narrowing gap and found his interposed body the point of best conductivity. He imagined his cerebellum sizzling in his brainpan and his carcass charred to coal. Where were his pursuing soldiers? Maybe they were warned to avoid the capacitor.

He felt the air around ionized with energy about to be released. The small hairs on his forearm stood up. Bradan couldn't run fast enough to get out from between the plates. He needed something to create a more conductive path than that through his body and hurled the javelin at the nearest plate. A vast bolt of blue-white light traced itself between the two plates, catching the missile in midflight. Bradan felt himself picked up and hurled to the floor. He lay in a stunned heap for a moment before levering himself up and moving toward the distant exit with the strong smell of ozone in the air from the massive discharge.

Off to his right in the dim lighting, he saw a dozen soldiers, grim golems moving toward him with tactical proficiency. Bradan hobbled as quickly as he could toward the exit sign, his labored breathing and footsteps echoing in the hall. Fuck, he'd never make it outside. By instinct, he ducked sideways as a sword blade sliced within millimeters of his neck, missing decapitating him by a whisker. He clambered over a display case desperately trying to avoid a dozen stabbing blades and fell headlong into the glass exit door.

Bradan fired twice at the lunging warriors, ejected the empty clip, and shoved his hip into the exit door's bar handle, cursed at the stab of pain that lanced through his side, hammered a full clip into the gun, and tumbled out onto the gravel path surrounding the museum. He fired several more times into the swirling mass of soldiers trying to jam themselves through the exit after him. Bradan felt bits of stone stinging him as debris sprayed him when lead met stone. He turned and fled around the pond toward the open field only to be confronted by still more soldiers filling almost the entire open space in ordered ranks, hemming him in completely. Overhead, the two swans circled to arrange the maneuver.

He was right back where he'd started before his worthless detour into the museum. Maybe not. The birds were confident and a little too stationary. Bradan snapped the laser sight on. The red dot centered on a wing of one of the swans. He fired twice and yelled in elation at the explosion of feathers that showered to the ground. The red beam now intersected the flight path of the other swan as it struggled for altitude and he pulled the trigger until the gun emptied.

Something sharp stabbed into his back between the shoulder blades. He whirled around and saw a blade in his face close enough to make his eyes cross. Two dozen soldiers stood within striking distance of him. The closest had extended his sword until it broke the skin on Bradan's back, but the warrior's arm had frozen mid-stroke. He felt blood trace its way down his backbone. The entire troop now stood inanimate in poses so natural that Praxiteles couldn't have teased stone into them. For a long moment, Bradan simply inhaled deeply, and then, guessing that he'd hurt the priests but not killed them, he gingerly backed away from the legionnaire's weapon and navigated his way hurriedly through the densely-spaced masses of statuary.

Running out to Beach Street, he looked back to see concentric circles of immobile figures improbably menacing a now empty spot in their midst.

He yanked open the Tesla's door and fell into the seat, too drained to think. Tintagel bounded out of the car to stand facing the Palace of Fine Arts, expecting more pursuers. Weakly, Bradan patted the seat next to him and the wolf clambered back into the Model S, stepping heavily on Bradan's bruised, glass-cut knee in the process. Bradan heaved himself upright in the seat and started the car. He'd made the seat sticky with blood. Then he realized that he'd been blocked into the parking spot by an Acura parked millimeters from his front bumper and a late-model minivan making love to Connie's trunk. He stomped on the accelerator, sending the Tesla smashing into the lighter car ahead of him.

"Ouch," Connie said.

Bradan shifted into reverse and backed up at fifty miles an hour, collapsing the van's nose and shattering its windshield.

"I'm sure that hurt," Bradan said.

"Felt like bad cosmetic surgery."

"I will make it up to you. When this is all over."

Now, with plenty of clearance, he pointed the Tesla out onto Beach and raced down the block to Divisadero with the sounds of two car alarms echoing off the elegant townhouses lining the street.

"Plan B?" the ghost asked.

CHAPTER 15

It's All in the Makeup

It should have been raining; the sun lit the Pacific's breakers on a cloudless December morning. The gorgeous weather didn't match Bradan's mood or physical sensations; every part of him hurt as he sprawled in the Tesla's back seat. Even the car's soft upholstery pained him where it touched his anatomy. He ran his hand through his hair. It was a doormat. He traced a finger along one cheek. A buffalo's hide must be smoother. He needed a shower in the worst way. He looked at himself in the car's mirror. Ocher-colored bruises and bloody cuts covered his body. Torn clothing left the damage clearly visible. Bradan pulled his socks off. He had giant blisters on both feet from his death race through Golden Gate Park. He looked at his watch. Fatigue numbed his brain cells. The wolf snored jammed into the front passenger seat on its back, paws lying loosely on its chest and canines showing through an open mouth. The priests were out there somewhere and they'd either butchered Claire already or would do it soon.

He hadn't defeated the priests; he couldn't locate Claire. He had no idea why he'd awakened. He closed his eyes.

In the netherworld between consciousness and sleep, Bradan grew aware of a spell's signature. This magic seemed to come from Angel Island. It was a reasonable place for the priests to use as a base of operations, centrally located, mostly uninhabited during the winter except for a few day tourists and undeveloped other than a park center and a grim immigrant detention facility from the previous century. Second-growth forest covered most of the island. They'd feel at home amid this natural environment. Could Claire be there, too?

"You up?" Connie asked.

"Maybe." Ennui clouded his voice.

"Let's leave town. These guys have all the aces. Plus, the police are after you. Stupid as they are, they'll get you sooner or later if the magicians don't."

"Nothing I've tried has worked," Bradan agreed. "Claire–"

"You don't even know where she is," Connie said.

"No. Yes. Maybe."

"Well, which is it?"

"She might be on Angel Island. Thought I felt Cynbel and Aennati out there, but I don't really know. Claire might be with them."

"Even if you knew she was, what would you do? Sometimes you got to fold 'em."

"My bag of tricks is empty," he admitted.

In an instant, fifteen hundred intervening years disappeared and Bradan was back in Tintagel. From a hundred rafters, dangled bodies suspended head-down twisting slowly. Cynbel shoved the poker's glowing tip into his face. Bradan squeezed his eyes shut trying to block the searing heat and twisted away from the poker, but Cynbel shifted the poker nearer and Bradan spilled his guts, giving away all the information that had slaughtered his friends, Merlin, Arthur, and their followers. Civilized life had crumbled. Far from restoring sylvan oak forests as the priests claimed was their goal, the ensuing decades of savage

208 PETER W. BLAISDELL

slaughter that engulfed the English countryside had corrupted both man and wilderness. Instead of reverting to nature, Britain had descended into chaos.

"So, let's get far away from here," Connie said. "They'll never think to look for you in Los Angeles. Or we could go somewhere in the Midwest. I come from there. Not even pagan priests would visit that part of the country—though they'd fit in pretty well if they did."

"We can go anywhere," he said listlessly. "Didn't Camus say: 'One can be right and yet be beaten, that force can vanquish spirit, that there are times when courage is not its own recompense'?"

"Cam—who? Some literature crap? We know all about life's futilities without taking an English class again. Time's a-wastin'. Let's go."

Bradan pushed himself upright. "I brought them here."

"One of your dumb clients brought them here." Connie sounded exasperated and impatient to flee. "When they did that ritual thing on Angel Island last Halloween."

"Danielle was the trigger, but I'm the real reason that they're here. If I hadn't kept the resurrection spell without hiding it properly, they wouldn't exist. I brought them to this place and time. They have a connection to me based on hatred."

"You've got a spiritual connection across the ages?" Sarcasm laced Connie's tone.

"Sounds idiotic, doesn't it? But hate is a durable emotion."

"So, why did this all happen now and not three hundred years ago or at any other time in your past?"

"I don't know how this shit works exactly. I've done this all my life and I know some of the rules, but I don't know all the theory or principles. I've tried to understand. It's sort of at the edge of physics."

"Now you're going to say that you're accountable," Connie said.

"Yes."

"You don't know that for sure. Maybe it was coincidence. Kept running into my ex-husband all over Indiana after the divorce, at weddings, funerals, and truck rallies even though he was the last person I wanted to see. It wasn't karma, it was bad timing. You kept that parchment not because you were proud, but because you wanted to bring your friend Merlin back. Sounds like a good motive to me. Things didn't work out. In my experience, they rarely do."

"I'm not leaving," Bradan said.

"You want to warn the city about what you set loose? They'll put you in prison and pin all this shit on you and nothing would be any better. You'd even still feel guilty."

"There's got to be something to do."

"How are you going to fight them? What are you trying to prove; you're not a knight in armor. You do have a plan?"

"I'm making this up as I go, but as long as I don't use a spell, I'll be undetectable. I need Danielle's phone. Besides my parchment, it's the only place the incantation exists—assuming I can find it after lying around on Angel Island outside during the last several weeks of rain."

"Great odds," Connie said. "You don't even have a boat to get out to the island."

His phone rang. Miraculously, it still functioned after last night's beating. He'd picked up a burner after demolishing his original phone

"Yeah," Bradan mumbled.

"Bradan, it's Jack."

"Who?" Bradan thought he recognized the voice, but couldn't

place it. His new burner phone shouldn't have been tracked so quickly, but life had changed and the police were no doubt mustering a lot technological effort to locate him. He almost disconnected as the voice at the other end spoke again.

"LaPlante. Jack LaPlante."

What did this son of a bitch want?

"Jack, when this is all over, I'm going to hunt you down and kick your ass right out your mouth. How did you get this number?"

"Bradan, I know you're in a bind now but listen a minute. Clearly, the cops think you're behind all these killings. That's good for my client, Danielle. Now they'll stop watching her. But you should be considering hiring quality legal representation and I have a name I'll pass along. It would be inappropriate for me to represent both you and Danielle under the circumstances, but we have another attorney at Fierstein and Marcotti who would be almost as effective as me—not quite as much trial experience as I have, but close—"

Bradan cut the line. He kicked the back of the driver's seat, eliciting a snarl from Tintagel. How would LaPlante's face look after being rubbed in broken glass? He looked at the phone and decided to hurl it into the sea. The police and FBI could easily triangulate on the device even with it turned off.

He was trying to use technology to destroy the Druids, but his phone might put him in prison. Maybe he should just paint a target on his back. Time to move.

The wind blew rough surf off the Pacific. He heard the breakers below. San Francisco and the Iron Age British coast felt akin at that moment.

He shoved the driver's seat forward and pushed open the door to heave himself out of the car. He stood unsteadily with one hand braced on the roof, feeling the ground on his bare soles, inhaling the smell of eucalyptus. Blood from the gash inflicted by a sword caked the small of his back, gluing the tattered shirt and sweater to his body. The wound itched incredibly and he reached around awkwardly to discover he couldn't scratch the irritation. Bradan collapsed into the front seat, drawing another angry growl from Tintagel who rolled over, curled-up tail covering his nose, and resumed sleeping. Then the wolf farted. Bradan hauled himself back outside to let the interior air out. A coat hanger from some past visit to a dry cleaner fell out of the car. No wardrobe cleaning for a while. He bent over beside the Tesla to pick it up and felt an unnatural creaking. His sinews had the same elasticity as rusted metal cable. The Tesla looked in no better shape with dents and a partially crumpled rear bumper after last night's adventures.

Bradan heard vehicles approaching on Lincoln. He'd hidden the Tesla well last night in a small service parking lot off Baker Beach far from any tourist destination. Trees screened the lot from the road with the trunks closely spaced so that it would take a very careful observer driving past slowly to spot the Tesla's dark, metallic shape. Bradan edged around the car and crouched behind the nearest trunk. His phone rang again. He ignored it. A police car drove past. So the phone had given him away. They might not know his position down to the millimeter, but they would know that he was in the vicinity.

A second cop drove by much more slowly than the first. *They know I'm close*, Bradan thought and hunkered down lower, putting the pine between himself and the main road. It was close enough to get sap on his cheek. He needed to camouflage the car. Bradan considered for half a heartbeat. He'd never before tried the sort of magic that he now had in mind and he wasn't sure what would transpire. Then, he uttered what he hoped were the appropriate stanzas. Immediately, he felt more bone weary. If they were close, the priests would detect his magic. Between Cynbel and Aennati using his enchantment to discover him and law enforcement tracking him using his phone, Bradan wondered who would get to him first.

The cop slowed almost to a stop out on Lincoln near the dirt access road to the parking lot. *He's going to come in*, Bradan predicted. Spraying gravel, the cruiser lunged down the access road. Meanwhile, washed by a giant magical paint brush, the Tesla's glossy blue paint job abruptly shifted to dappled tan and dark-green hues blending beautifully with the vegetation, dirt, and leaves scattered about the gravel parking lot.

The cruiser pulled into the lot, stopped twenty meters away at the far end. Bradan watched the cop scan the beach and then turn to look over the lot. He took his time. The camouflage had better work. Maintaining the spell was exhausting Bradan. He wouldn't be able to run if it came to that. Then the policeman picked up his car radio and spoke. For a second the man talked into it. The cruiser's emergency lights flared. Bradan stopped breathing. The police car made a tight loop, wheels spinning, and surged out of the lot back down the access road toward Lincoln.

Bradan moved out of the trees and staggered over to his car. The camouflage paint job vanished leaving the Tesla as it usually looked, give or take assorted dents and crushed metal. It took him three tries to force the door open in his vitiated, post-spell state.

"Nirvana." Bradan sank back into the upholstery.

"Pretty slick with the new makeup for me," Connie said. "Kind of tickled when you did the makeover."

"Glad you approve," Bradan wheezed. "Now let's lose ourselves."

He shifted the transmission into Drive and looked through the front windshield. Two white birds coasted in formation some distance above the Tesla's position and out over the beach. He pulled himself toward the windshield holding on to the steering wheel and watched them drift off over the surf until they were white dots. Gulls? He hadn't seen them clearly enough to tell. For a minute, he didn't move then, tentatively rolled the car down the dirt service road and bounced over the curb onto Lincoln, watching for the birds' return or police vehicles.

"Our friends?" Connie asked.

"Could be—trying to finish me off after last night. It isn't potent magic, but if they were in the neighborhood, the illusion I just worked tipped them off about where we are."

He accelerated down the quiet boulevard in the opposite direction the cop had taken. Bradan glanced at the glove compartment thinking of the .50 semiautomatic. He'd do the James gang credit. He pulled over to the side of the road.

"The fuck . . . ?" Connie said.

"Just a sec." Bradan pulled the gun from the glove compartment, jumped out of the car, and hobbled over to some pines along the roadside. With a stone he quickly dug a small trench and tossed the Magnum and clips in. Using the rock, he pounded his phone and its SIM card into oblivion. Any treasonous cards or chips in the phone would be too pulverized to be effective as trackers, then he pushed dirt and pine needles over the grave for tools he'd hoped would give him leverage over the priests, a burial for his impotent tech gadgets.

None of this had worked. What would? Ambushing Cynbel and Aennati had been worth a try and, if nothing else, it had startled the bastards. But not critically injured them. Until last night, he'd reckoned that he had two edges over the priests: intimate knowledge of the city and familiarity with modern technology—ephemeral advantages. His computer hadn't been any more useful despite a repository of thousands of spells. He was on his own except for the modest number of spells he'd committed to memory and his wits—rather paltry weapons against the focus and capability of his opponents. He got back in the car.

"Wally has a boat. Maybe I can convince him to ferry me—assuming he doesn't turn me in to homicide detectives. I can't call him now, so we'll have to actually meet him if he's home. We're heading down to the Haight where he lives."

Bradan hesitated—did he really want to know?—then turned on the news. How would last night's disaster at the old Exploratorium be explained by National Public Radio? Bradan waited with exasperation while a summary of national issues was breathlessly described.

The wars all sounded the same now. Immutable politics and duplicity, he couldn't be surprised by human behavior; that was longevity's true curse.

Next came local calamities, including the efforts of city authorities to track the brutal serial killer. California's governor had now gotten into the act, offering Sacramento's help to San Francisco and generally trying to undercut the city's mayor, a potential future rival for an open Senate spot next year. The multiple slaughters had become a cause célèbre and a copycat murderer had already been apprehended across the Bay in Hayward after clumsily hacking his neighbors to bits with an ax and then decorating the murder scene with poorly drawn symbols in the victims' blood and viscera copied from news stories.

"...and in an unusual item, last night the grounds surrounding the Palace of Fine Arts, San Francisco's nationally-known park and former location of its science museum, suffered some sort of environmental disaster. In a grim prank, illegal dumpers evidently unloaded hundreds of gallons of oil-based sludge and industrial waste into the lagoon, killing most of the plant life. Unpleasant odors have caused residents bordering the park to evacuate the neighborhood until city engineers can determine the material's nature. Members of the posh St. Francis Yacht Club have also complained. The mayor has requested assistance from both the state and the federal Environmental Protection Agency."

"They haven't linked that one to you," Connie said.

"Give them time."

"Wonder how they'll explain about the statues all over the lawn?" the ghost asked.

"Performance art run amok," Bradan said.

Traffic was light this Monday morning and he took less-traveled streets heading south and east toward the Haight. However, within a minute a white sedan pulled in behind him, crowding his rear bumper. Bradan resisted the impulse to floor the Tesla's accelerator. The car trailing him had the conspicuously nondescript look he'd expect to see in an unmarked police vehicle. A knot of tension formed in his stomach. Discreetly, he examined the driver who stared at the Tesla, his glare magnified by sunglasses. The sedan zipped past him. Bradan saw that the driver's expression reflected only the irritation that San Franciscans reserved for fellow commuters who respected speed limits.

Suppose Wally didn't want Bradan anywhere near him. Who else might help? His clients wouldn't be caught dead in his company. Attending spiritual healing workshops or back-to-nature seminars jolted them with all the adrenaline and endorphins they could handle. Bradan slapped the steering wheel. He had an appointment right this minute with Glen Atwood about transformational meditation. He could kiss that four-hundred-dollar hourly fee good-bye. The fellow would have a coronary if he saw Bradan now. Actually, he couldn't blame Glen. The entire city believed he was a deranged psychotic who would hack them to pieces after lulling their suspicions by counseling them about internalizing positive feelings toward their pagan souls.

The wolf sniffed its crotch in the back seat.

"Connie, before we get onto more crowded streets, I was wondering–"

"Let me guess. You'll give me another makeover."

"Something tasteful."

"Tasty I ain't. What sort of makeover?" Menace colored Connie's tone. "Besides, it won't work."

"Why the hell not?" Bradan demanded.

"We've already been made," Connie said.

Bradan looked in the rearview mirror. Fuck. One block back, a police car accelerated after him. The cruiser's top suddenly exploded in red, white, and blue lights.

Bradan stomped on the accelerator and the Tesla zipped down Lake Street. The wolf finally awoke after slamming into the door and growled at their pursuer as Bradan flew west on California toward Pacific Heights, one of the city's wealthiest neighborhoods. Glancing in the rearview mirror, Bradan saw that he was pulling away from his pursuer. The Tesla had torque and horsepower, if not brilliant handling. However, reinforcements would be converging and this neighborhood wasn't big enough to shed a dragnet. A few more cops on the scene and he'd be in a trap no illusion could get him out of. The timing of this interruption couldn't be worse. If he used even the smallest spell to ditch the cops, the priests would be on top of him, too. He was screwed.

Maybe he could outrun his pursuer before the rest of the cavalry arrived. The Tesla whizzed over a pothole, almost spinning out of control. In this neighborhood, the residents' aristocratic languor evidently mitigated against complaining about road conditions that would drive middle-class homeowners screaming for their city councilmen. Two blocks ahead of Bradan, he saw a second police car charging directly at the Tesla. In an instant, the cruiser had closed to where Bradan clearly saw the passenger-side cop pull his shotgun off its dashboard mounting. What was the jerk going to do, let loose a blast through his own windshield?

Bradan stood on the brakes and wrenched the steering wheel right at 29th, sending the Tesla's rear quarter panel into a fire hydrant. He caught a brief glimpse in the mirror as a geyser of water burst out of the pavement.

"Son of a bitch!" Bradan screamed out the Tesla's window as he swerved around a brown and gold Rolls-Royce backing out of a driveway directly into his path. Bradan took another sharp right onto El Camino Del Mar and slowed to check the driveways along the street, almost sending Tintagel through the windshield. He heard tires shrieking somewhere behind him and guessed that the cop must have braked hard to avoid the Rolls, too. Good. That would slow pursuit momentarily.

Bradan examined the homes along the street. Most of the dwellings were completely hidden behind solid stone fences or hedge ramparts pierced occasionally by gates, thick-barred and solid. These were all closed, preventing access to their driveways, but the owner of the fifth house from the corner had left the gate open. Construction material including a portable cement mixer and rebar clustered around the gate. Cursory inspection showed no signs of the residents or workers. The police would round the corner soon. Bradan slid the Tesla onto the slightly curving driveway leading to a garage. Briefly, he inspected the expansive Spanish Colonial home. Excepting the building supplies, the grounds looked so pristine it was hard to believe that anyone actually lived here. Maybe its owners simply visited to admire the place and check that the immigrant construction workers were making progress and the gardeners had pruned the hedges. The street was only visible through a narrow slot in the bushes. Nobody appeared to be around today, so Bradan pulled the car right up to the garage door.

"What the hell you doing?" Connie yelled. "Get back out on the street. We're faster."

"There are more of them."

Bradan hopped out of the car to regard the garage and its lock. It seemed to be an older mechanism, the type controlled by an automatic door opener activated as the driver pulled up to the home. A suitable spell would pop it open, but he had another idea. He ran back to his car and rummaged about amid the debris on the floor. He pulled out a wire coat hanger and untwisted and extended it to its full length. A police car zipped past.

It was in sight only an instant and Bradan heard it accelerate down the full length of the block. It would be back.

"Let's see if this takes six seconds," he said. "I saw someone do it on YouTube."

He hurried to the garage door and formed a hook at the end

of the stiff wire, then carefully jammed the wire through the poorly-fitted seal between the garage door and doorframe. He rammed his fingers into the small gap, creating enough space for him to see through and guide the hanger toward the rope handle controlling the door's manual backup locking mechanism.

"You're vandalizing the garage door?" The ghost sounded in the last stage of exasperation.

"Breaking and entering."

"You're not wanted for enough other felonies?"

The first try missed, but Bradan snagged the rope the second time then gently but firmly pulled the hanger and the rope. There was a soft thunk as the locking mechanism disengaged.

"No magic, no muscle, just sneakiness," Bradan said. "Some of the older automatic garage doors will open this way." The door had no exterior handle and Bradan stooped to slide his fingers between the smooth concrete and the lower lip of the garage door. The door rolled up easily and he drove inside.

The ghost hissed, "Magic would have been faster."

"Connie, half of being a magician is knowing when not to use magic."

Bradan pulled the garage door almost shut, rolled underneath it, and crept back down the driveway to the gate. He peeked around the hedge. At the end of the block, brake lights flared as a police car rolled to a stop. Two other squad cars pulled up nearby in the intersection. The three policeman conferred, shouting at one another through open windows, then one swung around and moved back along El Camino Del Mar, stopping beside each house while the cop examined it carefully. Blue-red light splashed mansions along the street and the loud squawk of the police radio echoed off the walls.

Bradan noticed several doors open and homeowners with

puzzled expressions peered out at the activity on the street. Two men and a woman strode across lawns, converging on the police car. One of the men gestured at a house. The woman pointed down the block. A terrier danced around her feet. Everyone, including the policeman, leaning out his car window, talked at once. Bradan moved back to the garage and rolled the door completely shut.

Almost the entire back of the garage had been removed leaving only a few studs in place to support the structure's roof. A large patio beyond the rear of the garage had been partially tiled with gravel covering the remainder. Past this, he saw the yard with still more construction implements neatly arranged along the far edge of the half-finished patio. There must be workers returning soon.

"Maybe the candy-ass cops will arrest the jerks out front, take some of the heat off us," Connie said.

"Not in this neighborhood," Bradan answered. "It's got to be a city supervisor or some hedge fund director complaining about the commotion."

"What now? Wait it out?"

"No. As soon as the neighbors find out why the police are here—mad killer on the loose—they'll get a lot more cooperative. Every house will be checked thoroughly. And this one is the only house with the gate open. Besides, someone's working on the place. They'll be back." Bradan hopped into the car.

"So we can't go out the way we came. What do we do?"

"You'll be sorry you asked. Connie, this is going to hurt, but I know you'll understand."

Without waiting for an answer, Bradan drove the vehicle directly out the open back of the garage, crushing a workbench in the process and scattering tile. Beside him he heard Tintagel clawing at the seat trying to stay upright.

The Tesla burst out into a beautifully manicured backyard with an incredible cacophony, heading toward a tall row of hedges and an extensive patch of roses. All the flowers had little signs planted beside them identifying the variety. Another row of hedges behind the roses formed the back perimeter of the yard. The grounds could have made a wonderful spread in *Better Homes and Gardens*. That was about to change.

"Close your eyes!" Bradan yelled as the Tesla roared into the roses, a rhino through a flock of flamingos. White and yellow petals flew into the air and briefly covered the entire car before being blasted away by the hedges that Bradan now drove the car through. He wondered if the vegetation concealed a chain-link or brick fence, but, carried along by its hurtling momentum, the car burst into a neighboring yard prettier than the first. Bradan cut right across, leaving behind long gashes in the grass. He swerved around a gazebo, threaded his way through a narrow gap between the house's side and a fence, and rolled down the front driveway. The gate slid aside and he pushed out onto the street.

He'd made it from one block to the next by going cross-country. Bradan looked up and down the street. No police . . . yet. He glanced into his rearview mirror and winced. His flight had been noisy and the path he'd left was obvious. An army tank couldn't have left greater devastation.

Three blocks away, Bradan pulled into an alley off Clement between a convenience store and the side wall of an apartment complex. He edged the car behind a maroon dumpster that partially concealed the car from pedestrians. The alley smelled of ginger and rotting chicken. Somebody directly above him on the second floor was taking a shower and singing a Verdi aria.

Bradan patted the Tesla's upholstery gently.

"That didn't feel at all good, sugar. I'm reconsidering a police crime lab. They couldn't do worse to me."

"I'll make it up to you," Bradan said. "New paint, body repair, the works."

"Do I get to choose the color?"

"Surely. In fact, what about a change right now?"

"And those things chasing you, can't they home in on us if you do a spell?"

"We don't have a choice. You look like a wreck. From here it'll take us about five minutes to get to Wally's, assuming light traffic in the Haight. If they're close, we're screwed; if not, we may make it."

The shower above shut off abruptly. Bradan paused a moment to consider the choice again, then recited the same rhyme he'd used back at Baker Beach with a modest variation added to the last stanza. Locating the source of a spell seemed to work like radar detecting an object. The more elaborate and closer the source of the enchantment to the person trying to find it, the easier it was to locate, and the priests were exquisitely sensitized to enchantment. Even a small, distant spell would impinge on their consciousness. The question was, how soon?

"Now, did that hurt?" he asked weakly.

"Didn't feel much at all, actually. Similar to when I was in bed with Earl."

"Your ex?"

"One of them."

Bradan smiled. He hadn't the energy for a laugh.

"I ain't got a mirror," the Tesla said. "How do I look? Inconspicuous?"

"No. That hasn't worked well so far. I'm trying a different

strategy. I'd like a lot of people to notice us. Can we have some music?"

"What kind?"

"Loud."

The Jefferson Airplane's "White Rabbit" swirled about him in the car's interior which served as a perfect acoustic environment for Grace Slick's thunderous choruses. Mad Hatters and White Rabbits indeed. "Feed your head"—an ideal refrain for evading Druids and police. Bradan rolled down the windows.

"Turn that down."

Bradan looked up to see a bare-chested, middle-aged man with wet hair leaning out of a window to stare down at him. Then the window slammed shut.

"Turn it up," Bradan said as he backed the Tesla out onto Clement. "Let's give the day a soundtrack." He was already tiring from keeping the illusion in place.

"It's your funeral," Connie said.

"That should have a soundtrack, too."

Nothing got the attention of jaded San Francisco drivers, but his car's music proved the exception this morning. Fully cranked, acid rock flooded out of the Tesla in a vast, multicolored tidal wave to spill over sedate luxury sedans and lap against polished, foreign sports coupes with pastel interiors. Well-dressed drivers shot irritated stares at Bradan as if he were some outré intrusion onto their Pacific Heights neighborhood's cloistered boulevards, a known sex offender paroled to a nunnery.

What was Connie playing now? Something from Quicksilver or Moby Grape? The song sounded like it came out of a Marshall stack rather than the Tesla's sound system, with power chords as pure as anything this side of Jimi Hendrix heaven. Notes stretched with taffy elasticity that ignored musical structure as feedback-soaked guitar riffs and a surging organ almost, but didn't quite, overwhelm lyrics urging the listener to dump bourgeois life for the wonders of narcotics. Bradan smiled at the juxtaposition of anthems to infinity with this staid, wealthy enclave of upscale mansions.

"Goddamn it, Bradan, what have you done to me?" The electric car cut off the music. "I just saw my reflection in a window. I look shit."

"Keep playing the part, Connie. If the police lock me up, it's just a matter of time before Cynbel and Aennati get us."

"They'll get you," the ghost said. "What are they supposed to do to me? I'm already dead."

"You'll be even deader? Cynbel will incinerate me and everything associated with me. You're in the line of fire, too."

"Making me look like a Volvo wagon is pushing it. I'm some tinny little piece of crap."

"That's the point."

"I could stand being a pickup truck for a while."

"I'll remember that next time," Bradan said. "You haven't really been changed. It's just a vision like the camouflage back on Baker Beach, poor taste masquerading as nostalgia for a dead era. You and I know you're still a Tesla, the classiest car in the universe."

"You're flattering me."

"Damn straight. You should be happy with the paint job. It's you, loud and proud, green and gold paisley. If it's any consolation, I've made myself over, too. As far as anyone can tell, I'm about sixteen, barely have a driver's license, and have a ton of pimples. Now, turn the music back up."

Bradan pulled onto Haight Street. En route from Pacific Heights, he'd passed a half dozen police cars. The wagon with the wicked sound system and surreal paint job pulled eyes like a neon sign and offended every instinct an authority figure might have. However, the police had more important things to consider and scanned the streets for a blue Model S driven by a thirty-year-old serial killer.

"I can't keep the spell going any longer."

He pulled up to Wally's apartment complex as the image dissolved.

"Damn, that's better," Connie said, a Model S once more.

Bradan draped himself over the steering wheel, ready to faint.

A boy on a bike pulled up to driver's side of the Tesla. "Did your car just change color?"

"Trick of the light," Bradan whispered.

"Some guy and a woman up the block just did a funny trick. Except they were playing with birds."

CHAPTER 16

Forests Ancient as the Hills

Bradan turned on the small Maglite and narrowed its beam to an ultra-tight blade that sliced the night like a razor. Dazzled, he blinked for several moments knowing he'd lost his night vision. Not good. To avoid the Druids, he'd need all five senses supplementing his magical intuition. Bradan pointed the beam down, creating a white spot on the grass. The ground now looked back at him with its new eye.

For better or worse, he was on Angel Island to look for Claire and the phone. He stood on the concrete Nike missile pad atop the hill where Danielle's husband and friends had been slaughtered on Halloween. The crime scene seemed the best place to start his hunt, though it would be pure luck if he found the phone at night, on unfamiliar terrain that had been combed by the police. Determining Claire's location would also be next to impossible. Assuming she was still alive and on Angel Island, Cynbel and Aennati could have sequestered her anywhere.

Bradan surveyed the surrounding trees. He didn't remember them being this dense when he and Julie had hiked here last summer. In fact, he didn't remember any trees at all near the pad. Then it had seemed refreshing and scenic—indeed, a bit too tame with battalions of park rangers, a grid of trails so well marked that a three-year-old could follow them, and masses of day visitors pacifying the park's natural character. Tonight the place looked primeval.

I'm intruding, he thought, and tried to quiet his breathing. The clearing resonated with the tiniest noises like a natural amphitheater. A puffball of a cloud momentarily blocked the half-moon, darkening the whole clearing. The world had just blinked. He was so tense that a breeze wracked his body with shivers. His tattered brown sweater and ripped slacks couldn't keep the cool out. Another gust off the Bay wrapped him in smells of leaves. He inhaled deeply and discovered that the air was supersaturated with odors. A faint charred fragrance mixed with the other smells. Had Cynbel and Aennati cast their victims' bodies into a bonfire after ritually killing them? Which of the Celtic pantheon had the priests sought to propitiate with the slaughter? Most of the gods were bloodthirsty enough to have appreciated the gesture. The priests only followed a long Angel Island tradition. Centuries before, if the park information center was to be believed, Native Americans had also used the island for seasonal human sacrifice.

Bradan stared about the hilltop. Yellow crime-scene tape attached to thin stakes, festooned the summit and fluttered in the breeze like old battle pennants. They'd been hammered into the earth a few meters from where he stood, cordoning off an area around the Nike missile pad. As at old battlefields, blood had watered this ground.

Trees enclosed most of the summit's little clearing, giving it a hemmed-in feeling except where a dirt path pierced their ranks on the southwestern summit overlooking the Bay and San Francisco. Three prosaic picnic tables, marred and stained by countless tourists' meals, reminded him of altars tonight, standing next to the pad awaiting more victims. Bradan thought that the area was off-limits to hikers, but someone, a tourist maybe, had left a Coke can on the nearest one. Even this modern token reflected the moon oddly; it was a ceremonial artifact from some unknown era. The summit had an archaic quality to it with the Bay's water not only isolating it from the city, but also creating a temporal separation from modern times. The setting looked identical to a deserted glade in old Britain, hallowed by the Celtic tribes two millennia back and far beyond the reach or knowledge of marauding Roman invaders who would have burned the entire area because of the implied threat to their rule.

The sensation of enchantment was strong enough to be palpable. Bradan had the impression of pushing his body through waist-high water. He knew it was the residue of Cynbel and Aennati's Halloween killings. Sensations crowded in on him, creating cognitive and psychic impacts on his mind like mescaline-induced imagery.

Bradan wondered whether he'd be able to detect Cynbel and Aennati against this intense background noise. He'd counted on being able to sense them if they arrived suddenly on the island. However, the missile pad was so permeated with malign magic, it might mask their appearance.

Tintagel stood beside him. In this forested place, the wolf was almost invisible, a shade among shadows, completely in his element. When the animal moved over the carpet of tinder-dry leaves and twigs, he didn't make a sound. The night and the windblown, wild surroundings aroused atavistic instincts in his pet that Bradan didn't notice in the city and was uneasy seeing here on the hilltop where the Druids had murdered five people in a primitive ritual.

Now Tintagel seemed inattentive to modern noises and

instead listened to echoes of times when he had been part of a swift pack that scavenged the edges of war, loping fleetly through the armored and tattooed fighters lying mingled together beside their shields and crushed helmets, the bloody flotsam of battle. The wolf and his companions hadn't sought carrion but instead chased the souls of dying warriors at the moment of release from their mortal remains.

Tintagel let loose a long, wailing howl, ineffably wild and eerie, that filtered out across the island and echoed against pine trunks. Bradan shushed the animal and stared about him. Would specters rise out of the ground responding to the call? The island seemed subtly to be transforming itself into something primitive with the presence of death heightening the metamorphosis. He remembered mostly eucalyptus trees from previous visits, but off to his left, he thought he saw clusters of oaks amid smaller rowan trees with blood-red berries. He remembered rowans well from his youth fifteen centuries back, though he'd never seen one in the Bay Area.

A branch perhaps weakened by November storms snapped and fell to the ground. Bradan froze.

Get on with the search and get the hell out of here. Odds were he'd find neither Claire nor the phone, and each second he stayed on Angel Island made it more certain that the Druids would give up their hunt for him in the city and return to find him here. Besides, Wally in his boat near the island's marina wouldn't wait for him forever. He'd told his friend he'd only be here a few hours and to retreat at any sign of trouble, with or without Bradan.

He probed around him with the light. The Maglite was bright but tightly focused and its tiny beam should be screened from observers by trees that surrounded the hill. He used the light to spear a patch of charred logs and sticks on the missile pad. Despite weeks of bad weather, the scars of Halloween's ceremonial fire remained. The heat must have been horrific because most of the surrounding pad was smoked black well beyond the circular pile of debris. Bradan walked closer and methodically quartered the ground. He didn't see any obvious traces of flesh or bone; the forensics team had had weeks to pick over the area.

He knelt close to the dead fire's edge. Danielle's husband and friends might not all have been dead when they were burned. Bradan suppressed an urgent need to vomit. Driving away macabre thoughts of the carnage that night, he swung his light out beyond the concrete. He pulled a pen from his pocket and nudged a piece of blackened material away from the other charred crud. The phone? A bone fragment? Despite his revulsion, curiosity overpowered fear.

"Mistletoe," he murmured. "They pulled out all the stops."

Deftly, he pulled the sprig out and reverentially blew blackened dust off it. Tintagel stretched his muzzle close to Bradan's hand and sniffed cautiously, then backed off as if he'd been burned. Mistletoe wouldn't have meant anything to the forensics team so they'd left it. However, the plant was an integral part of sacrificial rites. Supposedly, it had fallen from the heavens in a flash of lightning, a manifestation of celestial fire. By using it, Cynbel had enhanced the power of the forces that he called on. The fire would have been critical, too. Traditionally, a new fire was lit on the eve of November 1 so that its light could warm homes for the coming winter. The priest had perverted the ceremony's purpose.

Bradan glanced west out at the Bay. A plume of spray, small in the distance, rose out the water. Tail flukes broke the surface briefly then disappeared into the sea. The half-moon provided just enough light for him to glimpse the whale sounding. The leviathan must have lost its bearings and detoured into the Bay as it migrated south to winter in the Sea of Cortez.

Nothing else obviously related to the crime lay on the missile pad. Bradan stretched. His back muscles had cramped after hunching over the fire. Right now he'd kill for a cigar. He stood up and examined the circle of trees trying to guess the path Danielle might have used to flee down to the immigration center. If the damned phone wasn't here, maybe his client would have dropped it somewhere during her flight to the immigration center. He regarded the pines and eucalyptus skeptically. Surely, the poor woman couldn't have forced herself through the trees even in a panic. The only easy path down was the main trail connecting the hill to a partially-paved service road circumscribing the island. Someone as terrified as Danielle would have chosen the clearly marked main path. However, earlier that evening, he'd taken this trail himself up to the summit and hadn't spotted a phone. There must be other paths or game trails leading down from the hill.

He walked toward the tree line, stepping across the yellow police tape—the boundary of rational, bureaucratic inquiry. The transition between the clearing and the trees was as sharp as a knife with no brush to soften the change. The big trees jumped up from the earth forming an overhanging cliff, their bulk soaking up his Maglite's beam and preventing the light from penetrating the wilderness. The dark trunks marched in ranks away from him and down the steep slope. Some trees had shed patches of brown outer bark, leaving a white undercoating that gleamed as pallidly as a corpse's skin when his light hit them.

The beam jerked about erratically. Bradan stilled the light in his hand, working to quiet the tremor.

A foghorn changed into demon's howl among the trees as transplanted memories from another era found root in fertile ground recently sanctified by sacrifice. Brooding spirits around the island heard the call and echoed and reechoed it from one trunk to the next. A breeze blew through the trees, pulling down a cascade of red and brown leaves. The ground now looked like it was covered with rust from a million metal weapons representing man's wars, axes to missiles and lasers.

Bradan froze. Try as he might, he couldn't bring himself to move closer to the trees. Why continue his pointless search? The more he reflected, the less possible it seemed he'd locate the phone.

Bradan played the beam over the trees. There. It was a small path down the summit that seemed to lead east in the general direction of the old immigration center. Tintagel materialized at his side, nosed about in the leaves for a few seconds, then raced down the slope, flitting as a black ghost amid the trunks. In seconds the animal was lost from his sight. Now he had the missile pad to himself. Staying in the haunted clearing seemed worse than moving into the trees.

"Faith," he said.

A moment later he added, "In what?"

He edged into the woods and inhaled the musty-pungent smell of fallen leaves and tried hard not to think of Danielle's flight through the same trees serenaded by the screams of her husband and friends being sliced to pieces by the priests. The wind gusted and blew the branches together with clicking sounds, joining the bare limbs together in interlocking fingers. Through them, the wan half-moon limned shreds of bilious clouds. The cosmos seemed empty, sucked dry by some vampire leaving only a residue of black pitch.

Bradan pushed on, trying not to lose his footing on the steep incline. Despite strenuous efforts, he must have been making enough noise to wake the dead as leaves crunched with every step. Moving down Mount Everest's flank, he felt the steady jolts to his thigh muscles and tried to avoid building up lethal momentum, but the descent impelled him downward like a juggernaut accompanied by avalanches of debris and dirt. The forest demanded silence, for Bradan to hold his breath and listen and not disturb things. He rubbed his legs to return vigor to his burning muscles.

Abruptly Bradan sent his beam stabbing off to the left. What had he seen? He grabbed a trunk to stop his forward motion and stood for a second, leaning into the hill for balance, trying to crystallize the ephemeral vision he'd observed, perhaps a person, but it seemed to move with unnatural deftness and certainly. He knew it wasn't the wolf. Tintagel would announce himself. The animal wasn't coy. Perhaps the priests had returned from the city to stalk him. Even away from the summit, the pervasive residue from last Halloween's magic still muffled his ability to detect other enchantment. Cynbel and Aennati might have left a guardian spell in their absence to drive off intruders.

Bradan switched the Maglite off and listened intently. Wind sent the leaves skittering over one another and, in the distance, waves moved against the shore of the big, lonely island. He heard nothing else. If something followed him, it must have now been waiting noiselessly. Bradan stared around. Even with his pupils dilated, he still couldn't see the trunk that his hand rested on, and the foliage overhead blocked moonlight. He was blind. However, turning on the Maglite would give away his position.

In all of his long life, raw terror always felt the same. Christ, he needed friends by his side now. Bradan turned around. No matter how he shifted, something was just behind him. He stopped breathing and listened until his lungs ached. Nothing. It must have been a deer. The Maglite flared on, searing away his night sight. He moved on down the slope. Every now and again, he whipped the beam around to check behind him.

He emerged from the trees near a small wooden chapel. Its steeple was barely two stories high, too humble to petition God more ostentatiously. After checking carefully, he stepped out of foliage and moved along the perimeter road that circumscribed the island. From what he recalled of Angel Island's geography, the immigration station was close by. Maybe the center's more penitent staff and inmates had once worshiped here.

He continued until he spotted a cluster of stone buildings through the trees and turned off onto a side road, part dirt, part broken asphalt, to descend to a small field overlooking China Cove off the San Francisco Bay. The park service had rebuilt parts of the old immigration center, its barracks, and various administrative structures and the hospital as a museum to the vetting and detention of almost a million mostly Asian immigrants. Seen from a distance, the buildings had a phosphorescent quality that framed each structure with a faint halo. Bradan opened and shut his eyes. The strain of the beam's brilliance contrasting with the nighttime darkness must have been affecting his vision.

Hadn't the immigration/detention center been renovated? But tonight the facility seemed to be in various stages of restoration. Skeletal scaffolding surrounded some buildings and ladders were propped against walls. The biggest structure, a block-shaped, rectangular building, would have looked right at home on Alcatraz. Bradan stared at this edifice's high walls. He guessed that it had served as a dormitory for Asian immigrants passing through the camp in the early years of the last century. The entire complex was grim. Welcoming habitation had not been foremost in its architects' plans, and tonight despondency seeped out of every dark window. Bradan wished Tintagel would return, but the animal must be roaming the island's farthest corners, ecstatic over the wild setting. With no company, the place felt desolate to Bradan, and his senses seemed heightened by the empty wilderness.

As he walked, he probed the ground with his Maglite. The beam had gotten perceptibly dimmer. Now it wasn't a light saber capable of fending off his fears. He approached the dorm. He wasn't sure where Danielle might have hidden on Halloween, but this seemed a good place to start his search. He moved around the dorm, feet crunching on gravel, asphalt, and vegetation. Immediately he was disappointed. Fencing prevented easy access to ground-floor windows and doors to prevent tourists and vandals from wandering in. Despite the barrier, someone had written a name "Jim" in English along with several Chinese characters. He stood back and kicked at the obstacle once and then again. Nothing happened except for a tinny rattle.

He quit and continued his circuit. On the rear side of the building, the fence had a small tear in it. Inside this perimeter, the only entrance even remotely accessible was an improvised plywood wooden door about four meters off the ground. How in the hell had someone as unathletic as Danielle gotten in, assuming this been her point of access to the building? Maybe the park service had been repairing it last Halloween and put a temporary ramp in place. No ramp existed now.

He played his beam over the door. This, he estimated, might be forced without resorting to enchantment or a broken foot.

A stone landing and flight of stairs had once provided access to the entrance, but the staircase had been almost completely destroyed, leaving only the top three steps still attached to the landing. He didn't see any handholds that might allow him to climb up. Even with a running start, jumping high enough to catch the lowest intact step of the staircase would be impossible. But . . . there was an aluminum ladder beside an administrative structure forgotten by maintenance workers. The ladder reached the landing and he confronted the temporary plywood door at the top secured with a padlock. Flimsy hinges attached the other side of the door to the frame. Bradan clambered back down the ladder and located a thick branch. Using this as an improvised crowbar, he forced a gap between the door and frame and pushed inside the building's first floor wrenching his already cut shoulder in the process.

"Excellent," he breathed. "There's nowhere that I don't hurt."

"Bradan, I'm here."

He froze. The disembodied voice came from somewhere way above him. He swept the ceiling with the Maglite until he came to a rectangular opening. Through this opening he saw another similar hole in the floor above, like an Escher diagram showing geometric patterns retreating off to infinity. The shifting shadows cast by his light heightened the effect. Whoever had sealed the building had also destroyed the internal staircases between its three floors, leaving only large square holes where the stairwells had once been. Claire looked down at him from the third-floor attic. Her face shown palely in his light.

"You're okay?" was all he could think to ask.

"I'm alive." Claire's voice sounded at once frightened and fatigued. "How did you know I was here?"

"I didn't," Bradan said. "Just luck. We'll talk later. I don't think anybody followed me, but I'm not sure. I'm going to try to get a ladder up to you. Then we need to find something I'm looking for and leave."

"You have a phone? Let's call help, for Christ's sake!"

"No phone."

He ran back to the landing and dragged the ladder clumsily through the partially open plywood door. He made a racket. Bradan hoped the ladder would be long enough to bridge the distance between floors. He maneuvered it into place and climbed up to the second floor, then wrenched it up after him and pushed it up toward Claire on the third floor.

"Can you grab the end?" he said. "It's heavy."

Bradan lifted it upward toward Claire's waiting hand.

"Hate heights," she said.

"Don't look down, just at the next step. Keep moving. We may have visitors."

"The people who attacked me?"

"Yes."

"I had my Beretta," Claire said. "They didn't seem worried about it. I lost it."

"I've already tried guns. Didn't work."

Bradan watched as Claire leaned out over the opening, managed to grab the top rung, and almost fell down on top of him. Hanging on gamely, she regained her balance and laid the ladder on the lip of the former stairwell. Slowly, she half climbed, half crawled backward down to join him on the second floor. Bradan heard her panting echoing off the bare walls. The building itself seemed to breathe. Finally, she dropped down beside him and looked upward for a moment at the opening she'd just descended from. Then she closed her eyes, blocking thoughts of her incarceration.

"Thank God you don't have pneumonia." Bradan watched his neighbor shifting her weight from one bare foot to the other on the concrete floor. Outside, he heard the wind blasting past the building. He'd left the rear entrance ajar and swirls of chilly air gusted into the room.

Claire looked surprisingly good albeit quite cold. One of the lenses in her glasses was cracked and she shivered in her emerald-green silk pajamas. Even the buttons running down the front of her shirt were green. The pant cuffs and shirtsleeves were too long, hiding her feet and hands. The garment masked her athletic figure and turned her into a kid. She must have tumbled directly out of bed to confront Cynbel and Aennati.

"They lit a fire," she said. "But it died after they left. They haven't been around for hours. I've explored trying to find a way down. No tools, no rope, glass on the floor. It's too far to jump down, so I've been sitting in the dark. My family must be going crazy. Does anyone think that I was a prisoner?"

"Don't know. No one saw them actually take you, but the detectives must assume that you were abducted, but they'd have no clue where to look."

Bradan shrugged off his tattered sweater and tossed it over to her.

"Don't mind the blood," he said. "Let's move."

She examined the slashed garment at arm's length.

"Someone stabbed you?"

"Several times," he said.

Claire looked at him, then the chill conditions overwhelmed her repugnance and she pulled the sweater on.

"This leaves you with your T-shirt and pants. You'll freeze."

"We won't be here long. A friend with a boat is waiting. I'll last till then."

"You know the people who kidnapped me?" Claire asked. She ran her hand through her hair and straightened her glasses on the bridge of her nose, trying to adjust herself to the reality of freedom.

"Yes," he said shortly. "Let's get back down to the first floor. I need to look for something. Then we'll leave."

"Look for what?" Claire's voice didn't rise, but her tone was so brittle Bradan thought the words would splinter. "Let's leave. Now."

"Soon," he said. "I may be able to sense them coming, in which case we'll have a bit of warning."

"Sense them? What does that mean?"

"Long story." Bradan directed the Maglite down to the first floor below. "What I'm looking for—a phone—is important and it won't take long to check for it. There's something on it that I need. Badly need."

"Can we call for help when you find this phone?"

"Doubt it. It's probably dead."

"What are they?" she asked. He noticed that she'd edged away from him. "And who are you?"

"I'm housebroken," he said irritated. "And the least of your problems."

Claire grabbed one end of the ladder and together they maneuvered it over to the hole leading down to the first floor.

"I guess the man and woman who took me were part of the group who are killing people around the Bay," she said.

He nodded. "They're not part of a group. It's just the two of them."

"Is there a phone on your boat?"

"Yes, but calling 9-1-1 isn't an option. They aren't typical California psychos. Siccing the cops on them won't help."

Just how was he supposed to explain the priests to a modern strategic financial consultant?

Bradan slid the ladder down the stairwell to the first floor and heard it bang loudly on the floor below. He winced at the noise and clambered down.

"Bradan, it's someone else's job to track down killers."

"If I could delegate this to the SFPD, I would," he called up at her. "The cops are after me, though. They don't know anything about the people who are actually doing the killings."

"Where are the man and woman now?" she asked. "Still in the city?"

"In the Haight, I hope. I distracted them earlier."

"Would they . . . ?" She ran two fingers across her throat to mime slicing it open. "They'd have chopped my head off, right?"

"You catch on quick," Bradan said. He walked along the first-floor room's perimeter. "I'm not sure about the decapitation, though. That wasn't always appropriate. They might have garroted you instead, then sliced open your jugular to let the blood drain away."

"Why keep me alive at all?"

"I'm not sure." Bradan rubbed his chin where a beard grew. It itched hellishly. "Maybe because they thought you could tell them things they needed to know about the city and local customs."

"Not that it matters, do they have names?"

"Cynbel and Aennati," he said.

"Odd."

"They're more than odd."

While Claire descended, he continued his inspection of the first floor, sweeping the room systematically with the light. There weren't that many places a phone might be. The place smelled stale, of ancient paint, dried vegetation, and anxiety. Despite on-going renovation, tonight everything looked desiccated from years of raw weather; he'd wandered into Cheops's tomb. They stood on a cruddy, leaf-strewn floor and the room itself was featureless, a bare, expansive box with the ceiling supported by dozens of thin, rusted metal pillars. The walls were painted a grayish color. Perhaps the designer couldn't decide whether it was a penitentiary or an infirmary and had compromised with this institutional color.

Bradan kicked a pile of debris, sending dust motes swirling in the air lit by his beam. He tried to picture hundreds of Chinese immigrants jammed together, lounging on beds or gambling on the floor to pass time while they all waited weeks or months for interrogations that would determine whether the packed sea voyage from China's Guangdong Province for which they'd spent their life's savings would have to be repeated in reverse if the white American authorities found them undesirable. He could almost hear the voices and coughing from a century past and smell the day's meals being prepared in the dining hall.

"Bradan, where are we?" Claire peered about at the room.

He stopped his search for a moment in surprise then realized that she hadn't seen anything more of the center than its attic with no windows. He widened his light's beam so she could see more of their setting.

"Angel Island. The old immigration/detention center." He looked at her. "Are you okay?"

"My father took me here when I was eight and I'd pretty much forgotten the experience. I'm third generation so I should be a little detached." She stared about, perhaps remembering her grandparents' stories. "We were treated as opium smugglers. No white European immigrants were penned up. Cattle got

242   PETER W. BLAISDELL

better care. It was a prison, really, with barracks and restrictions and bad food. Many of the guards hated the Chinese. My grandparents were both very young children, but they remember the humiliation." Claire's monologue rushed out.

"If you want, wait outside while I look around," he said.

"I'll stay. It doesn't bother me to be here. It bothers me what happened here."

"What are the characters inscribed in the walls?" Bradan asked.

"Poetry." She walked over to a wall and examined the writing. "I'll translate this one. There is a formal structure to them. My meter and intonation won't do it justice, but here goes:

> *I left heritage and family behind in my homeland.*
> *Here I walk between close walls, and curse blue sky and*
> *bluer sea.*
> *On an island, I sit alone by a city of thousands.*"

Bradan said, "I wonder if he was one of the lucky ones they let into San Francisco?"

"Who knows? I remember my father was very moved when he saw words, poetry on our visit years ago. He knew it was here, but it wasn't real until he actually saw it."

"Let's get out," he said.

"Nothing to find?"

"Maybe it's here, maybe it's not." Bradan randomly ran his beam over the floor and walls of the room. "I've looked, but it's a big park. The police recovered it already or it's just so thoroughly lost that no one can find it. It's time to get back to the boat."

They moved toward the entrance. Claire reached out to the wall to trace the faint Chinese characters with her finger and laughed at an unflattering description of the detention center's food or the staff. Almost at the door, she grabbed his sleeve and pointed out the faint outline of a dragon some unsung artist had traced between the poems. Bradan played the Maglite over it. The creature's stylized body embraced the poems' lines with serpentine grace while a gush of faded fire blew forth from its mouth and flaring nostrils. Elongated chin whiskers floated about its head. The representation was abstract and mannered, but real rage blazed out of the dragon's eyes and, in the shifting light, the creature looked ready to pounce.

Almost at the entrance, Bradan's shoe kicked something. Startled, he stepped quickly back and directed the light downward. Amid decades of upswept dust and debris, Bradan saw a metallic rectangle. It lay half-buried. He stooped and gently extracted a phone from the detritus.

"This might not be it, but how many phones would be lost in a this place midwinter?"

"I'm amazed we found it," Claire said. "If it hadn't been for your love of poetry, we'd have walked out."

"Verses are the lifeblood of a nation of storytellers. The Celts were that once." He blew dirt off the silvery phone and tried to turn it on.

"No surprise, dead. There's a charger on the boat. Maybe this is the key to putting the genie back in the bottle."

"What are you doing up after lights-out?"

Bradan and Claire whirled around together. Three men stood at the far end of the room staring at them. One of them pointed a pistol at Bradan's stomach. Bradan's first impression was that they were Nazis, with belted uniforms and peaked hats, but half a heartbeat later he realized that the clothing was American from an earlier era. One of the men wore a dark civilian suit also dated by a century, with a broad tie held in place with a pin and a starched shirt jammed up under his chin. His reddish hair was short and parted neatly to one side with every strand in place.

"Are you park rangers?" Bradan asked. He knew they weren't. What were they?

"Turn that light off," one of the uniformed men said. "You'll wake the others."

"Didn't think they let Chinese women in this year, Exclusion Act and all," the second soldier said. He wore steel-framed glasses with round lenses accenting the circular chubbiness of his face.

"Who are you?" Claire shouted.

The demand hardened the trio's already grim expressions.

"She speaks English," the civilian said. The two soldiers radiated power while the civilian wore a look of reproach like a preacher chastising parishioners who'd strayed.

"And I'm telling both of 'em—in plain English—that we'll send 'em back where they came from," the guard with the gun said. "Is the guy with her white? What's he doing here?"

"Let's go," Bradan hissed at Claire. He grabbed her sweater sleeve and yanked hard in the direction of the door.

She struggled to free herself. "No one can talk to me that way . . . who the fuck do they think—"

Bradan managed to pull her toward the plywood door. Part of the doorframe disintegrated just above them, spraying wood splinters. He was deafened by a shot. The bastard with the pistol must have fired. Christ, the gun was loud. Claire's resistance instantly transformed into a running jump off the landing. No time for ladders. Bradan duplicated the feat, landed hard in shrubbery and was amazed that he didn't fracture an ankle from the fall. He saw Claire pelting away from the building. Bradan bolted after her, up the path toward the woods. He heard boots on the wooden floor in the building. Two more shots kicked up dirt and pebbles to their right and in front of them. Bradan didn't try to create a defensive spell. It hadn't worked outside the Paradise.

"Don't run straight," he shouted at Claire. "Dodge."

They both rushed up the hill toward the perimeter road. Bradan cut left then right. A searing pain scorched across his deltoid muscle. Someone had just cut open his upper arm and then instantly packed the wound with rock salt—worse than the javelin gash on his other shoulder. He hadn't heard the shot. He stumbled but managed to keep his feet and reached across to touch the damage. His hand came away bloody, but he now knew that the bullet had grazed him, not torn his upper arm off.

He looked over his shoulder and saw the three men almost on top of him, running with eldritch fleetness and certainty along the dark, uneven path overhung with trees. When he'd first seen them inside the immigration center, they'd looked heavy, ponderous with society's certitude. Outside, they moved adroitly and quickly after their wounded quarry. Bradan watched the soldier with the gun level it at him again. He lurched left to throw off the guard's aim, but they were too close. Bradan's back must fill the gun sight.

A snarl almost as loud as the gun shredded the air just in front of Bradan. A massive blur of teeth and black fur flashed out of the woods and down the path directly toward him, moving so fleetly that it barely touched the path. Shit, another threat? However, the creature agilely swerved around him and instead launched itself at the guards. The night was too dark to see any detail, but Bradan knew instinctively that it was Tintagel. This time he did hear the shot as the soldier with the pistol fired at the object hurtling at him, and then Bradan heard the clip emptying in a staccato burst of sound. One errant bullet zipping through the branches overhead nicked leaves on its flight. *Better to shoot at a shadow*, Bradan thought. He tried to slow enough to turn around, but tumbled clumsily to the ground and landed on his wounded shoulder. Bradan ground his teeth at the pain and rolled over to see what had happened.

Moving with the same unnatural speed they'd used to chase Bradan and Claire, the three guards now fled back toward the center, growing more spectral with each step. Tintagel pursued them relentlessly, moving like a hound on a mission from hell. As the wolf closed in, now within a bound of its quarry, the figures melted away, the bureaucrat last of all, his suit moving for a moment with a man's motions after the figure inside had vanished.

Tintagel overshot the spot where the eerie trio had just disappeared, carried along by his furious momentum, skidded in the dirt, regained his footing, and loped back to the point of disappearance. The wolf nosed about on the ground, then lay down, flipped over on his back, and rolled energetically in the dirt, quickly raising a cloud of debris and leaves.

"Pets," Bradan grunted.

"They're gone?" Claire stared fixated at the place where their pursuers had vanished and where Tintagel now undulated with carnal zest. She breathed heavily.

She looked down at him lying on the ground. "Are you hit?"

"I think so, but not badly." It hurt, though. A lot. Bradan inhaled lungfuls of air for several moments. He tried to sit up and discovered he could by levering himself into a sitting position with the arm that hadn't been shot. The javelin wound from the night before made this painful but not impossible.

The trees and path shifted before him. For a moment he sat in the center of the path letting the dizziness pass and collecting himself before trying to stand upright.

"You did get shot. Your arm's all bloody." She stared at his soaked T-shirt. "Bleeding like a stuck pig."

"What a pretty simile. It's not deep. I can move my arm . . . a little. Wally's got some alcohol on board. I'll clean it out."

Claire held out her hand. Using it for support, Bradan heaved himself to his feet. He tried to vomit, but nothing was in his stomach. How much blood had he lost? For that matter, when had he last eaten a solid meal? Amazingly, he still clutched Danielle's phone after the slug smashed into him.

"Off the path," he said. "Into the trees. Something else might come after us." He whistled at the wolf.

They pushed into the forest. Claire looked down the hill at the detention center seen through gaps in the foliage.

"What happened? How could Tintagel scare them off? They were some kind of phantoms?"

"All the better for the wolf. A long time ago, Tintagel and his pack chased down the spirits of warriors killed on battlefields. You could say he worked for a sort of collector."

Bradan wondered how to explain the god Gwyn in modern terms and decided it couldn't be done. Claire must already think he was mad. Maybe not. She'd been kidnapped and held captive by enchanters within the last twenty-four hours.

"And you thought Chinese mythology was strange," he said to her.

"What is Tintagel?" she asked.

Despite their circumstances, Bradan laughed. He pictured Claire thinking about her morning runs with this monster pacing beside her.

"I haven't a clue. I do know he's friends with me."

They threaded their way through the trees running as fast as they dared in the darkness, moving toward Angel Island's marina where a little dinghy was tied up. The size of Wally's vessel made an inconspicuous approach to the island impossible and he'd used a dingy to ferry himself and the wolf from Wally's boat to the island.

"Think we can get back to the dock through all this brush?" Claire ducked under a low pine limb half visible in the dark. "I can't see a damned thing."

"Let's try pushing through there." Bradan pointed to a faint path cutting diagonally across the slope. He thought he saw the marina ahead.

"Will we run into more immigration center guards?" she asked.

"Or something worse." Bradan wondered if the Druids had returned to Angel Island. Perhaps not. The guards might have been a manifestation of a spell left in place to ensure that Claire didn't escape.

"Your kidnappers can be creative," he said. "Using the guards to hunt us down seemed to be an amusing use of local color, given the setting. Cynbel and Aennati draw inspiration from their surroundings and use the psychology of their foes against them. It's also more economical letting the surroundings inspire enchantment."

"But Tintagel–" Claire began.

"Won't be able to fend off Cynbel and Aennati's next creation. If they have returned from the city, the bastards may be close enough to just will us dead. They don't get any points for that, but at this stage, we're a nuisance that's distracting him from bigger plans."

"Then why use those things back there?"

"They may have been just guards to keep you put or maybe they used them to flush us out. The priests probably know we were somewhere near the detention center—hell, I've been blundering about now for several hours—but they didn't know exactly where."

"Now they do?" Claire said.

"Don't be so pessimistic. Tintagel interrupted the plans. We might have a reprieve if we move."

"I hope your friend has a fast boat," she said.

———

"This is your boat?" Claire asked.

"Actually, it's Wally's boat," Bradan said.

"Yes indeed." Wally gestured expansively at the massive tug. He deftly caught the rope Bradan tossed up to him and secured it to a cleat. "Come aboard and welcome. She'll be a beauty once I get the rust removed."

"If anything's left once the rust is removed," Bradan said. "Wally, this is Claire. Claire, Wally. We may have company soon. Let's move. I'll winch the dingy onboard." Bradan helped Claire clamber up the ladder and into the tug. Tintagel leaped aboard with a single bound.

"Who's coming, the police?" the bartender asked.

"Someone else," Bradan said.

"Criminals?"

"Yes."

Wally nodded, picking up on the anxiety in Bradan's voice without understanding what might be chasing his friend. He swung himself up into the cabin perched above the deckhouse. Bradan watched Claire stare about curiously. Wally's boat smelled of tar, diesel, and rope. There were hoses and hawsers everywhere. Gears and the housing of some outsized piece of machinery lay scattered about the aft deck amid an oil stain as if a titan had decided to tinker with his watch and then given up halfway through the process. Every part of the boat's hull above the waterline was protected by a thick rubber fender and huge truck tires to buffer the shocks of contacts with other ships and wharfs; Bradan knew the boat had been a working tug until Wally had bought it from an Oakland salvage and towing company. To Bradan, the thing looked capable of pulling an entire city block up by the foundations. It did not look fast.

He listened as Wally powered up to the twin engines from idle to maneuvering speed. The whole process seemed to take forever. He breathed deeply several times trying to dissipate tension. The less time they spent exposed out on the Bay, the better. Bradan strode forward, skirting the nautical paraphernalia and an outdoor grill sitting incongruously near the bow. The wolf clambered after him nimbly. At last, the tug began to vibrate and he smelled diesel exhaust. For a few seconds, heat washed down from the funnel. He welcomed it. He'd move back to the cabin in a minute, but right now he wanted an unobstructed view of Angel Island to watch for pursuit.

The island bulked darkly before him. He heard the waves lapping against its shore. Off to his left, Tiburon's peninsula jutted out toward them. Despite the late hour, a few of the city's mansions nestled into the forested hillside were still lit. They hung suspended against a dark background, fireflies in a void. Bradan couldn't distinguish the borders between land, bay, and night.

"I can't believe we got away," Claire said. She'd joined him leaning against the metal railing.

"We haven't," Bradan said. "If the priests are on the island, they'll know we're escaping and there's only one nonmagical way to do that: by water. So they're waiting for us to show our hand. If I used some kind of spell to get us off island, then they'd know our location in a second. If we use a boat, we'll be visible, too. Nobody else is sailing now; we're pretty obvious."

"Magic?" Claire looked at him.

"We'll talk later," he said.

"I'm in something deep, aren't I?"

Nothing to hide now. "We both are. Let's go aft to the cabin. I'm freezing out here."

Inside, lit softly by glowing instrument dials, Bradan pulled up a stool and sat slumped against the bulkhead. Wally had decorated the small cabin with several of his photographs. Aside from that, there wasn't room for much. The bartender steered the craft holding the big wooden wheel tightly as if his craft might spin out of control at any moment.

"You've been trained?" Bradan asked him.

"Soon, my friend. Between the Paradise and my pictures, who has the time? I need to look into what's required for a master's license. Pretty much, you just point the boat where you want to go and be sure that you have a huge amount of room to stop. You want to take the wheel?"

Bradan shook his head.

They plowed onward in the dark. By default, it would be flight in this steampunk relic. Periodically, Wally shot anxious glances at Bradan. He must have picked up on his friend's anxiety but couldn't identify the source. Bradan had been as vague as possible when he'd persuaded Wally to ferry him out to the island, merely indicating that someone he knew was in mortal danger. The man was helping him based on friendship alone; Bradan had once again put a friend in the line of fire. Now they were all in harm's way.

Bradan rummaged about amid the cabin's clutter and located a first aid kit. Sheets of white light crossed his vision as he gently dabbed alcohol on his fresh shoulder wound that still oozed blood. God, he'd love to hit Cynbel and Aennati back hard. Right now, though, his best tactic would be to stay out of their way until he could inspect Danielle's phone. He had it charging now. Possibly, just possibly, the spell could be reversed, sending the priests back to oblivion. Otherwise he was as impotent as the vacant Nike missile pad on Angel Island.

Their tug pushed through the black, glistening waves without running lights, cutting a wide arc as Wally swung around toward Sausalito. To Bradan, they barely seemed to move despite shudders that shook the entire tug; the vessel sounded ready to tear itself apart at any minute. Their slow progress reminded him of a scene from Coleridge's *"Rime of the Ancient Mariner"*—their vessel sat becalmed in a sea of specters. It was a night for phantoms of all sorts. Moonlight and starlight provided faint visibility and everything seemed to float on one of Saturn's vast oceans where distance was a pointless concept.

"Where to?" Claire asked. "The city?"

"I have a berth in Sausalito," Wally said.

"Can't we pull into Tiburon's marina?" Bradan asked. "It's right over there." He pointed.

"No room, Bradan," Wally said. "There isn't an open slip big enough to hold us."

"The closest place possible, then," Bradan said. "Christ, it's dark out here. Can we even see the channel markers?"

"What are those?" Claire asked.

"They keep us from running aground," Bradan said.

"Imagine, me, a ship's captain," Wally said. "The markers have lights, so we'll see them." Bradan guessed he was trying to make conversation to take their minds off their circumstances. "I grew up in the desert and didn't even see a large body of water until I was twenty." He inhaled deeply. "Until I got *The Rubaiyat*, I'd never even sailed a rowboat."

He looked at Claire. "I couldn't interest Bradan, but would you care to steer?" He stepped back from the wheel with a gallant flourish. "Sailing's really rather easy, though docking is a little more of an effort."

"No, no, you're doing fine," she said.

A rush of wind, funneling off the winter Pacific and through the Golden Gate, caught them as they cleared Angel Island's shelter. Tiburon passed to their left.

For the hundredth time, Bradan turned to look behind them. A flash of fluid, silvery movement above the island's hills stopped his eye. Something floated behind them in the cold air. Bradan stared. A cloud? It was big and indistinct. He lurched off his stool and moved close to the cabin's rear window. He felt his intestines tighten. If it hadn't been a clear night, he might have suspected that it was an oddly shaped fog bank hanging low over the island.

"Wally, pick up the speed, will you?" he said.

"I'm going almost as fast as *The Rubaiyat* will go."

"'Almost'? We need everything this tub's got."

Wally swung around, keeping one hand on the wheel, to look back at the island. "I don't see anything."

Bradan pointed.

"Still don't . . . what do you think it is?"

"Damn it, let's move," Bradan said sharply. The engine speed picked up. However, he judged that it would still take them at least another fifteen minutes to reach Sausalito. Should they leave the boat on its course as a decoy, abandon ship, and try swimming for Marin's shore? Within minutes hypothermia would set in. The phone would get soaked, too.

Bradan watched the object better define itself as it floated above the trees. It rose over the island with the languid buoyancy of a zeppelin and seemed completely at ease in the wild night winds. As the object stretched and rotated, he noted a covering of mirror-bright scales that reflected the moonlight. A long serpentine neck supported a head filled with sharp tusks and, balancing the neck, an equally long tail snaked out behind the monster. Bradan estimated the creature must be at least fifty meters long. Folded legs ending in hooked claws hung under it. Though obviously very much alive, it had a stylized, almost mannerist appearance which mocked mundane biological principles and basic vertebrate anatomy.

"Shit, what is it?" Claire said.

"The detention center's painting of the dragon. They're still using local history for inspiration," Bradan shouted above the boat's roaring engine.

Wally spun the wheel wildly but despite frantic efforts, the tug seemed to be sitting stationary as the monster leisurely oriented itself. Even at the great distance, Bradan saw its napalm-yellow eyes staring into his, reptilian and amused. He wished he still had Rod's Magnum. It wouldn't scratch this son of a bitch, but he couldn't stand sitting lamblike waiting to be destroyed as they floated, a toy in the dragon's playground.

"What have we gotten into?" Wally screamed. He switched to Arabic momentarily then back to English. "It's a mirage, as in the desert?"

The dragon had spotted them and its wings flapped with a

fluttery, leathery sound, some gargantuan bat that had flown through an open window into a nighttime bedroom. After spiraling upward twice, it surged forward in their direction, angling down with a hawk's precision. Bradan saw its chin whiskers stream behind luminous in the night sky. The beast swept along over the waves as it rapidly closed on *The Rubaiyat*. Now the big creature's muzzle twitched violently. With a deafening bellow, the monster blew fiery clouds of smoke out of its mouth and nostrils and a sulfurous fireball shot down toward the tug. In a second, the frigid nighttime chill became the sun's core. Even protected within the cabin, Bradan threw up his hand to shield his face. He heard Claire's labored intake of superheated air. A pane of glass shattered. The mass of flame shot toward the tug as if the entire contents of a steel mill's blast furnace poured at them, deep orange with floating black motes of metal in its center about to dissolve into atoms. The fireball hit *The Rubaiyat's* wake twenty meters behind them. Steam exploded into the air as fire met water, turning the entire area into a giant boiling cauldron and pushing a wave of heat over everything. The heavy tug rocked wildly, pitching Wally into the wheel and throwing Bradan and Claire into each other hard. Something on the deck fell overboard with a splash. Bradan dragged himself upright, burning his hand on the cabin's wall, and checked the damage. The dragon's shot had fallen just short of turning *The Rubaiyat* into a pyre. However, the beast now maneuvered just above them and opened its mouth for a second blast of hell.

Bradan wondered fleetingly what spell would drive the monster off. Nothing ever worked right the first time, the rhyme and pace were inevitably wrong. He was reduced to his own stock of illusions, a paltry defense.

What gossamer weapons could he deploy?

If the priests could improvise, so could he. Bradan rushed through a series of rhymed couplets, looking not at the dragon but at Angel Island's highest hilltop. He heard a hissing whoosh that rapidly shifted an octave lower to become a sullen, almost subliminal roar that rumbled across the water and engulfed their boat. Then the sequence of sounds repeated itself twice more.

"It's two rockets . . . no, three," Claire said. She stood beside him staring first at their attacker, then at Angel Island. Bradan guessed what she'd said by her mouth movements. He couldn't hear. Noise pulverized the night air.

"Nike surface-to-air missiles," Bradan shouted. She couldn't have understood. He held his hands to his ears trying to block the deafening rumble as the three white streaks, two in advance of the third, surged away from the hilltop and angled out across the water leaving contrails as they moved toward the dragon. The beast heard, whipped its neck about, then tried to brake its momentum and struggle to turn and confront the threat. Instantly, the first two missiles homed in on the dragon and detonated with twin thunderous concussions and a huge wash of white light that lit up the dragon, their boat, and half the Bay. Flat echoes of the explosions rebounded back at them from surrounding landmasses; a giant had slapped the Bay.

Bradan knew exactly what to expect next: nothing. No shrapnel, no blast wave, no incendiary fuel or missile debris engulfing the dragon or their tug. Unlike Cynbel and Aennati, he couldn't make his illusions tangible. But he could make them distracting. The third missile followed the path of its brethren and homed in on the leviathan. Recovering its wits, the dragon, seemingly amazed to find itself undamaged, saw the remaining

Nike closing on it and dodged the incoming missile by dropping straight down almost into the water. The projectile overshot its target and then arced upward again, exactly mimicking a 1950s missile that had lost lock on a Russian MiG and now sought to reacquire its target.

The beast turned from *The Rubaiyat* and fled back toward Angel Island chased by an illusory anti-aircraft weapon. Its flapping wings created a windstorm powerful enough to shake the tug anew and drench the boat with spray that hissed on the stern's hot metal.

All about them, lights popped on from Tiburon and Sausalito's hillside homes, an audience in a darkened arena demanding an encore with their phones.

CHAPTER 17

Semiotics for the Semiliterate

Bradan's bed rocked, waking him. Where was he? He sorted cautiously through the last several days' jumbled and sleep-hazed memories, almost afraid of what he'd find as he probed. Recent events cascaded down on him like a ton of lead ingots: the Chinese dragon, the chase through the park, butchery in the city. He'd crawled into a spare bunk on Wally's houseboat, too bone weary to hide anywhere else.

The boat still shook. He felt along the walls, located a light switch, and picked his way through the little stateroom's clutter, tripping over a speaker. He pulled the door open and moved out onto the deck, steadying himself carefully to avoid being knocked into the bulkhead. Both shoulders ached and he felt as if half a pint of Wild Turkey sloshed around in his cranium.

"Claire, get on deck."

"Already here. It's another quake."

Bright midday sun poured down from the sky, searing Bradan's eyeballs. Through tears he saw her leaning against the railing still wearing emerald-green pajamas. She smiled at him and pushed her glasses further up her nose. The deck rolled and yawed beneath him coincident with a sensation of magic surging against his psyche. He grabbed for the boat's railing.

Water slapped loudly against the wharf's pilings as the force of the movement built rapidly until it felt as if he stood on top of a mattress while a big-league slugger smashed at the other side with a baseball bat. He felt a deep, sub-bass rumble as plate moved against plate. The priests were trying again. Bradan focused on the origin of Cynbel's energy—not Angel Island anymore—in the city, trees, steep drops to rocks and surf below, in sight of the Golden Gate Bridge. Bradan guessed the enchanters were in the Presidio near the cliffs. The seismic movement subsided. He intuited that Cynbel and Aennati hadn't quite mustered the precise leverage needed to catalyze the quake, but they were very, very close.

A telephone line ashore swayed wildly and then slowed gradually to droop, normally suspended between poles. Gulls that had circled above squawking cacophonously during the quake now settled back demurely onto the line.

He looked around. The far end of marina berthed well-maintained sloops and motor yachts, while Wally's tug inhabited a ghetto for a wild miscellany of watercraft ranging from houseboats to sampans and a square-rigged brig, any one of which would be idiosyncratic enough to send the Sausalito marina's slip rental rates plummeting were they not sequestered in the remotest part of the waterfront.

"Where's Wally?" he asked.

"Buying food," Claire said. "He'll be back soon."

Bradan heard a child crying on a boat nearby and smelled bacon frying. A moment later someone turned on a radio that rasped out news of the quake. Time to get inside. He needed to shed the conspicuously bloody T-shirt. Bradan still found it difficult to think of himself as a fugitive from the police as well as the Druids. A man laughed out loud on the deck of a houseboat adjacent to *The Rubaiyat*.

"Man, that quake came too close, too close." Their neighbor flipped long gray hair out of his eyes and wiped his hands on a leather vest and paint-spattered jeans.

Trying to affect a nonchalant manner, Bradan waved at him. He could be a former long-haul trucker who'd managed to save enough to retire in squalid splendor on a houseboat. The man munched a burger.

"You two Wally's friends?" he asked.

"We're on his boat for a couple of days," Bradan said. "We'd never been on one before."

Claire nodded.

Bradan checked over the neighboring houseboat. Stained-glass windows peeked through dense plant life. It was a floating jungle sitting atop a miniature of the Chartres Cathedral. Was it waterworthy? Bradan had trouble discerning the deckhouse though the flora. He did note several marijuana plants tucked amid the other greenery. The few exposed parts of the deck were thoroughly bombed with gull droppings.

"Did you people see that shit out on the Bay last night?" the man asked. "Lit everything up. The Coast Guard must have had a coronary." He bent to pick up potsherds where a fern had been tossed to the deck during the quake and kicked the dirt overboard.

"Weird stuff going on."

"I slept through the whole thing," Bradan said. He edged back to the door leading into the cabin. His T-shirt would be appropriate for someone who moonlighted as a butcher.

"There might have been fireworks," Bradan added.

"Fireworks? My ass. I was in Iraq. That sounded like a rifle company on a bad night in Fallujah."

"Early New Year's celebration?" Bradan suggested.

"Chinese New Year comes early this year," Claire added helpfully.

"Some party," the man said.

"I'd better pick up inside." Bradan thought the man looked too stoned to connect his new neighbors with recent mass killings. However, someone else was sure to notice him sooner or later as the dock shifted from post-quake stasis to agitated repair activity with people hustling about the dock to check on their boats and clean up the mess.

"Stuff fell everywhere," the man said. "One of my windows on the other side of my boat busted. Won't be cheap to replace the panes. Stained glass costs."

"We need to talk," Bradan said as he and Claire slipped inside.

"Yes, we do. How do I get my life back?"

———

"So, Cynbel and Aennati are magicians?" Claire said. "They're trying to destroy San Francisco? And you've survived since King Arthur's times? If I understand the story right, you were a sort of apprentice to Merlin?"

Bradan noted her deadpan tone. She stood next to a window in the houseboat's forward cabin with the sun casting her face into either deep shadow or warm light. The illumination sharpened her cheekbones, and her profile was composed of taut planes and long eyelashes. She neither smiled encouragement nor frowned disbelief.

"That's right," he said blandly. "I was the original sorcerer's apprentice." Ah, the innate skepticism of the educated modern. "That should be believable after what's happened to you these last few days."

"How long till the next quake?" she asked.

"Not much time. They came close a few minutes ago."

Bradan leaned back on a decrepit, overstuffed chair blowing wavering rings of smoke up at the ceiling. Wally kept a batch of cigars in a small glass humidor sitting on an old rolltop desk in the houseboat's forecabin. The smokes were cheap, but Bradan didn't care. Between puffs, he sipped strong black coffee, feeling almost human despite his wounds. The wolf slept soundly at his feet. Aside from the gentle slap of water against the hull, the cabin was silent. It might have been a sunlit sitting room in a Victorian London men's club where he'd been a member, hazed with cigar smoke, except for the artistic clutter and the smell of tar and paint. A Nikon with a telephoto lens sat on a stack of proofing sheets next to the humidor. Tall windows let light into the room and provided a view of neighboring boats.

"I always thought Arthur was a myth," she said.

"He was real enough. So was Merlin, though neither of them was chivalric in a storybook sense. They were just desperate men trying to beat back overwhelming odds. In the end, they lost. I see all sorts of uncomfortable parallels with our own situation."

"If you're a magician, let's see you work a spell," she said.

"Where do you think those missiles came from last night?"

"That was you?"

He nodded. "If I tried something big now, I'd give our location away. Besides, I'm too tired."

"They can sense you?"

"And I can sense them when they create complex enchantment."

Claire smiled. "Just a little spell, then?"

For a moment Bradan's caution fought with his pride. Hubris won and he looked around the room, now permeated with cigar smoke, seeking inspiration. He quietly recited three couplets.

"So?" she said. "The words sounded pretty, but nothing changed."

"Have a cigar," he said. He waved weakly in the direction of the humidor. "They're not bad smokes."

"Oh." Claire's voice was completely toneless. The cigar container floated about a meter over the rolltop desk.

"Go ahead, run your hand underneath it," he said. "Or try to put it back where it sat."

She glanced at him, then approached the glass humidor and circled it. In its new position, light coming through the windows made the humidor's steel lid shimmer and its glass glitter like leaded crystal. Claire didn't touch it. Bradan reversed the spell by transposing its first and third stanzas. The humidor settled gently back down to sit next to a stack of Wally's unopened bills and a darkroom supplies catalog on the desk.

"Industrial Light & Magic couldn't have made it look that easy," Bradan said.

Now Claire did pick up the cigar container, rendered mundane and safe by its restoration to solid support, and inspected it. Bradan noted a shiver pass through her.

"Could you teach me to do that?" she asked.

"Sure. You're a quick study. Now we need to come up with something a lot stronger than parlor tricks—though that's about all I'm capable of."

"You . . . we don't seem to hold many winning cards, do we? If Cynbel and Aennati are so strong, why don't they just will you dead?"

"They have to know where I am."

Claire's expression stayed unreadable when she moved away from the window to stand beside him, looking over his shoulder

264 PETER W. BLAISDELL

to survey Danielle's phone as if this might be tangible proof to corroborate what he'd just told her.

"What are Druids?" she asked.

"Celtic priests and spiritual leaders. They were teachers, too. They were from violent times and sacrifice was part of that world's creeds, but they weren't killers for their own gain or gratification. In fact, they helped the tribes remember their culture and traditions and how to revere nature." He let it sink in then asked, "Does that help?"

"Have you ever explained your history to anyone else?"

"Only when there seemed to be a good reason. I met a woman in . . ." Bradan paused. He enjoyed playing raconteur, but instinctively stripped references to specific dates from his stories. No need for that deception now. It felt refreshing.

"It was in tenth-century Córdoba," he continued. "I thought knowing about me might be amusing enough to win her favors. As it happened, I amused her. I tried the same trick a few decades later in Avignon and almost got burned at the stake. The Moors were more cosmopolitan than the French in those days."

"I guess I should feel honored that you've taken me into your confidence," she said. "I assume seduction isn't your only motive."

"It's nice having an audience. Given what I've put Wally through, I owe him the full truth too when he gets back."

"How did you get involved with Cynbel and Aennati?" Claire asked.

"My family lived in a small town—a collection of huts, really, by today's standards. At the time, though, it was considered civilized. My home was in an area that was being contested by Saxons who were fighting a loose confederation of Celtic tribes under Arthur. A Saxon band and some allied Angles torched my town and killed my parents. They weren't tough people, my parents. Father even knew a bit of Latin. I think we'd all gotten so used to order and civilization under the Romans that we forgot that it hadn't taken root in our country, not deeply, anyway. Arthur and Merlin kept the Celts together for a while, but eventually we went under. Cynbel decided his chances were better with foreign invaders because they were stronger. He sold us out." Bradan surprised himself with the anger in his voice. It had been so long ago, but his emotions were right there just waiting to be evoked.

"He isn't someone who consults a moral compass very often," Claire said. "Or the woman, either."

"I'm looking forward to meeting them when they're vulnerable."

"Can they be vulnerable?" Claire asked.

Bradan tossed his cigar into an ashtray. "Who knows? I'm barely fending them off unless I can reverse the resurrection spell and send them back to hell. But I'll have to sacrifice somehow to affect a spell this powerful, and I'm not killing anyone. So that leaves me with a puzzle." He drank deeply from the coffee cup.

"Is there anything I can do to help?"

"Call your family and let them know that you're okay, but don't say exactly where you are or that you're with me. Use Wally's phone. They won't associate that with me, so they probably won't bother to trace its location."

"I'll tell them to leave town before the next quake." Claire moved over to sit beside him on the chair's thick armrest.

"You'll never convince them of the urgency."

He regarded Danielle's phone screen showing an image of the parchment. He was very familiar with its structure and key phrases; he'd had the hard copy in his possession for fifteen centuries. As he traced his finger along a line of text, he was conscious of her muscled thigh beneath the silk pajama leg against his forearm. She looked over his shoulder at the phone. Trying to ignore the physical contact, Bradan scrolled through the calligraphy. Some of the ancient ink was smudged, but it remained legible. It filled two pages and one section had two versions, one to specifically bring Cynbel back and the other to allow Cynbel to resurrect anyone he selected. No preamble introduced the verses except for a brief handwritten notation indicating the spell would be most potent if used at Samhain. This seemed to have been added later than the spell itself.

"It's in Latin," Bradan said.

"Can you say a few words?" she asked.

"Return sleeper.
Do not muse on places you have passed through after your
death,
whether empty nothingness or paradise.
Hear my call now . . ."

Simply reading the passage created a surge of enchantment that hit him with the impact of a hammer. Claire looked startled by his reaction. She also seemed suddenly queasy.

"Someone just sucked all the energy out of me." He leaned against her shoulder. "This really takes it out of you."

"Can you get rid of Cynbel and Aennati now?" she asked.

"I don't have the strength to make it work," Bradan said. "It's too heavy. Also, I need to know where they are. I'll have to see them as I say the verses."

"Then how did Danielle bring those people back? She's no magician."

"She didn't have to be. By accident, everything somehow aligned that night. It was Samhain, the rituals were done appropriately, a family accidently burned to death in the Marina at just the right moment, though there was no ceremony associated with their deaths so maybe that wasn't the trigger. Resuscitation is a big deal and organized sacrifice is needed to make it happen. Possibly the killings of Danielle's husband and friends immediately after the spell somehow paid the energy debt. That's unique in my experience, but this incantation seems to have been written so that it could be performed that way."

Ironically, the spell Danielle had used to invite the priests to modern times also contained all the elements theoretically needed to return Cynbel and Aennati to eternity. The door could swing both ways. He'd experimented earlier this morning with rearranging phrases to achieve the desired effect. However, without actually doing the incantation, he didn't know if he'd revised it appropriately. This led to a bigger problem.

"You're wondering what I'm wondering?" Claire asked. "Do you have to kill people to make the spell work in reverse?"

He nodded. "I'm not sure how to get around that one."

He heard Tintagel growl. Generations together had taught him the nuances of the wolf's vocalizations. Something threatened them. Now the wolf jumped up, his claws scratching the floor for traction. Claire caught the tension and froze.

"Bradan Badon," an amplified voice sounded from outside. "Bradan Badon, you're under arrest. Come on out, hands in plain sight. Open the door slowly. Don't make sudden movements. To the other person in the room, follow the same instructions when we direct you to come out. Do not come out together. Leave any animals you have in the room. If they are aggressive, they will be shot."

Bradan stood up. The airy forecabin now was a cage. A fleeting image of Cagney in *Public Enemy* standing off an army of rifle- and tommy-gun-wielding police zipped through his mind. He considered rapidly. The vet in the neighboring houseboat wasn't as vacuous as he'd appeared. The son of a bitch had recognized him and phoned the cops. Now the man could sell his story to the media. There had to be dozens of journalists training their lenses on the houseboat. Locking him up would be wonderful closure on a frightful string of murders over the last several weeks during holiday season. Bradan might escape with some spell or other, but anything powerful enough to get himself, Claire, and the wolf out of harm's way would only alert the priests to their precise location.

The police warning was repeated word for word, echoing throughout the marina. He made a decision. Get arrested and see what happened.

"Do what they say," Bradan snarled. He stuffed the phone into his pants pocket and walked over to the door. Perhaps they'd give him warm clothing in jail.

"Bradan, open it slowly," Claire said from behind him.

He pointed at Tintagel and said, "Sit still. There are too many to get away from."

He eased the door open just as the warning from the police was repeated a third time. The huge voice sounded impatient. Bradan stepped into the sun and, half blinded, dimly saw guns, police boats, and a Coast Guard cruiser hovering before him. He tried not to think about how many tense forefingers might exert just a little more pressure on triggers. The slips around Wally's houseboat had quietly been cleared of anything he might use for cover if he made some sort of doomed effort at flight. His stomach burned with acid.

"Walk straight toward us."

Bradan did. He'd only gotten about five meters from the door when the same voice yelled, "Get down. Face down on the ground. That's right, on the deck. Keep your hands in sight, away from your body."

He guessed they were trying to keep him off balance with the rapid-fire demands though he knew that he was already putty in their hands thanks to dozens of shotguns, several assault rifles, and scores of pistols pointed at his head and chest. The verbal games were superfluous bullshit. Maybe the cops felt themselves justified because he was a psychotic. He slowly eased himself down onto the deck. He lay atop a large oil stain. Maybe the jerk with the megaphone had intentionally directed him to this spot. His cheek was in the oil, a repugnant, slick tactile sensation reminding him of last Saturday night outside the Paradise. Life had fallen into predictable and unpleasant patterns.

"To the second person in the boat, same drill, come out slowly, hands in plain sight. Do not go near Badon."

Bradan heard steps approaching him, but off to his right. His head wasn't turned in the right direction to see Claire. He shifted slightly to watch Claire's progress.

"Don't move. Do not move." One of the cops screamed at him. "We'll fuck you up good."

This was all being played out for the media crews and news bloggers. They'd have to delete any vulgarities for the major networks. Whoever manned the megaphone already pictured themselves giving a seemingly offhand, post-arrest interview to the news anchors describing how they'd masterminded the arrest. He caught himself mumbling the first words of a spell and stopped himself. There would be a better time.

He watched Claire dressed in her rumpled pajamas march

out along the narrow dock, face set with tension. Did the army of police facing her look any different than the detention center guards who'd chased them last night? The cops instructed her to lie prone.

That left Tintagel. Did they know his pet hid in the tug? The vet hadn't seen the wolf, but that hardly mattered. The police would get around to searching the boat. Then they'd shoot Tintagel out of hand without trying to capture him. Nobody would quibble about a killer's feral pet.

"Stay just as you are," the voice shouted. Bradan saw several flak-jacketed men edge forward from behind the cover of pilings and storage lockers with weapons extended. Other cops lifted themselves and leaned across car roofs or deckhouses to better sight in on Bradan and Claire and support the advance group that moved down the wharf toward them.

Suddenly, cops raised their weapons. Bradan stopped breathing. What had they seen? A shotgun blast deafened him, followed by several rapidly spaced shots popped off by cops with AR-15s. Glass broke in Wally's houseboat. If these morons decided to use full auto, the entire marina would be Swiss cheese. Bradan tried to sink into the boards. What the fuck was happening? The cops shot at something behind him. An object moving so fast and erratically that it was a black blur crossed his field of vision. Tintagel. The wolf leaped from the tug to the deck of a houseboat just as a potted plant exploded behind him, sending a fountain of soil into the air.

Tintagel briefly charged along the wharf, then leaped back onto another boat before making a phenomenal leap to shore and threading himself between two unmarked police cars as bullet holes materialized in the vehicles' fenders and car windows and headlights disintegrated under the fusillade. The beast ran fluid as water. Had the police hit the wolf? Bradan struggled not to lurch upright and sprint over to where he'd last seen his companion. The animal had gotten him out of too many jams during their centuries together for him not to help.

"Stop! Everyone stop firing." The guy on the megaphone finally managed to make himself heard above the din. The shooting died away. Bradan saw why. Now weapons pointed in every direction. The police would hit one another. Tintagel had vanished.

Slowly, everyone's attention returned to him. The SWAT team moved cautiously forward looking tenser than ever. One squat fellow with a crew cut kept looking over his shoulder expecting the wolf to rematerialize and attack him from the rear. A tall, black cop in body armor pushed his pistol down to within centimeters of Bradan's temple. Crewcut stood by Bradan's side pointing his assault rifle at his neck. A half dozen other SWAT team members and several plainclothes detectives now surrounded him. Everyone wanted to be in on the fun today.

"Put your hands in the middle of your back," someone said. Moving very deliberately, Bradan obeyed.

"My dog, what happened?"

"Shut the fuck up," Crewcut shouted at him. "You have the right to remain silent . . ."

Bradan ignored the perfunctory recitation of his rights. His world had been reduced to staring at black military boots. There were too many of these for him to see Claire now. Bradan breathed out two brief enchantments.

"Praying isn't going to help a lot," the black SWAT officer said.

"Can't hurt," Bradan replied.

Someone grabbed his wrist and wrapped a cuff over it, then yanked his other hand and snapped the cuff shut, but not over the wrist. Only one of his wrists had been confined. No one noticed the dangling cuff. To anyone who looked, it would seem that both of his hands were securely manacled. The illusion was a small spell and wouldn't drain him too quickly but would allow him to keep one hand free. Hopefully, they'd get him into a van soon. Hands slapped his torso and legs checking for concealed weapons, but no one noticed the phone. Good, his second spell rendered the thin phone undetectable.

A brief, piercing howl from several hundred meters away cut through the noises of men and machinery. Everyone froze for a moment before resuming the process of arresting him with stolid professionalism.

"Your poodle is going to be history when we find it," the black cop said.

Bradan couldn't repress a small sigh of relief. Tintagel had gotten away. Only the wolf's incredibly quick reflexes had saved it. Bradan knew Tintagel could survive even if they used dogs to track him. Sausalito's high-walled and widely spaced mansions were set amid dense foliage and trees that would make ideal concealment. The wolf would be as difficult to corral as a passing breeze. After issuing his challenge, he would already be a kilometer away. Bradan hoped that Tintagel wouldn't supplement his diet by dining on the city's wealthy residents.

"She's the Chang woman who went missing," Bradan heard a cop say a little distance away.

"It's Chan, not Chang," Claire said.

Good, someone had recognized Claire even if they'd gotten her surname wrong. Bradan didn't think they'd release her right away but guessed the police wouldn't cuff her because they'd assume she'd been Bradan's captive. He hoped Claire would have the sense to look confused, feign shock and blame Bradan for her unexpected appearance amid the dragnet. Instead, a short argument ensued in which Bradan clearly heard Claire's angry voice rising above several male voices. It did not sound like she was playing the bemused naïf. Christ, they'd drag her off in chains, too.

A compact Asian approached Bradan's group. "Take him over to the van. Power's down in Marin including the county lockup thanks to the quake, so we haul psycho killer here down to the city."

"It's their jurisdiction," the black cop said.

"Just saves the trouble of moving him later is all," Crewcut said.

Two large policemen grabbed Bradan's arms and hauled him upright. He winced involuntarily as his shoulder wound sent a lancet of pain through his upper arm.

"He get that during the shooting?" the Asian asked. He looked incuriously at Bradan's bloodstained T-shirt.

"Not us. Had it already, I think," Crewcut said. "Maybe someone else took a shot at him."

They were at the van now on a little service road leading down to the wharf. A dozen other police vehicles sat parked nearby. Further back, a crowd stared at the drama. The black cop pulled open the van doors to let the two big cops shove Bradan inside. So far, nobody had noticed the dangling cuff. Bradan couldn't repress a smile. Parlor tricks had their uses. In fact, he now needed another trick. Bradan mouthed several lines quietly. He wasn't sure it would have the effect he wanted, but he felt the third spell go into effect and simultaneously a downward drag on his mental and physical energy levels. Would the priests catch on? He was working minor-league spells, but the cumulative effect of enough trivial magic must sooner or later alert them.

One of the big cops who'd lugged Bradan over to the vehicle laughed and told his partner, "Save us all a lot of trouble if we just ran a hose from the tail pipe into the van compartment with this jerk. What do you want to bet they let him off with ten years? He'll be out in no time and prowling around your neighborhood–"

Thanks to his spell, the closing van door slammed, but didn't quite latch and lock. He heard the outside door handle being turned and hoped no one saw that the door wasn't completely shut.

Someone slid a small panel open between the driver and guards sitting in front and his compartment. Despite the cops' gallows humor, they wanted him alive and kicking for the trial. He sat down on a low metal bench that lined van's side. Aside from the benches and narrow windows overlaid with heavy-gauge mesh, there wasn't anything to see. The vehicle smelled of piss. Bradan looked forward. He didn't recognize the man who stared expressionlessly back at him. Evidently, he hadn't been part of the team who'd made the arrest.

Bradan kept his hands behind him, shielded from easy view by his body and stopped the spell. Involuntarily he sighed aloud in relief as he felt the psychic drain vanish. The cop staring at him didn't react. Perhaps he thought Bradan was relieved that the chase was finally over.

Bradan heard other engines start nearby and then his van edged forward, lurched to a stop, then moved forward and picked up speed. He must be sitting in the center of a convoy of marked and unmarked police vehicles. Getting out of the van would only be the first of his problems. What then? Bradan was pondering that when he noticed the van slowing.

"Jesus, look at this shit."

Bradan turned forward again to see the cop who'd observed him in profile looking at the van's driver who'd evidently just spoken.

"Problem?"

"There must be an accident on the bridge," the driver said. "Can you check your traffic app or radio for a status?"

The cop riding shotgun now turned completely away from Bradan to stare through the windshield. Discreetly, Bradan sat up straighter and stared through the slit out the van's front, too. Cars, lots of cars. He tried to orient himself. They must still have been in Marin approaching the bridge.

The driver picked up a mike and spoke too softly for Bradan to overhear. A staccato response came back a few seconds later.

"Save the what?" the driver said loudly into the mike. The second cop snorted. A different voice rasped something back over the radio.

"That's what I thought she said, 'Save the oceans.' Can't CHP get these guys out of there? They are the highway patrol, after all. We've got a prisoner plus escorting vehicles. Move 'em the fuck out of our way. They can protest on the Bay Bridge instead."

The van came to a dead stop. Bradan stared out through the dense mesh at the brake lights surrounding them. Traffic snaked ahead seamlessly and endlessly, hugging the curves of 101 as the highway moved south past the final Marin County exits, winding its way through Marin's hills. Between the bluffs he saw San Francisco lit from the east.

"They're in all six lanes?" the cop on the passenger side said.

"Who the hell knows? Yeah, that's what she said. There are

only about two dozen of 'em, supposedly around mid-span. Inbound and outbound lanes stopped cold."

The radio chirped again.

"Oh Jesus," the driver said. "They're trying to work some units over from the city side, but of course they can't get through the traffic so they'll have to hike out to arrest the assholes."

Bradan watched drivers in some of the closer cars speaking into phones to tell bosses, spouses, lovers that they'd be hopelessly late. Horns sounded further back in the growing crush of traffic as motorists who couldn't see where the snag was vented their frustration blindly. At least the Golden Gate was in sight, seen end-on, impassive and massive rust-orange towers above the bluffs and looming over the mushrooming clot of traffic.

One of their escorts ahead turned on his emergency lights, which blossomed orange, blue, and white.

"Attaboy, Kevin," the driver said sarcastically. "I'm sure they'll all get out of your way now. Try the siren, too." A piercing wail cut through the sporadic blare of horns. The two cops exchanged glances.

"What's he in, Fourth Precinct?" the passenger-side cop asked.

"Transferred in last summer. Can't leave soon enough for me."

The cop on the passenger side turned back to stare at Bradan. "We could save ourselves a whole bunch of trouble by shooting you right here, bro. How 'bout that? Commuter execution?"

"Sounds wonderful," Bradan said. "But the media coverage would only make traffic worse."

"Good point. Guess that's out, then."

At the moment Bradan's impatience mounted with that of

the cops. Cynbel and Aennati were right across the bridge. If the packed span collapsed now in a quake, it would pull down thousands with it. He shifted position on the metal bench slightly. Both cops stared ahead at the traffic. It was now or never.

Bradan lunged for the van's rear doors. He smashed his left shoulder into the metal that buckled outward slightly but didn't pop open as he'd hoped. What happened? He knew it wasn't locked.

"Shit!" the driver shouted.

Damnation—how both his shoulders ached. Scrambling to his feet on the metal floor, Bradan barreled into the door again—no resistance whatsoever this time—and tumbled out of the van carried by his own momentum to fall onto the hood of an unmarked police vehicle that hugged the van's bumper. For half a heartbeat, he stared into the startled expressions of two SWAT officers and then they both scrambled to open their doors, one of them grabbing a dashboard-mounted shotgun. The cop on the left banged his door into a tractor-trailer rig idling in traffic almost flush with the unmarked police vehicle.

Bradan rolled left off the hood underneath the trailer, hearing the other detective vault onto his car's hood after him. Bradan hunched over to run under the trailer, ducking away from a rusted spare tire clamp and a loose air-brake hose to jump upright again on the other side of the truck. A spell? He'd never get it out smoothly enough to be effective. Behind him he heard a cop bash himself on the clamp beneath the truck.

"The prisoner is loose . . . I said the prisoner is . . . through the rear door . . . running south toward San Francisco . . . in traffic."

Bradan heard the police van driver shouting in the distance above the truck engine's harsh growl. He squeezed between a white Mercedes convertible with a license plate spelling "OUTAHIR" and another tractor-trailer with a big Confederate flag plastered across the bug-covered grill.

Bradan noted a cluster of colorfully dressed Indian and European tourists staring dumbfounded at his helter-skelter dash with plainclothes detectives and SWAT team members in pursuit, but the Bay Area drivers couldn't have cared less, ignoring him and the law to continue cursing traffic into their phones or opportunistically relaxing in their seats to review the morning's schedules and business plans.

Bradan clambered over a Jeep's fender with a cute brunette sitting in the driver's seat working on her phone before he reached the heavy steel and concrete railing separating the sea of stalled vehicles from the sidewalk. On the sidewalk, he sprinted in the direction of San Francisco, pushing his way past more tourists, Chinese—as intrigued as the Indians—and a half dozen bicyclists all walking or cycling along the sidewalks flanking the six-lane bridge.

A paint crew in white overalls worked above him removing a skin of oxidized metal that had materialized on the suspension cables since they'd last ministered to this section. Bradan smashed into a strolling couple, sending them both sprawling. Ah, and here was the cavalry now. Bradan saw two cops on motocross bikes threading their way between the cars toward him. The masses of vehicles were so tightly packed that even the cycles couldn't move quickly; nonetheless, their progress was inexorable. He also saw the two cops whose hood he'd landed on sprinting after him, encumbered by body armor, while further back a platoon of uniformed police, having abandoned their vehicles, swept through the bemused tourists.

Just ahead of him, a young man in bicycle shorts and a jersey transparent with sweat bent over a woman's mountain bike examining its tire. The woman looked irritated at the flat. The man's bike sat propped against the steel railing. It was black and looked clean, well-maintained, and high-tech with disc brakes as well as full-suspension. Bradan guessed it was rugged enough to jump curbs and fast enough to make great time on smooth pavement. Bradan huffed up to the couple, unceremoniously grabbed the guy's bike, and leaped aboard. He grunted from the pain in his wounded shoulders as they absorbed the shock of gripping the handlebars, but he managed to hang on clumsily as he picked up speed.

"Jeff, he got your bike," the woman yelled.

Bradan pedaled away, glancing briefly over his shoulder. Jeff stood up, realized that his wheels were fast departing, and ran after Bradan followed close behind by the police. However, pedaling furiously, Bradan shifted into a taller gear and pulled away from the group, zigzagging amid clusters of strollers and flanked by the immobilized river of cars.

Ahead, faintly at first, then louder, he heard chants and the massed tones of a crowd. Then the clusters of pedestrians on the sidewalk coagulated into a solid clot watching the demonstration in the bridge midsection. The people blocked further progress along the sidewalk. Bradan dodged between several bunches of spectators, jumped off his bike, and pulled it over to the railing separating the sidewalk from the bridge deck. The cars were tightly spaced now but not as packed as the pedestrians. Bradan looked over his shoulder again. Because of the bike, he'd put space between himself and the score of police who followed him, some of whom didn't seem to be in shape for a foot race.

"Is this real?" a balding guy in a resplendent white Porsche convertible asked a companion. "What's the point? All the otters are already dead, humpbacks too."

Just ahead of Bradan, beyond a row of cars, fifty protesters shouting in unison had arrayed themselves across all six lanes of traffic. About a dozen lay end to end with handcuffs linking them to the next person in the human chain, forming an unbroken barrier. Despite the living roadblock, one enraged commuter had rolled his Ford F150 forward, crushing a grey haired woman protester's forearm beneath his front tire. She shrieked in agony with her arm pinned under rubber. Now two television crews covered a pitched brawl that had ensued as environmentalists and several car and truck drivers punched and clawed at one another.

Bradan ducked under a McDonald's milkshake cup thrown into the crowd. Several of the protesters lobbed paint-filled balloons at the mass of cars, creating a psychedelic palette of splatters on windshields and gleaming chrome grills. He watched a teamster bodily haul a collegiate-looking environmentalist past a paint-smeared cab toward the railing preparatory to tossing him over the edge and into the water sixty meters below. The protester flailed away ineffectually with his placard. Other commuters sat on the hoods or roofs of their cars and watched the donnybrook.

Hefting his bike, Bradan worked his way up to the line of prone bodies and stepped over them. They shouted at him to stop and reached up to grab at him. A tall blond man accompanied by a willowy brunette confronted Bradan. Killer whales frolicking harmoniously with seals danced on her shirt amid a blue-green, underwater kelp forest.

"We're not letting people get through for another hour," the man said.

"I'm late for my counseling in the city," Bradan shouted

above the din. He dangled his handcuff in front of the blond man. "Solidarity. I was going to have joined, but I forgot my appointment. Brothers and sisters, we are either part of the problem or we are part of the solution." Bradan lifted his stolen bike above his head. "This is my solution."

"Jan, the guy has a point," the woman dressed in whales said. "I'm in therapy, too. It's made all the difference. I used to work for Exxon before counseling."

"Exxon?" Jan stopped glaring at Bradan and stared at Whales. "We need to reevaluate our relationship."

Bradan heard a police radio crackle in the background. Without waiting for Jan to muster more arguments against his passage, Bradan, as discreetly as he could, stepped past them, and hopped back on the bike and raced south toward San Francisco.

CHAPTER 18

Ephemeral Nature

Hit the priests hard and their apocalypse would be stillborn. Through pine trees, Bradan saw Cynbel and Aennati standing side by side thirty meters away on the Presidio's narrow cliffside path overlooking the Golden Gate Bridge. The priests were right around a bend in the path, but didn't appear to have seen him; their chanting continued. Where could he position himself to get an unobstructed view of them without being spotted himself? To his left, the cliffs dropped eighty meters straight down to rocks and little pocket beaches only big enough for a mermaid to recline on. The late-afternoon sun illuminated everything, turning the Pacific into a hard, coppery surface with the depth of a mirror.

It was a gorgeous postcard with the priests at the cliff's edge, two figures intent on their surroundings, natural elements in the scene rather than intruding humans. A trio of pelicans flew past in formation heading toward the bridge. The setting's wildness would be conducive to the malign concentration required to perform the enchantment needed to tear apart the Earth's crust. They wore dark-gray cloaks that blended in with the earthen hues of the path and tress. Modern clothing would seem perverse to them.

Bradan eased himself off the path, into the trees, and up

the steep slope on his right as he crept closer to Cynbel and Aennati. The sun was in the west behind him. That would be one small advantage, as it masked his approach. For the last hour, he'd felt the priests making magic intermittently and had thereby located them. Even wizards as accomplished as Cynbel and Aennati had to experiment with construction, rhyme, and meter to catalyze a quake, but the Druids would get it right soon. They'd had weeks to practice.

The strength of the enchantment the priests mustered buffeted Bradan almost physically and he grabbed a pine branch to keep his balance. He was a tiny magnet trying to force itself closer to a much more powerful electrical field of the same charge. He pulled the phone out of his pocket, almost dropping it. He felt frail and wondered if the stiff wind would push him over the cliff's edge. The modified spell on the phone's screen and such skills as he possessed seemed forlornly inadequate to take out the priests, but he clutched the phone to his chest and continued to work along the slope paralleling the path toward the sound of their voices. Cynbel and Aennati were out of sight for the moment, masked by vegetation. He hoped the priests' concentration would blunt their acute sensitivity to opposing spells.

Now Bradan saw them again, no more than ten meters away with their backs toward him as they faced east toward San Francisco. The fault shifted beneath him, almost tumbling him to the ground. He'd moved into position for a magical ambush, close enough so he'd have to whisper the spell or they'd hear him. He could almost touch the coarse wool of their cloaks. Abstract tattoos ran down the length of Cynbel's exposed forearms, one depicting an elongate prancing stallion enmeshed in ivy, another showing a pack of wolves pursuing human prey. Bradan noticed a small fire to the wizard's right. He hadn't seen that before. Aennati's black hair flowed out behind her. Bradan heard clearly the old Celtic language, poetry even when describing prosaic events, hypnotic beauty when used in a ritual. The priests held hands.

Bradan considered simply rushing forward and shoving them over the edge, but the instant he conceived the plan, it seemed unworkable. Cynbel and Aennati appeared twice normal size; he once again confronted them in a boy's body as he'd done fifteen centuries before. Even lost in the intimacies of their spell, they'd notice and crush him. Holding his breath, Bradan knelt behind a tree trunk. The sunlight and branches shadowed the phone's screen in Byzantine patterns making it almost impossible to read. This was the lone option, his magic against their vision. Reading an untested incantation, as he was about to do, risked botching it. He might send the enchantment crashing to bits like a crystal toy kicked down a flight of concrete steps. He'd been unable to give it any kind of test.

Bradan recited the passage. His efforts would become noticeable to the priests as the spell took shape. At that point it would be a race between his ability to ensnare them in the enchantment's web and their retaliation blasting him to a cinder.

Bradan's momentum slowed and he breathed more deeply as the magnitude of the edifice he struggled to create sapped his energy. He expected this. He had to offer something in return for what he intended to do. Cynbel wheeled to face him. The sun caught the wizard full in the face and he shaded his eyes as he intoned several verses. Bradan desperately threw himself aside as a flash of light detonated in front of him, on top of him, inside his mind. He heard no explosion.

Bradan felt surprised when he sensed pebbles and branches

against his skin. A hundred-thousand-watt halogen light glared directly onto his optic nerves and he thought his eyes must be open. He tried to shut them. They were shut. He struggled to bring his arm up to block the light but couldn't make his arm move. Giving up, he attempted to shift his head. He felt his cheek scratch against dirt. So he lay on ground. He slowly tucked his chin into his chest, diminishing the light's intensity and allowing him to focus on what was going on around him. He heard voices in the background that tripped a series of memories and he realized he'd lived through Cynbel's attack. Probably Cynbel had been partially blinded by the sun when he'd struck at Bradan. That had been the margin of his survival.

Had the quake occurred? Bradan opened his eyes to stare straight down to rocks and breakers below. For half a heartbeat he looked over the cliff. If he shifted a millimeter to his right, he'd plunge right over the edge. The voices behind him resolved themselves into the priests' familiar chant. The quake had not happened yet.

Did he still have the phone? He'd never be able to do his spell without it. He felt something in his grip. This time his arm responded and he was able to drag it into view. The hair on his forearm was singed, but otherwise Bradan was amazed to see himself unhurt. The phone was still there. He mustered the titanic energy needed to shift his head to bring Cynbel and Aennati into view.

Bradan began again, quickly reaching the point where he'd been forced to halt before. The momentum carried him along. The time for the requisite sacrifice had come. He inserted three stanzas into the spell: the offering. Bradan sucked air in but inhaled fire. The ground's sensations against his skin changed from mild irritations to the sensation that he was being flayed.

All his teeth felt as if they'd been simultaneously extracted. He struggled to keep reading through a red haze and mouthed the spell's words, trying to hear if the sounds he made were still audible. Then he realized he'd run out of words; the spell was finished.

He stared at the priests. Their chanting had stopped, but otherwise they appeared unaffected. Cynbel's expression looked at once mystical and focused. Aennati was a dark angel limned by the sun's purple-red illumination. They still held hands. Bradan blinked. Both vanished in that flicker of his eyelid.

Night set in and Bradan became conscious that he was cold. He heard a short bark from down the path and saw Tintagel loping toward him, a large black shape against the dark surroundings. Bradan heaved himself into a sitting position and let his legs dangle over the cliff edge. He patted a section of ground next to him and the wolf ambled over to sit down by him.

"You're late to chase down their spirits," he said. "But then, maybe they didn't have souls to catch, anyway."

Tintagel ignored him and energetically scratched his flank.

The priests were gone, but he still had problems. Simply giving himself up to the police—if he decided to go that route—would take dexterity; they might be inclined to shoot him down. No doubt, his escape across the Golden Gate would cement their conviction that he was the serial killer. Nonetheless, a good lawyer should be able to prove that the state had a weak case against him. Maybe it wouldn't even get to trial. He'd been in Miami when most of the killings happened. A dozen relatives and friends would swear to that, though dragging his Florida brood into the case was sure to raise awkward questions about his age. He'd finesse that somehow as he always had.

Unfortunately, he'd undeniably been near Stow Lake just after the most recent slaughter occurred. His guilty flight was all recorded. However, no blood or DNA existed that placed him at the exact spot of the butchery. None of the shoe prints at the site would match his. In fact, human tracks merging seamlessly into Irish elk hoofprints would only confound the case for the prosecution's forensics experts. He'd have to cook up some story to explain what he was doing in Golden Gate Park in the first place. Keep it simple: he'd been there to walk Tintagel, he'd heard screams by the lake and investigated, but run into some sort of wild animals instead. No one in Homicide would believe him, but what could they do about it? The news tape might also show two Irish elk, known to be extinct for ten thousand years. Any reasonably astute attorney would use these apparitions to call the credibility of the entire news footage into question.

Bradan half-smiled as he watched the sky darken over the Bay and city. A modern wizard had to be as adept at the rituals of contemporary law as with fifth-century Celtic ceremony.

———

Bradan sneezed. He reached for a tissue, blew his nose, then let the tissue drop to the floor. A little pile surrounded his chair, snow at the base of a tree during in winter.

"I don't remember the last cold I had," he said to Claire. "I'd forgotten how miserable you feel. I picked this one up while I waited to be bailed out of the city jail."

"I didn't think you got sick." She sat across the kitchen table from him sipping a cup of tea. Claire poured a cup for him. "Another one of Granddad's blends."

She'd replaced her glasses that had been cracked on Angel Island. After her first day back at work, she looked composed and professional in a short, blue wool skirt and a white blouse. Except for a guarded expression, the events of the last several weeks seemed to have affected her no more than drops of rain leaving evanescent dimples on a pond during a fall shower. Undoubtedly, the biggest impact of her kidnapping wouldn't be visible, though.

Bradan reached for another Kleenex. "Something had to be sacrificed so I could make the magic needed to get rid of the priests. I wasn't going to kill anyone. Giving up my longevity was the only other option."

He upended the little hourglass Claire had given him to time tea brewing. "Time has unfrozen for me. It'll take a while for that to sink in. Knowing that I have a lot less time alive, it's not that I've died, but it's the death of future possibility."

He looked about his home at the paraphernalia of more than a millennium, the Gainsborough ever so gradually yellowing, the Edo-period Japanese folding screen developing tiny cracks as the decades passed. The mementos had always been susceptible to time while he'd floated along detached from chronological consequences. Now he'd age with them.

And he wouldn't be able to see the artwork of coming centuries.

"I don't see any gray hair," Claire said.

Involuntarily, Bradan touched his right sideburn then checked his wrist. "Thanks. My scars are gone."

"The Bay Area owes you thanks—if they only knew it."

He looked at the picture of Arthur and Merlin. Had the wizard just winked at him?

"Nobody owes me," he said. "It's a debt paid up. It was my fault that the priests were revived. I kept the parchment securely, or so I thought, but it would have been best destroyed centuries ago. I wanted to resuscitate Merlin with it, but frankly, I also kept it simply as a reminder of my past like the artwork."

"Someone wants to see you," his condo's dulcet tone informed him.

"My lawyer again, maybe another journalist or the police." With a sigh, Bradan got up and walked through his condo.

"You've got a lawyer?" Claire followed him into the living room.

"Tony recommended a good one. She's the one who kept the bail within reason." He activated the intercom. "Yeah."

"Mr. Badon, my name is Sonja. Danielle referred me to you. I'm interested in help with dream interpretation. She said you were very intuitive about that kind of thing."

"You're not scared off by the media shit I've gotten?"

Sonja's voice became impatient. "Why should I be? Danielle said there was no way you could be a mass murderer and, even if you were, that it would just make your spiritual guidance more authentic."

Bradan thanked her for the endorsement and, pleading illness, scheduled an appointment with his new client for the following week. He'd assumed that notoriety would make him a pariah, but instead business had doubled. He was almost to the point of turning away customers and no one seemed the least fazed by his steep fees.

"I'm getting people contacting me hourly," he said. "Claire, just how bored are you with life in a big-eight accounting firm?"

She shrugged. "Pretty tired of it, actually. I've been in my current office for seven years plus two years at another firm. What were you thinking?"

"That you might consider a few months' sabbatical from your position and join New Age Counseling. Besides psychological and spiritual advice, my clients almost all need personal financial planning. Maybe we can provide full-service support to these folks."

Claire dropped into his couch. "I minored in psychology at Stanford so it's not a big stretch. Would you teach me a few more spells?"

"We'll pick up where we left off with the levitation spell."

"What do you charge per hour?"

"Depends." He regarded her lazily. "Three hundred to four hundred an hour. A bit more if the problem is difficult. I peg my rates to inflation, so they go up every year. The profit margin is close to ninety percent, since my living expenses are the only fixed costs."

"Music to an accountant's ears. All right, you've got a deal. If it doesn't work out, I think I can get back into a firm without too much trouble."

He sat down on the sofa next to her. "Interested in a date with an older man?"

"I'll be ready after I change clothing. Anything but Chinese food. Most of the restaurant stuff is toxic." She walked over to his door and paused.

"I'd drink a bit more of that tea if I were you. The Celts weren't the only ones who experimented with longevity. Granddad turned 102 last November. Also, I'm doing financial and operational consulting for a biotech down the peninsula that's working on extending life. They've made some real progress recently in early-phase testing. They've got a follow-up trial going to further test their gene editing technology. You should join."

ACKNOWLEDGMENTS

During the early part of the twentieth century, poems were inscribed by Chinese immigrants on the walls of the Angel Island Immigration Station relating the émigrés' hardships. Their poignancy can't be matched by the few modest stanzas that I've crafted, but maybe readers' curiosity will be piqued to explore this fascinating part of California's cultural history.

ABOUT THE AUTHOR

Peter Blaisdell lives in the LA area and has spent many years in San Francisco. He has a PhD in Biochemistry and has conducted postdoctoral research in molecular biology as well as publishing peer-reviewed research papers in these fields. He has also published business articles on managing research in technology companies. None of this has much to do with the literary side of his life, where he is an active reviewer of fantasy, science fiction and magical realism. *The Lords of Oblivion* is his debut novel.

blaisdellliteraryenterprises.com